# HONOR AND GLORY

## ABOUT THE AUTHOR

A California native, Michael Newton has published 215 books under his own name and various pseudonyms since 1977. He began writing professionally as a "ghost" for author Don Pendleton on the best-selling Executioner series and continues his work on that series today. With 104 episodes published to date, Newton has nearly tripled the number of Mack Bolan novels completed by creator Pendleton himself.

Newton's first book under his own name was *Monsters, Mysteries and Man* (1979), a survey of unexplained phenomena for younger readers. While 156 of Newton's published books have been novels—including westerns, political thrillers and psychological suspense—he is best known for nonfiction, primarily true crime and reference books.

# HONOR AND GLORY

## THE BUREAU BOOK FOUR

MICHAEL NEWTON

WOLFPACK
PUBLISHING
— EST 2013 —

Copyright © 2018 by Michael Newton
All rights reserved.

Published in the United States by Wolfpack Publishing, Las Vegas.

Wolfpack Publishing
6032 Wheat Penny Avenue
Las Vegas, NV 89122

wolfpackpublishing.com

Ebook ISBN: 978-1-64119-275-0
Paperback ISBN: 978-1-64119-276-7

Library of Congress Control Number: 2018953247

*For Sibel Deniz Edmonds (1970- )*

## DRAMATIS PERSONÆ

- *Aloysius Gantt*: agent of the Federal Bureau of Investigation.
- *Gwendolyn Gantt* (Née Blake): Gantt's wife.
- *Colby Gantt*: their son, agent of the wartime OSS.
- *Devon Gantt*: their son, agent of the FBI.
- *Eileen Gantt* (Née Brisbois): Colby's wife
- *Camille Gantt* (Née Perry): Devon's wife
- *Declan O'Hara*: agent of the FBI's Special Intelligence Service
- *Abigail O'Hara* (Née Monahan): Declan's wife.
- *Nolan O'Hara*: their son; U.S. Marine Corps infantryman
- *Keely O'Hara* (Née Prewitt), born 1923: Nolan's wife
- *Fiona O'Hara*: daughter of Declan and Abigail, born 1925.
- *Gregory Jordan* (Né Gregorio Giordano): legal counsel for the Giordano crime family.
- *Angelina Jordan* (Née Barbieri): Jordan's wife.
- *David Jordan*: their son, born 1924; member of the U.S. Army Rangers

- *Gemma Jordan*: their daughter, born 1927.
- *Isaac Sawyer*: agent of the Federal Bureau of Narcotics.
- *Talitha Sawyer* (née Boudreaux): his wife.
- *Payton Sawyer*: their second son, born 1929.
- *Keisha Sawyer*: their daughter, born 1933
- *Frederick Douglass Sawyer*: their third son, born 1938.
- *Leonid Babin*: Soviet intelligence officer, once deported from the United States.

## AUTHOR'S NOTE

*The Bureau* is a work of fiction, but real-life public figures, institutions and events often appear within its pages. Where that occurs, personal conversations and actions are the author's invention, except where drawn directly from reliable nonfiction sources. Timelines of historical events, likewise, may be rearranged, compressed or extended as required for dramatic effect. Anachronistic terms now often deemed offensive—"Negro," "colored," "Indian," "Japs," "Krauts," "queer" and the like—are used within these pages as they were applied during the years portrayed. Obsolete geographical names—e.g., "Canton" versus "Guangzhou," etc.—are used as they were normally applied during the years of 1941 to 1946 inclusive.

# HONOR AND GLORY

## PROLOGUE

FATHERS AND SONS. Across America, thousands, likely tens of thousands, sat down in the wake of the Pearl Harbor raid to talk about their options and the interruption—very possibly the end—of private dreams.

Before the bombs stopped falling, long before the smoke cleared, Tokyo declared war on the U.S. and United Kingdom, invading Thailand and British Malaya, launching aerial attacks against Guam, Wake Island, Hong Kong, Shanghai, Singapore, the Philippines. Canada and Australia instantly declared war on Japan, while Parliament and Congress would require a bit more time.

No one would pass unscathed before the end.

———

*FAIRLAWN, Southeast Washington, D.C.*

I

"HAVE you considered what your mom will say?" Declan O'Hara asked.

"She'll hate it," his son Nolan answered. "But she'll ultimately go along with our decision."

"*Our* decision?"

"Well..."

"You've thought about your options, I assume."

"Of course. I've graduated from George Washington and plan on law school, but a student deferment won't stretch another three years in a national emergency. I'd rather beat the draft."

"Suggesting that you've got a branch picked out."

"The Corps," Nolan replied.

"Ah. 'First to fight,'" Declan quoted from the *Marine's Hymn* and recruiting posters that were popping up around the capital already.

"Right."

"They're tough. I had a friend in the Marines last time around. He fought in France and got shot up. He seemed okay when I ran into him a few years back, by accident, but who knows, after what he saw and had to do?"

"Dad..."

"Have you thought about the Bureau?"

"After law school, absolutely. That's still what I want, but as it stands—"

"Before I leave, I could put in a word with Mr. Hoover. In the circumstances, they'll be expediting applications. You'd be serving just the same as anyone in uniform."

"Like you in South America?"

"Well, not at first. You'd have to train, then be assigned a field office."

"No, thanks." A hesitation, then, "I need to ask you something?"

"Go ahead."

"Did you ever regret not joining in the last war? I mean going 'Over There'?"

"Not for a minute," Declan lied. Then, "Did I ever tell you how I joined the Bureau?"

"No. I asked you once, when we were living in Chicago, but you said we'd talk about it later."

"Busy times. You want to hear it now?"

"I do."

"Three of us, fresh out of law school, went to sign our lives away at the Selective Service board before the deadline. There was me, your uncle Gantt—"

"Fake uncle," Nolan interjected.

"Right. And then the guy I mentioned earlier. Greg Jordan. On the way, who comes along but J. Edgar Hoover, with a plan to beat the draft and serve our country at the same time, joining up with Justice."

"Dad, I *know* you served."

Declan waved that away. "Beside the point. So Ally Gantt and I gave it a shot. We've been there ever since, starting before I met your mother. Greg went on, joined the Marines, and came back with some medals, plus some scars. Today, he's a big lawyer in New York—" shading the truth of that for Nolan's sake "—and doing fine, as far as I could tell, the few minutes we talked in '34."

"So, either way's all right with you."

"It's your life," Declan said. "I'd rather that you end up in one piece. Your mother, well..."

"You'll talk to her?"

"We both will. I believe you owe her that."

"Tougher than boot camp, eh?"

"I wouldn't be a bit surprised."

3

———

*TENLEYTOWN, Northwest Washington, D.C.*

ACROSS TOWN, Aloysius Gantt sat with his twin sons. Both had graduated in the spring from Yale, Colby *summa cum laude*, Devon *magna*. Both had planned on law school when Hideki Tōjō threw the world a curve.

Sipping a glass of scotch, their father said, "it's time to think about a strategy. You don't have any time to waste."

"Student deferments while they last," Devon suggested.

Aloysius shook his head. "Think *past* the war. When it's all done, a man who sat it out will look like damaged goods, no matter what diplomas say."

"You're saying we should join up?" Colby asked.

"Join *something*. You don't have to wear a helmet, with a rifle on your shoulder. I've been thinking."

"There's a shocker," Devon said, and both twins laughed as one.

Their father smiled and forged ahead. "Government service at another level spares you from the draft and you could still be in the thick of it, distinguishing yourselves without sleeping in foxholes."

"You mean join the Bureau," Colby said.

"Why not?"

"We're not lawyers or accountants," Devon said.

"Waivers can be arranged for the duration of the war. Whichever one of you goes with the FBI, start picking up night classes when you can. Show your initiative."

"Whichever one of us?" Now Colby seemed confused.

"I'd recommend separate paths. Divide and conquer, you might say."

"What are we conquering?" Devon inquired.

"The future, Son."

"And what's the other path, Dad?" Colby asked.

"Sign on with Colonel Donovan."

"Wild Bill? At COI?" asked Devon.

"Right," his father said. More properly, the OCI: Office of the Coordinator of Information. "He'll have an office up and running soon in London. After that, the world's his oyster— and whoever's working with him goes along."

"And Hoover hates his guts," Devon chimed in.

"So what? As long as Donovan is tight with FDR, the Chief can't do much damage to him. Think about it: one of you at COI, the other in the Bureau. Neither boss can stop twin brothers from communicating, if you're cagey and don't leave a paper trail. Help one another, help your agencies collaborate—or minimize the damage if they won't. Meanwhile, whatever COI turns into down the road, whoever's there will have an inside track. Grow with the group and who knows where you'll finally end up?"

"And at the Bureau?" Colby asked.

"I'm confident that I can further an emergency exception. Mr. Hoover doesn't mind a bit of nepotism if it benefits the Bureau. Anyway, something to think about."

The twins exchanged a glance and Colby said, "we need to talk it over."

"Absolutely. But I wouldn't take too long. Who knows how long this war will last?"

"Dad, Japs just sank the whole Pacific Fleet—or most of it, at least," Devon replied.

"And roused an angry giant in the process. They'll regret it soon enough, the Germans, too."

"We'll have an answer for you by tomorrow morning," Colby said.

"Sounds good. Whatever you decide is up to you." Gantt eyed each of his sons in turn. "Before you go, another drink?"

# CHAPTER 1

*MARINE CORPS BASE CAMP PENDLETON, SAN DIEGO: DECEMBER 12, 1941*

THE TRAIN BEARING recruits was late arriving, which did nothing to improve the surly mood of the drill instructors waiting on the platform for their latest crop of "boots" to bully and abuse. The shouting started on arrival and would not abate for six more weeks.

Nolan O'Hara knew construction on the base had started back in 1919, under Colonel Joseph Pendleton, retiring as a major general five years later. It was a former Spanish *rancho grande*, roughly 123,000 acres, purchased by the Corps for $4.2 million. Nolan also knew he'd be part of the 2nd Marine Division, commanded by Major General Clayton Vogel, blooded at Shanghai four years ago, during the Second Sino-Japanese War.

Upon arrival, though, acceptance didn't enter into it. With the other boots, Nolan was cursed, divested of civilian clothes and other personal belongings, shorn of hair down to his scalp, and dressed in a "utility uniform" of heavy sage green cotton herringbone twill. The jacket had three flapless pockets, while the trousers had a button fly and four pockets. Lace-up leggings chafed his ankles, and it seemed his feet would have to grow before they fit his boots. Helmets, at least for now, were still the World War I style issued to recruits in 1917.

Nolan's drill instructor—Sergeant Ethan Savage, who appeared intent on living up to his birth name—informed his boots in no uncertain terms, obscene whenever possible, exactly what they could expect over the next six weeks. They would be working seven days a week, and any Bible-thumpers in the group could make fucking appointments with the chaplain on their own time, thank you very much. If they survived to morph from "maggots" into bona fide marines, they would be learning everything from military courtesy and discipline to proper care of weapons ranging from .22-caliber rifles to .50-caliber machine guns, hand grenades, mortars, flamethrowers, and field artillery. If something new should come along before they graduated, they could goddamn well learn that on top of all the rest, including first aid, field maneuvers, forced marches and night maneuvers, unarmed combat, knife fighting, and all the calisthenics any superman could bear.

And they would fucking love it, bet your sorry asses, or they'd be washed out and left for some inferior outfit to pick over; maybe the army, navy, or the Coast Guard, where there was no frigging premium on excellence and no one gave a shit.

So said the Savage Gospel, and Nolan O'Hara pledged himself to make the grade.

———

*MEXICO CITY: December 14, 1941*


DECLAN O'HARA SAT in a dim corner of Café Victoria on Avenida Bucareli, three blocks from the U.S. Embassy, eating an unfamiliar but delectable breakfast: *huevos rancheros* with a seafood enchilada, refried beans, and rice seasoned with jalapeno peppers. He wolfed it down, thankful that after three days on the first stage of his journey south, he'd still managed to dodge a dose of the *touristas*.

In an hour, he was scheduled for a meeting with a consular official at the embassy. It should've been America's ambassador, but none was currently available, since the withdrawal of Josephus Daniels on November 9, with no replacement yet appointed by the president.

*A lucky break,* O'Hara thought, and kept on with his breakfast, wondering how bad it might have been.

Throughout Latin America, ambassadors so far were skeptical or downright hostile to the thought of SIS agents roaming unleashed around what most regarded as their quasi-private turf. That attitude was mirrored by some bureaucrats back home, at State, except for one who'd come to a surprise *détente* of sorts with J. Edgar Hoover on his own.

That one was Adolf Berle Jr., a key member of FDR's "Brain Trust," appointed Assistant Secretary of State for Latin American Affairs in March 1938. Berle didn't always see things Hoover's way, but he had opted for a *laissez-faire* approach that gave the SIS free reign up to a point, installing G-men at various embassies and consulates as "legal attachés" while they pursued their undercover work with one eye on discretion and the other on their goals. The postings carried diplomatic status, theoretically exempting SIS agents from interference by the governments they were observing—sometimes undermining—but that wouldn't help with Axis operatives, rogue authorities, or others who desired to see the *Yanquis* swept away.

Legal attachés could send correspondence back to Bureau headquarters in State Department diplomatic pouches, but it was a leap of faith. Whose prying eyes might peer inside, either before they left a given country or after the pouches got to Washington? Berle did his best to oversee the process, but he was a busy bureaucrat himself, and might be gulled by unreliable subordinates. One slip could get an agent killed thousands of miles from home, and there was nothing headquarters could do about it afterward but try to track the slayers down.

That said, not all of Hoover's headaches from the SIS were traceable to State. The U.S. Army's MID launched one such thrust in February 1941, seeking to edge the SIS out of its New York City headquarters. Hoover sat down with Berle and General Sherman Miles before the Interdepartmental Intelligence Committee, delivering an ultimatum to the army: either FBI headquarters would remain in charge, or Miles could have all regions covered by the SIS. Confronted with a bitter choice of all or nothing, Miles reluctantly backed down.

Seven months later, Hoover had to blunt another charge, this time from William Donovan, Edgar's longtime foe and FDR's Coordinator of Information. Unlike General Miles, Wild Bill *wanted* responsibility for all spying below the Rio Grande. That time, Hoover had played it cool, informing Berle that "the Bureau has no feeling one way or another as to whether this transfer should be made." That dropped the ball in Berle's court, and he told the president that SIS had done "an excellent job", prompting Berle to add he was "opposed to having it transferred into untried hands." Donovan tried again before Pearl Harbor, and again Berle used his influence with FDR to shut it down.

So here sat Declan, staring at his empty breakfast plate and waiting for his embassy appointment, fairly certain he'd hear nothing new except complaints of Bureau interloping. That was fine. He'd let the flack's grumbling go in one ear and out the other, file the usual report with headquarters, and go on with the preparations for his next move, farther south.

———

*Moscow: December 17, 1941*

LEONID BABIN HAD DISCOVERED that going to war would be a waste of time. He merely had to wait at NKVD headquarters and let the battle come to him.

Germany had launched "Operation Typhoon" on October 2, running headlong into defenses organized by General Georgi Zhukov, decorated as a Hero of the Soviet Union for his campaigns against Japanese troops in the Russian Far East, and more recently at Leningrad. One patrol reached Khimki, twelve miles northwest of Moscow, but the Nazis would advance no farther. Zhukov had the brutal winter on his side—a lesson Hitler could've learned by studying Napoleon's campaign from 1812—with temperatures dropping below -31 degrees on December 4. General Walther von Brauchitsch, Commander-in-Chief of the German Army, halted his offensive the next day, prompting Red Army troops to counterattack during a heavy blizzard.

One week after the Pearl Harbor raid, temperatures dropped again, immobilizing German tanks. Von Brauchitsch persevered with an advance on the fifteenth, most of the Russian government evacuating to Samara on the Volga River, although Stalin stayed behind to supervise construction of tank traps as the offensive failed once more. Red Army reinforcements landed from Siberia on the eighteenth, one day before Stalin declared a formal state of siege, imposing martial law. The Nazis stalled again, and this time Babin reckoned there would be no coming back.

The same could not be said for Leningrad, besieged by German forces under Field Marshal Wilhelm von Leeb since September 8. Finland was helping the Nazis, with seven divisions led by Marshal Carl Mannerheim. Against them, General Markian Popov commanded thirty-five divisions, six regiments and two brigades. Two weeks in, resistance proved so stubborn that Hitler planned to occupy the city sometime "early next year."

In the meanwhile, what could be done with Leningrad's civilian population of some 3.4 million? Evacuations to the Volga area, the Urals, Siberia and Kazakhstan began in July and would continue sporadically as opportunities presented themselves. But while the city's year-round residents were gradually shuttled out, more than 300,000 refugees arrived from Pskov and Novgorod alone, by late July. Nazis did their best to thin the herd with aerial and artillery bombardment, killing or wounding thousands, destroying Leningrad's largest food depot, the Badajevski General Store, on September 12. Ten days later, Hitler stated what the world already knew: "We have no interest in saving lives of the civilian population." On November 8, in Munich, he proclaimed that Leningrad "must die of starvation."

Supplies were certainly a problem, eased only slightly

since November 20, when Lake Ladoga iced over to create a perilous "Road of Life," soon dubbed by truckers as the "Road of Death." By then, food rationing limited citizens to 125 grams of bread per day, 50 to 60 percent of it sawdust and other indigestible ingredients. NKVD filed its first report of cannibalism in mid-December, listing thirteen cases that included a plumber killing his wife to feed his sons and nieces, plus a mother who suffocated her toddler to keep three older kids alive.

Where would it end?

Only with ultimate annihilation, Babin realized. He'd prefer elimination of the foul *nemtsy*—Germans—but above all else, he must preserve his own life, or the whole of it to date would be a shameful waste.

And that, he knew, might well require every under-handed trick he knew.

———

70 GROSVENOR STREET, *Mayfair, London: December 18, 1941*

COLBY GANTT SAT in the outer office of COI's London head-quarters, cooling his heels twenty feet from his new boss on site. They hadn't met, but Colby knew his man was Frederick Plumber, thirty-six, from Iowa, recruited from the army's Military Intelligence Division after Wild Bill Donovan pulled strings at the Department of War's Munitions Building on Constitution Avenue in Washington.

Gantt *had* met Donovan when he applied to COI and was accepted, days before his transatlantic military flight, expecting to be strafed by Messerschmitt fighters or barraged with ack-ack fire from German ships below. When neither of those things transpired before touchdown at Great West Aerodrome southeast of Heathrow, Colby took it as a sign.

Of what, he couldn't say.

His meeting with Wild Bill had been a revelation. Donovan was in his late fifties, clear-eyed, no spectacles, his white hair parted slightly off-center to the right. He'd worn a double-breasted suit, no sign of his Distinguished Service Medal with an Oak Leaf Cluster from the First World War, no limp from either of the two leg wounds he had received in France. He shook hands like a farmer cracking walnuts, or as if their lives depended on an instant bond—which, Colby supposed, they might someday.

During his application interview, Gantt learned that Donovan had met his father once, when he'd been an assistant to Attorney General Harlan Stone, hanging around the first Justice headquarters on K Street in Washington. If he and Colby's father spoke, Donovan didn't bother going into details, but he did remark that J. Edgar Hoover was "a piece of work."

"They call him Speed, Sir," Colby said.

"That way he talks?"

"Something from high school. Maybe football."

"Huh. I would've thought he was too small." And skipping straight from that to business, "so, you want to join the COI?"

The interview was brief, with Donovan explaining he expected COI to undergo some major changes soon, expanding exponentially now that the country was at war. He'd offered no details, but clearly judged Colby by observation, intuition or whatever. After ten short minutes, he had welcomed Gantt aboard.

Now here he was in London, doing nothing much so far.

As if on cue, the door to Agent Plumber's office opened and the man himself emerged: six foot two at least, his slicked-back hair already thinning at the temples, snazzy in a three-piece sharkskin suit, smelling of cigarettes. He personally ushered Colby into his *sanctum sanctorum*, took his place behind a busy-looking desk, and waved Gantt to a single facing chair.

"So you're the new guy." Plummer's accent came from Brooklyn, maybe from the Bronx.

"Yes, Sir."

"You want to be a spy."

Not asking; telling. Colby answered back, "or whatever you have for me to do, Sir."

"That's the question, isn't it? When you imagine this job, what are you *prepared* to do?"

"Whatever helps the country, Sir."

"Right answer, but I hope you've thought it through. You know, most bureaucrats and diplomats hate spies. Ask them, they'll tell you gentlemen don't read each other's mail or sneak around with whores and burglars, cadging secrets on the sly. They certainly don't *murder* anyone, no matter what the provocation."

Colby saw his opening. "Is killing during wartime murder, Sir?"

Plumber smiled. "What kind of training have you undergone so far?"

"Reading a manual. Beyond that, nothing, Sir."

"Forget the manual. It's a plan laid out for stodgy congressmen who don't read other people's mail and haven't got the first idea of how to win a war. Of course, that doesn't mean they won't *use* spies, but they'll feel guilty while they're sipping chilled martinis at the country club."

Colby allowed himself a smile but said nothing.

"Are you enjoying London, Agent Gantt?"

"So far, Sir, what I've seen of it."

"Well, have yourself a night out on the town if you can manage it. Tomorrow, you fly back."

"Back, Sir? You mean the States?"

Plumber frowned thoughtfully. "Let's wait and see about that, Gantt. You have a lot to learn before we drop you in the shit."

———

*FBI Headquarters: December 19, 1941*

Aloysius Gantt was swamped with information flowing to the Bureau from Pearl Harbor and environs in Hawaii, where the Honolulu field office had suffered through a hit-and-miss existence for the past decade. Opened in April 1931 with a single agent, Joe McFarland, the "office" handled fugitive and immigration matters till it closed in 1934, reopened in '37 with the same one-man staff, then closed again in '38, finally rebounding for good in August 1939 under SAC Robert Shivers.

Despite his stated wish to safeguard the Japanese residing on the islands, Shivers got permission from the Chief to start detentions on December 7, while bombs were still falling on Pearl. Before day's end, generally without warrants, he'd arrested some 1,200 *Issei*—first-generation immigrants—whose names were on a list of suspected enemies. Those caged included priests, teachers in language schools, newspaper editors and community organization leaders, slated for evacuation to detention camps on the mainland. Second-generation *Nisei* weren't being arrested yet, merely subjected to restrictions on their travel, social gatherings, and work hours.

Meanwhile, the butcher's bill was mounting at Pearl Harbor. The latest word: more than 350 Japanese bombers and fighters had staged a two-wave attack, damaging seventeen ships that included all three of the Pacific Fleet battleships, one ex-battleship used for training, three cruisers, three destroyers, and four auxiliary ships, with an estimated death toll of 1,800. At six nearby airfields, where planes were cunningly parked close together from fear of creeping saboteurs, 328 military aircraft were wrecked or damaged, another 244 men killed by bombs or gunfire.

Against those stunning damages, the Japanese lost twenty-nine planes, with another seventy-four reportedly damaged by antiaircraft fire. Fifty-five airmen died in the attack, plus nine submariners—and one unhappy ensign was caught alive after his disabled craft was stranded on Oahu's Waimanalo Beach.

Five days after the attack, Secretary of the Navy Frank Knox landed in Hawaii bearing FDR's command: find out what happened to the fleet, and how. Thirty-six hours later, Knox—an ex-newspaperman and failed Republican vice presidential candidate in 1936—issued a report that minimized the damages, praised U.S. heroism under fire, and blamed an unsubstantiated "Japanese fifth column" for the raid. Still questioning how Pearl was taken by complete surprise, just yesterday the president had named Supreme Court Justice Owen Roberts chairman of a full commission to investigate further.

Which wouldn't be the end of it, Gantt realized. Not even close.

And J. Edgar Hoover, true to form, had yet to mention Duško Popov's prescient warning of the raid, delivered and rejected four months in advance. He had an eye on someone he could blame, though; namely, James Lawrence Fly, chairman of FDR's Federal Communications Commission since September 1939. They'd clashed the first time over wiretapping in September 1940, five years after the practice had been banned by federal law. Hoover didn't care, and wrote a bitchy letter to the president complaining, but Roosevelt ignored him. Next, in February 1941, Alabama congressman Sam Hobbs introduced a bill to authorize government taps if agents "suspected" felonies in progress. Attorney General Robert Jackson supported the bill, but Fly opposed it and Congress defeated it in May, leaving Hoover to the only other tricks he knew: building a dossier on Fly and publicly smearing his patriotism.

Ex-judge Francis Biddle replaced Jackson at Justice in August, wielding the Espionage Act of 1917 in a bid to silence "vermin publications" such as Father Charles Coughlin's anti-Semitic weekly magazine *Social Justice*. At the same time, he created "The Biddle List," a roster of eleven organizations he deemed subversive. Curiously, despite Biddle's distaste for Coughlin, only leftist groups were listed, branded as fronts for the Communist Party.

*Nothing to rile J. Edgar Hoover there,* Gantt thought, and turned back to his stack of files.

———

*Little Italy, Manhattan: December 20, 1941*

If there was one "good thing" about Pearl Harbor, Greg Jordan decided, it was that the shock distracted nearly all Americans from focusing upon the trials and tribulations of the Syndicate. It knocked Abe Reles off front pages citywide, diverted curiosity from Lepke's ongoing appeals, and generally made Americans forget about the Mob. The drifting smoke from Pearl even obscured a press release from Albany, three days after the raid, when New York's Court of Appeals reversed Irving Nitzberg's murder conviction for killing stoolie Albert Shuman in 1939 and ordered a new trial by a vote of four to three. The problem, as they saw it: Judge James Wallace had suspended a sentence of seven to fifteen years on witness David Price, convicted robber, to make Price corroborate testimony from Reles, Allie Tannenbaum, and Blue Jaw Magoon.

Last but not least, Isidore Juffe, linchpin in Special Prosecutor John Amen's botched frame-up of Joe Adonis and Sam Gasberg, had died on December 18 in what the *Times* referred to as "obscurity." It was no less than he deserved, in Greg's opinion, and the sooner he was underground, the better.

Jordan had more pressing matters on his mind these days, with gangland warfare temporarily on hold. The global war was threatening his family, with the Selective Service Act amended in November to permit induction of eighteen-year-olds. Next year, Jordan's son David would attain that age, as would his nephew Dominic, son of his elder brother Carlo. Jordan was already looking into angles for deferment. David would be entering Columbia University as a freshman one month before his birthday, and if student deferments were canceled, there was still the IV-F angle for registrants deemed unacceptable due to some "physical, mental, or moral defect."

The "moral" part might cover Dominic, who'd logged a couple of street gang-related juvenile arrests, but David had a clean record, and as a high school athlete couldn't be considered physically unfit. As for the mental aspect, Jordan had no doubt that he could dig up a psychologist to furnish any diagnosis he desired, but that would be a blot on David's record that could dog him to his grave, blighting his prospects for employment anywhere outside the Syndicate.

Something to think about and worry over for the next ten months, along with anything the feds or various D.A.s devised in the meantime to make his life a misery.

———

*FEDERAL BUREAU of Narcotics Manhattan Field Office: December 22, 1941*

IKE SAWYER COULDN'T CLAIM Pearl Harbor took him by surprise. Ten years of Japanese expansionism in the Far East clearly pointed to a global war, and Tokyo always enjoyed a sneak attack. Was it an accident the Japanese ambassador only delivered Tōjō's declaration of hostilities *after* the raid on Pearl?

Hardly.

The only bright spots: Ike was too old to be drafted, while Payton, the eldest of his three surviving children, wouldn't turn eighteen till 1947. No war in the country's modern history had lasted that long, and Ike saw no reason to believe this one would set a record.

At work, Harry Anslinger's flood of articles attacking weed had tapered to a dribble lately, only four published within the past two years. That said, the FBN was still enthusiastically pursuing any marijuana case that fell within its jurisdiction, 39.8 percent of federal drug prosecutions for this year.

Elsewhere, Generalissimo Chiang Kai-shek had ordered "complete suppression" of opium poppies in China, mandating the death penalty for cultivation, manufacturing of opium, or selling it. That might impress the U.S. State Department, but to Sawyer it was just another smokescreen masking the illicit trade that kept Chiang and his Green Gang backers flush with cash. That took a lot of sales, since one *yuan* these days was worth some fifteen cents American.

One FBN agent who'd turned into a star was Garland Williams, first ever to train dogs for sniffing out narcotics. He'd been wooed away by the Army War College in January, presently teaching counter-espionage courses in Chicago. Another standout, George Hunter White, reminded those who met him of a Buddha statue, pudgy to a fault, but he possessed a knack for posing as Chinese that would've made Lon Chaney envious. In that disguise, he'd wormed his way into the Hip Sing Tong, taking its oath in fluent Cantonese. In 1937, based on his collected information, FBN agents had jailed seventy-five Hip Sings for smuggling and related charges. One year later, working undercover, White had gunned down Gotham dealer Albert "Tuffy" Jackson.

Sawyer knew the coming war years would provide no shortage of pursuits for FBN agents. As far as conflict overseas went, he had trouble understanding any Negro who enlisted voluntarily to dig ditches or serve as stevedores for the United States. Granted, it was their country just as much as any white man's, theoretically, but thirty-five out of the forty-eight states still had Jim Crow statutes on their books. The Deep South seemed hopeless, and Mississippi worst of all, scorned the First Amendment with a law that punished any written matter "urging social equality" between races.

Even cutting Dixie from the picture, though, that still left twenty-five states that discriminated legally against minorities. Fifteen outlawed miscegenation, twelve boasted "separate but equal" schools, five restricted voting in defiance of the Constitution, four segregated housing, four banned interracial adoptions, two had separate railroads and streetcars, and two divided all public accommodations and recreational facilities. California restricted the hiring of Asians. Kentucky segregated nursing homes, and Oklahoma went all-out with Jim Crow hearses, phone booths, and locker rooms for miners.

Even in the nation's capital, where FDR had created a Fair Employment Practice Committee in June and First Lady Eleanor Roosevelt met with black groups the FBI deemed "radical," Negroes faced discrimination in public schools and recreational facilities, still battling back from the bad old days under Woodrow Wilson.

Worse yet, in Sawyer's view, were 1941's five lynchings to date, reported from four southern states since February. The most startling had occurred on Georgia's Fort Benning, where nineteen-year-old Negro Private Felix Hall was found hanging on March 28, six weeks and three days since his white civilian boss on the base had threatened Hall's life. When found, Hall was in uniform, hands tied behind him, feet bound with baling wire, hanging by his neck from a sapling. A military doctor certified Hall's death as homicide, but now army "investigators" called it suicide. G-men identified two likely suspects at Fort Benning, but the case was going nowhere fast.

*My country?* Sawyer asked himself, and was disturbed to say no ready answer came to mind.

---

*Camp Pendleton: December 29, 1941*

"THIS IS MY RIFLE, this is my gun! This is for fighting, this is for fun!"

Nolan O'Hara paused while spit-shining his boots to watch the boot who'd barged into the barracks in full field gear, brandishing a rifle overhead, his trouser fly open, clutching his penis with his free hand. Nolan felt an urge to laugh but swallowed it, knowing this punishment was standard for marines who made the critical mistake of calling service-issued rifles "guns." The blushing boot would have to shout this litany in every barracks on the base, for screwing up the Creed of the United States Marine.

It was one of the first things they had learned in camp, compelled to memorize the words, ready to parrot them for any DI who demanded it.

*THIS IS MY RIFLE. There are many like it, but this one is mine. My rifle is my best friend. It is my life. I must master it as I must master my life.*

*Without me, my rifle is useless. Without my rifle, I am useless. I must fire my rifle true. I must shoot straighter than my enemy who is trying to kill me. I must shoot him before he shoots me. My rifle and I have love knowing that what counts in war is not the rounds we fire, the noise of our burst, nor the smoke we make. We know that it is the hits that count. My rifle is human, even as I, because it is my life. I will keep my rifle clean and ready, even as I am clean and ready. We will become part of each other. Before God, I swear this creed. My rifle and myself are the defenders of my country. We are the masters of our enemy. We are the saviors of my life. So be it, until there is no enemy, but peace. Amen.*

THAT WASN'T ALL they'd learned, of course. Other training ranged from indoctrination and military courtesy to inspections, interior guarding, drills and marching, scouting and patrolling, sanitation and first aid, defense against chemical warfare, unarmed combat, fighting with pugil sticks, and bayonet training with shouts of "Kill!" as they skewered dummies.

Nolan was surprised to find that his best times in camp were on the firing range. He'd seen his father's gun at home but hadn't handled one before, discovering he had an unexpected taste for it. As promised, they had worked their way up from small .22s to the same .30-'06 MI917 Enfield rifles that had seen American fighters through the last World War, fitted with vicious sixteen-inch MI905 bayonets. Aside from that, they practiced night and day with Winchester trench guns, Browning Automatic Rifles, .45 Colt automatics, Tommy guns and Reising submachine guns, on up to the whole line of Browning machine guns: the water-cooled MI917AI, air-cooled MI919, and their big brother, the ass-kicking .50-caliber M2HB.

For variety, the boots lobbed "pineapples"—the Mk2 antipersonnel grenade—and learned to handle MI flamethrowers, weighing in at seventy-two pounds, including five gallons of fuel, with a top range of sixteen yards. For longer range and targets out of sight, they mastered the M2 60-mm mortar, capable of launching three-pound shells over a mile.

For hand-to-hand combat, their trainers specialized in dirty tricks, reminding boots that there were no fair fights unless you won and walked away. Aside from bayonets, their only cutting weapon was the Mark I trench knife from the last World War, its brass knuckle-duster grip weighing a pound and fitted with a pommel meant specifically for cracking skulls.

At night, if they weren't rousted from their barracks for surprise patrols or moonlight runs, boots listened to the radio and wished—some more than others—they could jump into the action overseas.

Japan had not been idle since Pearl Harbor. On the very next day, they'd captured the Gilbert Islands, bombed Clark Field in the Philippines, attacked Thailand, Hong Kong, and British Malaya. Two days later, they sank the British warships HMS *Repulse* and *Prince of Wales* in the South China Sea. Marines repelled them at Wake Island, while invaders penetrated Burma, stormed Borneo, and landed on the southern Philippine Islands. A second attempt on Wake failed two days before Christmas, as General Douglas MacArthur declared Manila an "open city," retreating to Bataan Peninsula. Mitsubishi bombers, code-named "Betty" by the Allies, dumped their loads over Rangoon. Hong Kong surrendered to the Japanese on Christmas Day, and paratroopers had descended on Sumatra only yesterday.

*I'm missing out on all of it,* thought Nolan. *When do we start fighting back, and will I even be a part of it?*

Patience. He had to graduate from boot camp first, become a sure as shit gung-ho marine, and maybe then he'd get his taste of blood.

And if his luck went south, maybe he'd choke on it.

# CHAPTER 2

DEVON GANTT LOVED workouts at the firing range with other FBI trainees. The *pop-crack-boom* of pistols, rifles, shotguns, and the nonstop rattling of automatic weapons always gave his blood pressure a boost. Above all, he liked punching holes in man-sized silhouettes, each with a mugshot of John Dillinger scowling down range.

Devon was vague on details, but he knew Director Hoover had negotiated terms with the Marine Corps back in 1934 to use their base southwest of Washington for firearms and other physical training, then leased space to erect a three-story training academy building on the main section of the base in 1940. Gantt enjoyed the thirty-five-mile early-morning drive from D.C. and had taken naturally to the classes, poring over crime statistics, court cases, arrest procedure, and whatever else the teachers threw at him.

His father had been right about finessing Hoover into an appointment for the war's duration, while Devon kept up his night school classes at GW's law school. It was a come-down after Yale, but what the hell. The FBI's Director was a graduate and couldn't really bitch.

The bad part about night school was the time he missed with his fiancée, Camille Perry, daughter of a chef in Arlington whose restaurant had weathered the Depression, and now was considering a second spot in Alexandria if he could swing the financing. Camille was twenty, raven-haired and willowy, demure in conversation but a tiger in the sack since Devon had proposed—as long as they were careful and he didn't knock her up before the wedding, scheduled for this coming Saturday at First Presbyterian. Gantt loved her to the best of his ability, and reckoned it was time to settle down.

Whatever that meant.

Anyway, barring some really dumb mistake, he had a good career lined up, a brother who was going places in a varied but related field, and all the opportunities a global war could offer.

Who could ask for more?

---

*FBI Headquarters: January 24, 1942*

Agent Aloysius Gantt closed the newly issued report of the Roberts Commission, assessing the Pearl Harbor raid, and wondered whether its verdict would withstand close scrutiny.

Aside from Justice Roberts, the report was signed by four other presidential appointees: ex-Admiral William Standley, Chief of Naval Operations from 1933 to '37, now ambassador to the Soviet Union; Admiral Joseph Reeves, Commander-in-Chief of the U.S. Fleet from 1934 to his retirement in '36, recalled to active duty in May 1940; General Frank McCoy, interim commander of the First United States Army in 1938, retired that October, recalled in 1941 to serve on the commission; and Brigadier General Joseph McNarney, chief of a special U.S. Army observer group in London before Pearl Harbor.

The commission had questioned 127 witnesses in Washington and Honolulu, including code-breakers involved with "MAGIC," a decryption program shared by the Army's Signals Intelligence Service and the Navy's Communication Special Unit. On December 6, 1941, they'd intercepted a fourteen-part message sent from Tokyo to Ambassador Kichisaburō Nomura in Washington, predicting the strike against Pearl, but the crucial sections hadn't been decoded till a week after the raid. On top of that embarrassment, MAGIC was top secret and couldn't be exposed to anyone outside the "need-to-know" intelligence community.

So, who to blame?

There were the Japanese, of course. As the report declared, "there were, prior to December 7, 1941, Japanese spies on the island of Oahu. Some were Japanese consular agents and others were persons having no open relations with the Japanese foreign service. These spies collected and, through various channels transmitted, information to the Japanese Empire respecting the military and naval establishments and dispositions on the island."

All nice and vague, perhaps including Caucasians hired by Japan's *Tokubetsu Kōtō Keisatsu* intelligence service. In fact, Gantt knew one's name: Takeo Yoshikawa, fingered by Duško Popov in his fruitless meeting with J. Edgar Hoover in August 1941—a revelation still suppressed by the Director.

Guilt must be assigned, however, and in the commission's eyes it settled on Admiral Husband Kimmel, Commander in Chief of the U.S. Pacific Fleet, and Lieutenant General Walter Short, responsible for the defense of U.S. military installations in Hawaii. As the commission spelled it out: "In the light of the warnings and directions to take appropriate action, transmitted to both commanders between November 27 and December 7, and the obligation under the system of coordination then in effect for joint cooperative action on their part, it was a dereliction of duty on the part of each of them not to consult and confer with the other respecting the meaning and intent of the warnings, and the appropriate measures of defense required by the imminence of hostilities. The attitude of each, that he was not required to inform himself of, and his lack of interest in, the measures undertaken by the other to carry out the responsibility assigned to each other under the provisions of the plans then in effect, demonstrated on the part of each a lack of appreciation of the responsibilities vested in them and inherent in their positions."

Both commanders were relieved of duty and would soon retire, Ford to head the traffic department at a Ford Motor Company plant in Dallas, Kimmel to work for another ex-admiral turned civil engineer, Frederic Harris in New York.

Call it a ritual hand washing or a human sacrifice, but Gantt was confident he hadn't heard the last about Pearl Harbor yet. Would Hoover ever fess up to his blunder with Popov that might have foiled the sneak attack?

*Sure thing,* Gantt thought. *Just like a snowball's chance in Hell.*

———

*RIO DE JANEIRO, Brazil: January 29, 1942*

DECLAN O'HARA WASN'T PLEASED to be leaving the Copaca-bana Palace Hotel, but the place cost a mint and SIS Chief Percy Foxworth kept a sharp eye on expenses from his office in New York.

Besides, O'Hara's work was done, at least for now.

Just yesterday, President Vargas had severed relations with the Axis powers, paving the way for creation of a Brazil-United States Political-Military Agreement to discourage Axis influence in South America. Under that treaty, Vargas granted the U.S. permission to establish air bases, while Washington "encouraged" creation of a Brazilian iron industry, handsomely profiting both native investors and their bankers Stateside. The blowback: German and Italian submarines were already retaliating, sinking Brazilian merchant ships and running up a butch-er's bill that ran into the hundreds.

Not that that was *bad,* entirely, since the deaths at sea were pushing Vargas and his National Congress closer to all-out war with the Axis. What could Brazil contribute in the scheme of things? Soldiers to fight in Europe, maybe, while the navy and air force pitched in to help the Allies with the ever-growing Battle of the Atlantic.

Adolf Berle and the Director were still more or less simpatico in Washington, despite Hoover's aversion to working closely with State or any other government depart-ment. When Berle expressed concern that SIS intelligence collection was overlooking South America's lower classes, Hoover had fired off a memo reading: "Take steps at once to cover this aspect." Above all else, the Chief feared personal embarrassment after spending the past decade promoting the Bureau as an agency that always got its man, woman, whatever. In a recent meeting with FBI Assistant Director Quinn Tamm, Berle had declared himself "more than ever convinced of the absolute necessity for so handling this situation as to insure the continuation of SIS operations in the Western Hemisphere solely and exclusively by the Bureau."

Problem solved.

Now all they had to do was win the war, while Declan and wife Abigail—4,800 miles apart and usually out of touch—worried about their son in the Marine Corps and whatever might await him on some foreign battlefield.

———

*FEDERAL BUREAU of Narcotics Field Office, Manhattan: March 5, 1942*

EUGENIO GIANNINI WAS SWEATING like a pig, and with good reason. Facing him across a wooden table scarred by cigarette burns, bolted to the floor of a ten-by-twelve interview room, Ike Sawyer knew he had the *mafioso* by the short hairs and he was prepared to twist.

Giannini was thirty-six, a product of Calabria, raised in the Bronx after his parents immigrated. As a boxer in his teens he'd had an admirable record, but by 1927 he had drifted into crime, serving time for robbery and packing a concealed weapon. In 1934 he pulled another holdup, killing a cop and wounding three bystanders in the process, but he'd skated on those charges and become a soldier for Tommaso Gagliano's Mafia family. Gagliano had his hands full, navigating choppy waters on *la Commissione* against an alliance of the Mangano and Magaddino families, and the last thing that he needed was a federal narcotics prosecution.

But here sat Eugenio, caught red-handed with a load of Chinese heroin and looking at hard time. Looking at worse, perhaps, if Gagliano got pissed off enough to put him on the spot.

Which meant he might be open to a deal.

"You don't know what you're askin'," Giannini whined. "I ain't no rat."

"You won't be anything," Sawyer replied, "if Tommy gets his back up over this and takes you out."

"That how you play this game? Blackmail?"

Ike snorted. "Says the paragon of law and order."

"Hey, how do I even know you got the juice to swing a deal? Gimme a *white* fed, maybe we work somethin' out."

"Fuck you!" Ike spat at him. "You either deal with *me,* or I go drop a dime to Tommy. What's it gonna be, Eugenio?"

An anguished moment's hesitation, then: "Awright. Whadda you want from me?"

"Not much," Ike said. "Just everything you know about the family."

If only it could always be this easy. Six weeks ago, in Chi-Town, FBN informant Dorothy Sullivan had been scheduled to testify against two heroin peddlers but she never made it to court. Instead, she'd fallen—screaming and on fire, a "flaming bundle of rags" as one witness described it—from an eighth-floor window of an office building on South Dearborn. Who had struck the match and pushed her to her death remained a mystery.

Some other things in FDR's America weren't so mysterious at all. On the same day Sullivan became a plunging comet in Chicago, "Imperial Wizard" James Colescott had been gently—*very* gently—questioned by the Dies Committee. They were looking into fascism but didn't mind the Klan's homegrown variety, especially since Colescott lauded the committee every chance he got. It must've stung, admitting that he only had 10,000 Kluxers paying dues these days, but part of that was due to purging all "extremists" from the ranks. Dies criticized the Klan for bashing Catholics, but Alabama's Joe Starnes praised the order for being "just as American as the Baptist or Methodist Church, as the Lions Club or the Rotary Circle." Soon afterward, reporters spotted Colescott in the audience at an Atlanta Elk's Lodge, avidly applauding speaker Martin Dies.

Lynchings still continued, most recently in Sikeston, Missouri, where police accused a Negro, Cleo Wright, of invading a white woman's home and doing his best to eviscerate her, though she managed to live. Cops shot Wright four times during his arrest, then drove him to a hospital where doctors wouldn't treat black folks. From there, they took their prisoner to jail, expecting him to die, but local lynchers couldn't wait. Before noon on that Sunday, they'd stormed the jail, dragged Wright outside, killed him and torched his corpse in full view of the worshipers at two adjoining Negro churches in the town's ghetto.

Meanwhile, Detroit's Housing Commission had opened a Negro project called Sojourner Truth, after the famed 19th-century black woman abolitionist, on the outskirts of an all-white Polish neighborhood. The racist residents turned out in force, attacking Negroes, scuffling with police while Mayor Ed Jeffries tried to keep the peace. The press reported forty injuries and 220 arrests—all but three of them Negroes, which even the *New York Times* found bizarre. A federal grand jury finally indicted Eugene Sage, founder of the Klan-like Black Legion, and Garland Alderman, a leader of the pro-Nazi National Workers League, for conspiracy to incite rioting, then gave up and dropped the case prior to trial.

In short, business as usual.

And how long would it be before the Ike felt the flames of racial violence closer to home?

────────

CATOCTIN MOUNTAIN PARK, *Maryland: April 7, 1942*

FRED PLUMBER HADN'T BEEN KIDDING when he'd told Colby Gantt he had a lot to learn and must prepare himself for any kind of duty with the COI. He'd already been to "Camp X" in Canada—officially British Special Training School No. 103 on the northwestern shore of Lake Ontario—where future U.S. agents were welcomed to train with Allied and foreign firearms while learning sabotage techniques, subversion, intelligence gathering, lock picking, demolition, radio communications including Morse code, silent killing and unarmed combat, plus recruiting techniques for anti-fascist partisans. Run by Britain's Secret Intelligence Service, Camp X was so hush-hush that Canadian Prime Minister William King was reportedly kept in the dark on its operations.

Now, toughened considerably and aware of what he might be called upon to do for God and country, Colby was at COI Training Area B in the Maryland wilderness, studying cryptography, more demolition, and more hand-to-hand combat. The daily regimen began with calisthenics and moved on from there to perilous climbing exercises and scrambling around on a huge timbered jungle-gym dangling from ropes forty feet in the air. Obstacles included sheer cliffs, rushing rivers, live machine-gun fire, and explosive booby traps like the one that had recently broken recruit William Colby's jaw when he snagged a tripwire.

Others had also fumbled on their early exercises, like Moe Berg, ex-catcher for the Boston Red Sox and other teams that dated from the Twenties. Sent to infiltrate a Baltimore defense plant, he'd been captured by the FBI and had to start all over, red-faced, at square one.

And then, there was the "house of horrors." First, recruits learned instinctive gunfighting, ducking and "double-tapping" human targets in lieu of lining up like ancient duelists on the firing range. When they had mastered that, to their instructor's satisfaction, they were called out individually in the dead of night, presented with a .45 and two full magazines, instructed to locate and kill a Nazi soldier hiding somewhere in a log cabin that proved to be a maze, where dummies in Axis uniforms rushed toward them randomly, propelled by wires. Failure to "kill" the enemies in residence meant failure period, with repetition of the course, of simply washing out.

Colby had passed with flying colors his first time around.

Soon, he'd be headed for advanced training Area A; sprawling over 15,000 acres in the western sector of the Chopawamsic Recreational Demonstration Area, adjacent to Virginia's Marine Corps Base Quantico where his twin brother Devon was earning his place as an FBI agent. They likely wouldn't see each other there, but that was fine. They could catch up another time, compare notes.

For now, Colby was focused on becoming the best spy and killer he could be.

He knew, without too many classified specifics, that the COI had penetrated China in January but was facing opposition both from General Dai Li, Chiang Kai-shek's chief of internal security, and from Captain Milton Miles, commander of U.S. Naval Group China. At the same time, Bill Donovan had established offices in Stockholm and in Cairo—covering Syria, Lebanon, Palestine, Transjordan, Iraq, Saudi Arabia, Iran, Afghanistan and Turkey. Efforts in Spain and Portugal were lagging, thanks to U.S. Ambassador Alexander Weddell, who condemned as "un-American" the act of spying on "friendly" fascist nations. Even so, agents in Lisbon and Madrid had safe houses set up, arranging passage for Frenchmen en route to join Free French forces in North Africa.

Another dicey spot was Burma, where COI Detachment 101 was gearing up for action behind enemy lines. Led by Captain Carl Eifler, an ex-Customs agent recruited from the U.S. Army Reserve, the unit instantly collided with General Joseph "Vinegar Joe" Stilwell, U.S. Chief of Staff to Chiang Kai-shek and Commander-in-Chief of the Allied forces in the China-Burma-India Theater. Stilwell disdained guerrilla action as "illegal shadow boxing," telling Eifler at their first meeting, "I didn't send for you and I don't want you."

Stilwell, however, had more pressing problems on his mind. In May of 1942 he had evacuated Burma with 114 Americans, leaving behind a Chinese force that Chiang considered his "best army" for a grueling nine-day trek to India. Finally arriving in China, Stilwell settled into an unpleasant rapprochement with Chiang and Dai Li. Chiang professed "full confidence and trust" in Stilwell, while habitually countermanding his orders to Chinese generals. Stilwell kept a diary of Chiang's corruption—380 million stolen Allied dollars and counting—while code-naming Chiang "Peanut" in official transmissions and dubbing him "the little dummy" in private conversations. Tiring of the dance, Chiang complained to U.S. diplomats about Stilwell's "recklessness, insubordination, contempt and arrogance," demanding his recall after Stilwell urged collaboration between Nationalist forces and Mao Zedong's communists. Washington demurred and kept the money flowing, even as 60 percent of Chiang's recruits failed basic training, 40 percent deserting and another 20 percent starving to death before they could complete the course.

It was a world of hurt out there, and Colby would be muddling through the middle of it soon. Whatever happened when he hit the ground running, wherever he was sent, he meant to be among the COI's survivors when the smoke eventually cleared.

———

*LITTLE ITALY, Manhattan: May 13, 1942*

GREG JORDAN COULDN'T OPEN up a newspaper these days without finding acquaintances in trouble with the law. It was the nature of his business, granted, but it still chafed on his nerves, particularly when the blows fell close to home.

In California, Ben Siegel and Frankie Carbo went to trial in January for the Harry Greenberg murder. Widow Ida Greenberg testified against them, though she hadn't seen it happen, while a movie studio employee fingered Carbo fleeing from the scene. Allie Tannenbaum also appeared, admitting that he brought the murder weapons from New York. Despite all that, Judge A. A. Scott dismissed Bugsy's indictment, citing insufficient evidence. The jury dead-locked over Carbo, after he produced a hotel reservation from Seattle for the murder's date, his presence there confirmed by manager and maids. Judge Scott scheduled a retrial, then dismissed that count as well, when Bill O'Dwyer wouldn't let star witness Tannenbaum fly out a second time.

That was the end of Greenberg's case and Allie Tannenbaum as well, fried with Happy Maione at Sing Sing on February 19. Max Golob, on the other hand, escaped the reaper, pleading his Brooklyn murder charge down to second-degree assault with the D.A.'s approval.

Four days after that charade, the Syndicate finally caught a break. The French ocean liner SS *Normandie,* launched in 1935 and was seized by the U.S. Navy for conversion to a troop ship five days after Pearl Harbor, caught fire at Pier 88 on the Hudson River. Firefighters failed to save it —or a watchman whom the blaze consumed—and the debate was still ongoing as to whether it had been an accident or Axis sabotage.

Backing the latter claim were Nazi submarines lurking offshore, sinking twenty-three merchant ships between the Pearl attack and February 6, dooming 157 tons of cargo and 581 seamen without a single U-boat lost. With all the talk of spies and saboteurs, impending strikes and thefts of vital war supplies, where could the military turn for help?

Who ran the docks? The Mafia.

It started with a random thought, half serious, from Commander Charles Haffenden at the Office of Naval Intelligence security unit in Gotham. Captain Roscoe MacFall, chief intelligence officer of the Third Naval District, reached out to Joseph "Socks" Lanza, Mafia boss of the Fulton Fish Market, the East Coast's top wholesale source for seafood, seeking cooperation. A member of the Luciano family, Lanza replied that only Lucky could deliver on the promise sought by ONI, but it would have a price.

Specifically, Lucky hated the spartan life at Dannemora

and desired a transfer to some penitentiary more civilized and closer to Manhattan. After touching base with D.A. Frank Hogan and the NYPD, the two sides struck a deal. "Operation Underworld" would be headquartered at the Hotel Astor on Times Square, and Luciano would be moved to Great Meadow State Prison in Fort Ann, 127 miles south of Dannemora and 211 miles north of Manhattan. It wasn't perfect, but still a better lockup and a shorter drive for Luciano's friends including Meyer Lansky, Frank Costello, his attorneys and the ONI.

Meanwhile, Socks got busy with the aid of Albert Anastasia and brother Tough Tony, planting extra spotters on the waterfront to sniff out spies, suppress "radical" labor leaders, direct ONI break-in teams to hotel suites that needed searching, and eliminate suspected saboteurs by any means available. At least two Nazi agents—if they *were* Nazis— were treated to a one-way ride by Cockeye Dunn and his thugs from the International Longshoremen's Association, and it didn't hurt when mobsters joined the local fishing fleets, to make damned sure no one was radioing U-boats out at sea.

While that went on, persons unknown lifted the "WANTED" cards on Anastasia and accomplice Anthony Romeo from police files on the order of D.A. O'Dwyer. Romeo didn't last, found murdered for squealing in Delaware one day before Anastasia joined the army as a private assigned to Camp Upton, New York. He was later promoted to private first class, then staff sergeant and technical sergeant, finally landing at Pennsylvania's Indiantown Gap Military Reservation, where he used his only skill, aside from theft and murder, training future stevedores. In return, a grateful government made him a U.S. citizen.

Vito Genovese, the former acting boss of Luciano's

family, had gone his own way as a fugitive in Italy, snuggling up to Mussolini's son-in-law and foreign minister, Count Galeazzo Ciano, donating $250,000 for construction of a new National Fascist Party headquarters. He also curried favor with *Il Duce* by placing a transatlantic contract on the head of Carlo Tresca, an immigrant newspaperman and leftist labor leader who never tired of publicly counting the ways he despised Mussolini. In return, Vito trusted the fascists to ignore his lucrative black market trade and guarantee he didn't share the fate of other *mafiosi,* jailed or shot by Mussolini's firing squads.

Whatever worked, the Mob would find a way.

Greg Jordan hoped he and his family would have the same good fortune as the global war dragged on.

———

*FBI Headquarters: March 18, 1942*

Aloysius Gantt had seen it coming from the day the Robertson Commission published its report, but he hadn't envisioned how the action would play out, the scope it would involve. Remembering the First World War, his own role in the "slacker raids," he now supposed he should've known.

It started on the West Coast, naturally, nearest to Japan, where Governor Culbert Olson said of his constituents, "They feel they are living in the midst of enemies. They don't trust the Japanese, none of them." It hadn't started out that way: immediately after Pearl, the *Los Angeles Times* opined that most *Nisei* and *Sansei*, their children, were "good Americans, born and educated as such," loyal to the USA.

That changed within six weeks, when "native sons" began campaigning for removal of all Japanese—and, incidentally —sale of their property at drastic cut-rate prices to prospective white buyers. Director Hoover made light of "fifth column" fears at first, but there was nothing he could do when Washington demanded that all "enemy aliens" first register at local post offices, then surrender their cameras, short-wave receivers and transmitters, while carrying "enemy alien registration cards" at all times. Attorney General Biddle defended those moves with statistics from Justice: 1.1 million enemy aliens occupying America, including 92,000 Japanese, 315,000 Germans, and 695,000 Italians. Oddly, given that disparity, most of the 2,972 arrested by then were Japanese, versus 231 Italians, most of them journalists, language teachers, and members of veterans' groups.

On February 19, FDR had signed Executive Order 9066, authorizing the Secretary of War to prescribe "military zones" from which "any or all persons may be excluded." In short order, that included all of California plus parts of Oregon, Washington, and Arizona. One month later came Executive Order 9102, creating a War Relocation Authority led by Milton Eisenhower, Director of Information for the Department of Agriculture, empowered "to provide for the removal from designated areas of persons whose removal is necessary in the interests of national security."

Where would it end? Behind barbed wire, if Gantt's surmise was accurate.

Some mostly-barren states were willing to have camps erected on their soil; others were not. Wyoming Governor Nels Smith had cautioned FDR, "If you bring Japanese into my state, I promise you they will be hanging from every tree."

Meanwhile, the Bureau was compiling files on 1.2 million German immigrants, plus 11 million with one or two German-born parents. Italians were another problem, clear-cut enemies swiftly arrested under the Sedition Act of 1918, others awaiting review on a case-by-case basis. Removal and internment of suspects required no concrete evidence of any crime, as Japanese Americans were swiftly finding out.

Gantt hoped he wouldn't have to lend a hand in the removals, but with war fever sweeping the nation, who could count on anything? As for his sons, Colby was off to new adventures with the COI, while Devon was among the new recruits at Bureau headquarters, awaiting his assignment to a field office once he'd been through the training course.

Something to think about, while the whole planet went to hell.

———

*Moscow: March 31, 1942*

Spring took its time breaking the Russian winter, and for many it would not come soon enough.

News bulletins at NKVD headquarters told Leonid Babin that the siege of Leningrad was killing off an average 100,000 citizens per month, most of them starving to death. In early January, Stalin had tried to relieve Leningrad with the ill-conceived "Lyuban Operation," resulting in destruction of his 2nd Shock Army and capture of its leader Andrey Vlasov, recruited from his prison cell by Heinrich Himmler to become a Nazi propagandist. At the same time, "Operation Spark" had likewise failed to lift the siege, inflicting heavy losses on Kirill Meretskov's 8th Army, compelling him to blame subordinates and leading to their execution by the NKVD in late February.

News from Moscow was slightly better—with the emphasis on "slightly." General Georgy Zhukov had launched a major offensive on January 5, pushing the battered, freezing *Wehrmacht* back 150 miles from the Soviet capital before the advance stalled two days later. A week after that, the Red Army captured Kirov and Medya, breaking the spine of Operation Barbarossa, but Hitler's henchmen were distracted by a meeting in the Berlin suburb of Wannsee, where SS *Obergruppenführer*'s Reinhard Heydrich spelled out details of the "final solution to the Jewish problem."

*Sheer insanity,* thought Babin, while the Red Army prepared to meet "Operation Fredericus," an Axis counteroffensive around Kharkov, in eastern Ukraine. That battle could go either way, with *Generalfeldmarschall* Fedor von Bock's Army Group South boasting 350,000 men, 447 tanks and 591 aircraft, but Semyon Timoshenko's force had the Nazis outnumbered on all counts: 765,300 men, 1,176 tanks and 926 planes.

If numbers alone could win battles, the war would be won in short order, but Babin had already seen too much to think that math alone solved anything. He guessed the struggle would continue for at least another two years, likely three, changing the landscape and the demographics of its principal participants.

Who would emerge victorious when the smoke cleared?

Guesswork accomplished nothing, and he kept his private plans foremost in mind. If he could slip away, avoiding contact with the enemy and spies serving Lavrentiy

Beria, the time had come for yet another visit to the Coastal Monastery of Saint Sergius, outside Saint Petersburg.

This time, Babin would put his plan in motion, though it likely wouldn't come to full fruition while the war went on.

Still, there was no time like the present to begin.

————

*MANHATTAN: April 29, 1942*

GREG JORDAN KEPT a close eye on the news these days, watching for federal moves against fellow *italiani* in New York or nationwide. So far, approximately 1,900 had been taken into custody, chiefly diplomats, businessmen, and Italian nationals studying in the U.S. In January, spokesmen for 200,000 Italian American trade unionists had petitioned FDR to "remove the intolerable stigma of being branded as enemy aliens" from Italians and Germans with pending citizenship applications. A month later, the Italian American Labor Council voiced opposition to "any blanket law for aliens that does not differentiate between those who are subversive and those who are loyal to America."

So far, the War Relocation Authority had established a fifty-mile-wide exclusion zone on the West Coast, adversely affecting Italian fishermen and longshoremen, but nothing similar along the Eastern Seaboard. And how could they, given Italian numbers on the docks or the prevalence of politicians, including Vito Marcantonio in Congress and New York Lieutenant Governor Charles Poletti? Hell, Gotham's mayor was half-Italian, and he never let the world forget it for a second.

Not that political *paisani* had done much to help the

Gotham Syndicate of late. Jurors convicted Irving Nitzberg at his second murder trial in March, then saw it overturned again by the Court of Appeals in a squeaker four-to-three vote. Vito Gurino went the other route, pleading guilty to three counts of second-degree, receiving consecutive eighty-year terms. Reminding the judge of his age, Gurino asked how he could serve that kind of time—to which the judge replied, "Just do as much as you can." Harry Maione might be dead and gone, but brothers Carlo and Louis—aka "The Duke"—remained locked up on charges of obstructing justice in the Brooklyn murder trials.

So far, nothing had stuck to Jordan or his family. With brothers Primo and Carlo Giordano, he'd been born in the U.S. and personally had a sterling record from the First World War to head off any doubts about his loyalty. As for the rest...well, he would have to wait and see. Some stoolie facing prison time might still link him to Salvatore Maranzano's murder, carried out eleven years ago, and every day he went to work committing or concealing new crimes by his two *fratelli*.

How much longer could he walk the highwire without tumbling down?

———

*Aboard the USS* George F. Elliott, *Mid-Pacific Ocean: June 10, 1942*

"I do."

Nolan O'Hara spoke those words on a brisk, sunny morning at San Diego's City Hall, before a tired-looking judge and his paunchy bailiff. He meant the pledge with all his heart, but at odd moments still wondered what brought him to that pass. A young man on his way to war halfway around the world, as likely to return inside a casket if he made it back at all, instead of coming back to see his bride.

Her name was Keely Mae Prewitt, two years O'Hara's junior, with a face to die for, auburn hair, a body that...well, never mind. She hailed from Mississippi, more specifically Mound Landing, where the Great Flood of 1927 had destroyed her parents' home and store while killing some 500 citizens and leaving 700,000 homeless. Rather than lamenting it, the Prewitts had moved west to California two years before the Wall Street crash and started over with another store in San Diego. A car wreck killed them both in 1940, whereupon Keely quit school and found the waitress job where Nolan met her, at a café on West Broadway—nothing like its namesake in Manhattan—where it crossed North Harbor Drive beside the docks. They'd hit it off at once, and Nolan thought her given name—Gaelic for "rare" or "beautiful"—was accurate on both counts.

Their first time together, winding up their second date when Nolan had liberty from Camp Pendleton, was spent at her apartment, a second-floor walkup on Front Street, six blocks from her job. She gave herself to Nolan without reservation, asking nothing in return, and by the time he realized that it was love, there seemed nothing for him to do except propose.

And she'd agreed.

They chose a civil ceremony with no guests, her parents gone and no siblings, while Nolan's father was somewhere in South America, unreachable beyond leaving a message with the Bureau, and his mother was stuck in Washington with his sister Fiona, not quite seventeen. The lack of family on hand didn't appear to bother Keely, and O'Hara was surprised to find he didn't mind it either.

Now the honeymoon was over and he was aboard the *George F. Elliott*, commissioned by the navy as a transport during World War I, retired, then brought back as a troop transport for the Pacific Theater. Its top speed was a hair over ten knots—twelve miles per hour to landlubbers—so the trip to Brisbane, New South Wales, should take them roughly ninety days to span 7,200 miles of open sea.

That was, if they avoided all of the 190 known Japanese submarines prowling along their chosen path. Radio silence all the way might help, but every time the aging *Elliott* unleashed a groan or shudder from below decks, Nolan kept his fingers crossed.

In truth, he liked it better up on deck, despite the green boots heaving every bit of chow they ate over the rails. Below, the ship was foul with sweat and diesel fumes, tobacco smoke and the effluvium of heads that didn't function very well. It also bore a close resemblance to a flophouse, with its stacked-up bunks and hammocks slung from every pole or beam available.

Commercial radio and lectures from Marine Corps officers were Nolan's only contact with the world they'd left behind and what might lie ahead of them, both of them in equally dramatic tones. He knew the Japanese had seized the Solomon Islands, the Dutch East Indies and Malaya, Borneo, Burma, and they were making headway in New Guinea, drawing close enough to bomb Western Australia. They'd seized most of the Philippines, driven "Dugout Doug" MacArthur to escape with relatives and his precious piano, while Bataan had fallen and Corregidor was clearly next in line. On Banka Island, near Sumatra, they had slaughtered twenty-one Australian nurses. Naval battles went no better for the Allies, in the Java Sea and Coral Sea.

The only bright spot in that carnage, dim as it might be, was the Doolittle raid in April, sixteen B-25 Mitchell medium bombers launched from the USS *Hornet* to drop their loads on Tokyo and Yokohama before fifteen planes went down, the last one landing safely in the USSR. At that, sixty-nine of the eighty airmen survived, allowing Washington to claim a propaganda victory it sorely needed.

But from here on out, it would be soldiers and marines tramping through jungle, storming beaches, routing suicidal adversaries out of caves and pillboxes. Nolan could only wonder whether he was up to it, or whether he would be among those who survived.

———

*Nazira, Assam, India: July 25, 1942*

The COI was dead; long live the Office of Strategic Services.

The change by FDR on June 13 had not been wholly unexpected, either by Bill Donovan or any of the agents under his command, including Colby Gantt. The president had gotten antsy about covert operations, seeking to separate "white" and "black" missions, so he'd divided COI, sending half its staff to the new Office of War Information, where they'd handle public—albeit censored—press releases. What remained was strictly covert, still with Donovan in charge, although a recent car crash had exacerbated his leg wounds from World War I.

On top of that, the military and the State Department

blocked OSS from using their MAGIC system for Japanese code intercepts and its counterpart for Nazi codes, dubbed "ULTRA." Another slap in Donovan's face; the FBI would handle all domestic security work *and* the whole of Latin America—but that still left the new outfit with Europe, Africa, Asia, and most of the Pacific, if they could negotiate agreements with a list of prickly admirals and generals.

So far, in fits and starts, it seemed to be working. The OSS had already established its own counterintelligence branch, tagged "X-2," and had a dozen agents working as "vice consuls" in major North African ports, gearing up for an invasion in November that was christened "Operation Torch." Recruitment for the agency was booming, both civilians and enlisted military people signing on—and they had even snagged a real-life movie star, Sterling Hayden, who'd retired from Hollywood for the duration, joined the Marine Corps as "John Hamilton" to shun publicity, and graduated from Officer Candidate School before switching to Donovan's outfit. He was tall, rugged, a man's man, but could he make it as a secret agent when he'd starred in two films during 1941?

No skin off Colby, either way.

The OSS was busy coming up with schemes, and some of them were frankly ludicrous. A case in point: "Project Capricious," using flies to spread anthrax among German troops in Spanish Morocco, thus deterring Spain from entering the war. That plan flopped, but others proved more practical, including creation of a Labor Unit that recruited European trade unionists as spies, and a corresponding Ship Observer Unit using seamen. The Operational Swimmer Group started training at a hotel swimming pool in Washington, D.C., using an oxygen rebreather unit rejected by the navy in 1939, then moved to Toyon Bay on

Santa Catalina Island, becoming the Maritime Unit trained in coastal infiltration and underwater sabotage.

The OSS had offices around the world, from London to Honolulu, where it labored despite ardent opposition from General MacArthur and Admiral Chester Nimitz. Vinegar Joe Stilwell and General Dai Li—lately nicknamed "China's Himmler—still made trouble in their part of Asia, but Stilwell had finally accepted the necessity of sabotage, telling Captain Eifler, "All I want to hear is booms from Burma jungle."

Colby Gantt was presently assigned to Eifler's Detachment 101, operating from a tea plantation near Nazira, in the northeastern Indian province of Assam. His cover was malarial research. His real mission: recruiting Burmese refugees and expat military personnel to fight against the Japanese invaders of their homeland. Eifler was particularly interested in the Kachin people, natives of a district neighboring southeastern China's Yunnan Province. He was anxious to create a group of Kachin Rangers who would raise hell with the Japanese, but in the meantime, Colby struggled with the local dialects while steering weapons and equipment drops to rebels in the Burmese countryside.

Turns out you didn't have to join the U.S. Navy if you longed to see the world.

He wondered, sometimes, what his father and twin brother might be up to with the FBI, but he had little time to spare for daydreaming. When they met up again—*if* they met up—there would be time enough for sharing war stories.

Right now, stuck in the midst of it, 8,000 miles from Washington, what mattered was survival and success.

———

*WASHINGTON, D.C.: August 8, 1942*

"IT'S DONE, THEN?" Devon Gantt inquired.

"As done as it can be," his father said.

The sat hunched over hamburgers in a café three blocks from Bureau headquarters, preferring it to brown bag lunches at the office, where the walls had ears.

"I'm still surprised he let two of them alive," said Devon —"he" being the president, and "them" a group of German saboteurs arrested in July.

The *Abwehr* plan—dubbed "Operation Pastorius," after the 17th-century founder of Germantown, Pennsylvania— had probably looked solid on the drawing board. Eight Nazi agents who had spent time in the States, two of them U.S. citizens, were handpicked for the mission, prepped to hit a list of targets that included hydroelectric plants at Niagara Falls; aluminum plants in Illinois, New York, and Tennessee; locks on the Ohio River near Louisville; a crucial railroad pass and Pennsylvania Railroad repair shops at Altoona; a cryolite plant in Philadelphia; Manhattan's Hell Gate Bridge; and Newark's Pennsylvania Station. They'd come ashore from two U-boats in June, one at Amagansett, Long Island, the other at Florida's Ponte Vedra Beach, equipped with civilian clothes, explosives and detonators, counterfeit birth certificates, Social Security Cards, draft deferment cards, drivers' licenses, and some $175,000 in U.S. currency.

The plot was meant to span two years, but hadn't made it through a month. First thing, an unarmed Coast Guardsman had caught the New York team burying their gear in seafront dunes, whereupon team leader George Dasch threatened the kid, then stuffed $260 into his hand and fled with his cohorts to Manhattan via the Long Island

Rail Road before reinforcements arrived. The Florida landing came off unobserved, leaving the infiltrators to meet up in Cincinnati on Independence Day.

But they never made it.

Instead, on June 15, Dasch called cohort Ernst Burger to his Gotham hotel room, confessing that he'd never meant to carry out the mission, hated Nazism, and was planning to alert the FBI. If Berger balked at that, Dasch warned, "Only one of us will walk out that door. The other will fly out this window." Burger agreed on the spot, and Dasch called the Bureau at once, failing to tip his six clueless accomplices. All were arrested in the next two weeks—but what to do with them?

Fearing that a civilian court might be too lenient, FDR had issued Executive Proclamation 2561 on July 2, creating a military tribunal to try the invaders on charges of conspiracy to violate the Articles of War laid down in 1806, pertaining to spies in disguise. Trial convened on the fifth floor of Justice headquarters, with all eight defendants convicted and condemned by August 1. FDR commuted Burger's sentence to life and Dasch's to thirty years for betraying the plot, but the other six had fried that very morning in the D.C. jail's electric chair.

Homegrown fascists also had their share of trouble waiting in the wings. On July 21 a federal grand jury had indicted twenty-eight defendants for sedition. As listed alphabetically in the indictment, they included: Court Asher, publisher of the Klan's *X-Ray* newsletter; far-right gadfly David Baxter, organizer of the fascist Social Republic Society of America; anti-FDR cartoonist Otto Brennemann; patent attorney and Silver Shirts member Howard Broen-strupp; D.C. resident Oscar Brumback; Prescott Dennett, chief of the pro-Nazi Columbia Press Service; Constantine de Aryan from San Diego, publisher of *The Broom,* an anti-Semitic newspaper; Hudson de Priest of Wichita, a writer for "Jayhawk Nazi" Gerald Winrod's publication, *The Defender*; German-born Hans Diebel, ex-member of the German American Bund and owner of the Aryan Bookstore in Los Angeles, already jailed as an enemy alien; Elizabeth Dilling, best-known leader of the women's isolationist movement; anti-Semitic pamphleteer Robert Edmonson from New York; Elmer and James Garner, father-son publishers of *Publicity* in Wichita; William Griffin, publisher of the *New York Evening Enquirer* and a leader of the Keep America Out of War Committee; Nebraskan Charles Hudson, employed by the Nazi press agency *Welt-Dienst* ("World Service") and author of *America in Danger!*; Ellis Jones, head of the Peoples Day Committee, a contributor to *Publicity* and *The Broom*; Nazi astrologer William Kullgren, publisher of California's *Beacon Light Herald* magazine and the newspaper *America Speaks*; Detroit ex-boxer William Lyman Jr., a member of the National Workers League and Social Republic Society; Chicago dentist and anti-FDR cartoonist Dr. Donald McDaniel; Robert Noble, a realtor and radio commentator, founder of The Friends of Progress, described by California Attorney General Earl Warren as "subversive in character and designed to destroy our war effort and with it our country"; Silver Shirts founder William Pelley; Eugene Sanctuary, anti-Semitic lobbyist for the American Christian Defenders; German immigrant Herman Schwinn, Western Director of the German American Bund, stripped of his U.S. citizenship in 1940; Edward Smythe, national commander of the Protestant War Veterans Association and publisher of *Our Common Cause,* who'd arranged a Bund-Klan rally at Camp Nordland in 1940; ex-diplomat Ralph Townsend of Oakland, already serving two years on a guilty plea to violating the Foreign Agents Registration Act to aid Japan; James True Jr., cofounder of America First, Inc. and holder of the patent on "Kike Killer" truncheons, available in men's and women's sizes; George Viereck, a German-American propagandist who'd registered as a foreign agent in World War I but hadn't bothered this time around; and Gerald Winrod, a great fan of Hitler and cheerleader for the fraudulent *Protocols of the Learned Elders of Zion,* invited to Berlin in 1935 "to study social, political, moral, economic, and prophetic trends."

Could any of them be convicted in the present atmosphere? Perhaps, but Aloysius Gantt would have to wait and see.

Another tempest in the capital surrounded J. Edgar Hoover's adversary Larry Fly. Despite the Bureau's opposition and some irritation at the White House over Fly opposing wiretaps, FDR had nominated him for another seven-year term as FCC chief, confirmed unanimously by the Senate. Hoover had been livid, and Fly's dossier was growing thicker by the day.

"What do you think about this Meyer taking over the WRA?" Devon asked.

"Too soon to say," his father answered back.

Milton Eisenhower had resigned his post at the War Relocation Authority on June 17, telling friends the work no longer let him sleep at night. Replacement Dillon Meyer had been assistant chief of the Agriculture Department's Soil Conservation Service and took the new job with some trepidation, but vowed to stick it out for the duration. Despite the fact that he'd determined General John DeWitt's reasons for Japanese evacuation from the West Coast "were phony and many of the rumors which were used to justify the evacuation which came out of the attack on Hawaii were proven to be completely untrue." A prime mover behind evacuation was Earl Warren, lusting to be governor of California in 1943 and riding on a wave or racism to get there. Attorney General Biddle initially opposed mass removal of Japanese Americans, but he'd caved in to political pressure and reluctantly signed off on FDR's plan.

"We'd best be getting back," Gantt told his son. "Tolson keeps track of tardy agents straggling in."

"Tolson." It sounded like a snort, coming from Devon. "What's it take to get rid of that guy?"

"I'm working on it. Don't say anything to anybody else. Too dangerous."

"Don't worry, Dad. I know the score."

———

*MARACAIBO, Venezuela: August 23, 1942*

THE DOMINOES KEPT FALLING in Latin America, which pleased Declan O'Hara even if it took some time. Eight nations—Colombia, Costa Rica, Cuba, the Dominican Republic, El Salvador, Guatemala, Haiti and Nicaragua—had declared war on the Axis powers following Pearl Harbor, and Venezuela had severed diplomatic relations while remaining officially neutral. Peru and Uruguay had cut off diplomatic contact in January, again without declaring war, but Peru *had* proclaimed a "state of belligerency" toward Axis ships approaching the Panama Canal. Mexico had declared war on May 28, after U-boats torpedoed two of its tankers, drowning twenty-three crewmen.

*Bad move, Adolf,* O'Hara thought, and smiled.

Most recently, just yesterday, Brazil had declared war on Germany and Italy but omitted Japan, perhaps in deference for its 17,000 Japanese immigrants.

There were still certain problems for SIS agents, of course. Ambassador George Messersmith was being a royal pain in Mexico City, trying to keep the Bureau out of his bailiwick, insisting on personal supervision if he allowed an SIS short-wave radio to operate from the U.S. Embassy. His reasoning: "The FBI representative in this Embassy is a very good man, but I do not like the idea of communications between the State Department and this Embassy on all sorts of matters passing through his hands." Adolf Berle was trying to finesse that contretemps but hadn't pulled it off so far.

Meanwhile, O'Hara was in Maracaibo, keeping a close eye on Venezuela's oilfields, anxious to abort the kind of sabotage that Germany had recently attempted in the States. When not engaged in that pursuit, he thought of Abigail and Fiona in D.C., with Nolan God knew where by now, somewhere in the Pacific, probably, and walking into Hell on Earth.

Declan wasn't a praying man, but he' begun to wonder if it wouldn't hurt to try.

---

LITTLE ITALY, *Manhattan: September 19, 1942*

"YOU GOT A BIRTHDAY COMIN' up, *cugino*," said Dominic Giordano

"You beat me to it, cousin," Dave Jordan replied.

"Older and wiser, eh?"

"I wouldn't go that far."

They sat outside the Napoleon Café on Worth Street, sipping Coca-Cola out of green glass bottles. Dominic drained his and belched, an act that seemed to please him.

"You're just jealous cause I'm older."

"By a minute, maybe."

"Yeah, yeah. Anyhow, I wanna ask you what you're gonna do about the draft."

Jordan frowned at that but figured there was nothing to be gained by lying, with his mind already set. "I'm joining up," he said, after a moment's stalling.

"What? You fuckin' kiddin' me?"

"I'm deadly serious."

"Deadly is right. You wanna go and get your ass shot off by fuckin' Japs or Krauts? For *what*, Davy?"

"Maybe to help the country."

"Ah, screw that. Take care of Number One, or let somebody help you."

"Help me how, Dom?"

"Since you're askin', hey, my old man knows a doctor. Say's he'll get me IV-F guaranteed."

"How's that?"

Dom aimed an index finger at his temple, twirling it. "Guy's some kinda psychiatrist or somethin'. He'll write up some paperwork and get me out on what they call a Section 8. On top a that, I got those juvey charges from a year or two ago."

Arrests, he meant. Jordan said, "You'd pretend to be a psycho? Are you telling me you'd be okay with that?"

"Why not? Man, it beats dyin' young, ya know? Your dad could fix the same thing, easy."

"No. I won't do that."

"Awright, then. Have you told 'im what you're plannin' for your short, dim future?"

"Not yet. I intend to have a talk with him today."

"Good luck with that, *cugino*. Good luck with your mama, too."

"But think about your future, Dom. That shit will follow you around forever. How'll you ever get a decent job?"

"Jesus, will you listen to yourself? What's that, a 'decent job,' some kinda nine-to-five shift at a factory or in an office? Fuck that, man. I've got a spot saved in the family business."

"Meaning?"

Dominic shrugged lazily. "Book bets or run some numbers. Put a little money on the street. Don't play the fool with me."

"That isn't what I want, either."

"So, be a lawyer like your old man. Wallow in that filthy lucre."

"What law school would take me with a psycho record hanging over me?"

"Well..."

"I'll make it easy for you. None."

"Okay, your mind's made up. I get it. Which branch do you wanna join?"

"Army, I guess."

"It's better than the navy, catchin' a torpedo up your ass, sharks snackin' on what's left."

Dave set his bottle down, rose from his wrought-iron chair. "I'd better get on with it. No time like the present for bad news."

Behind him, not quite taunting. "Yeah. Be sure 'n tell me how it works out, soldier boy."

———

*MANHATTAN: November 2, 1942*

GREG JORDAN FINISHED up his breakfast, tipped the waitress generously, and stepped out into bright sunlight. He didn't need the cashmere overcoat that he was wearing, but you never knew about November in New York. It could turn frosty when you least expected it.

Just like at home.

Greg figured Angelina would forgive him someday for not helping her prevent their son's enlistment, but he couldn't guess exactly when that might happen. Meanwhile, he left early for the office, ate breakfast at any random place he passed, and made it through another day. Dinners were mostly silent, and although he still slept in the same bed as his wife, "slept" was the operative word.

David was in the army now, specifically the 1st Infantry Division or "The Big Red One," after its shoulder patch. He'd mustered in ten miles from home, Fort Hamilton in Brooklyn, then a troop train had transported him with other new recruits to Fort Devens in Massachusetts. Beyond that, Greg knew nothing, and wouldn't until David made contact again.

Or till an army telegram informed him that his son was dead.

While waiting for his life to change, Greg occupied his mind as best he could with other things. On Columbus Day, symbolically, the feds had lifted most restrictions on Italian nationals living long-term in the United States. They could own cameras and firearms, travel freely, and were not required to carry special I.D. cards. Those already confined to camps were staying there, of course, and FDR's decree did nothing for the Japanese or Germans.

As if Jordan gave a damn.

Closer to home, there was a whiff of gunsmoke in the air and premonitions of disaster for one Syndicate bigwig. In early August, someone killed Lepke associate Morris Wolinsky and a buddy, Robert Greene, at a Seventh Avenue card club. Twelve witnesses fingered the shooter as Max Fox, Greene's former partner in the club, and he was facing first-degree indictments, but the D.A. hadn't looked too closely at the circumstances, unconcerned that "Moey Dimples" was a trusted friend of Lepke who—some said— had lied about the consequences of surrendering in 1939.

Revenge? Why not? Word had it that when Lepke heard the news, he'd grinned to beat the band.

But these days, that was all Lep had to smile about. The state Court of Appeals had disappointed him, a rude trick on the eve of Halloween, upholding his conviction and death sentence by a vote of four-to-three. His last hope now was an appeal to the U.S. Supreme Court or the ultimate long shot: a fantasy of White House clemency.

Dream on.

At least David had left the sordid trappings of his family behind, for now. As to the cost he might incur for breaking free, Greg Jordan couldn't bear to think.

———

*FEDERAL BUREAU of Narcotics Field Office, Manhattan: December 13, 1942*

IKE SAWYER SCANNED a memo posted in the office bullpen, heralding FDR's signature on a new Opium Poppy Control Act, restricting cultivation of *Papaver somniferum* or "any other plant which is the source of opium" without a license from the Secretary of the Treasury.

What licenses? A memo from the FBN to newspapers across the country—also posted on the office corkboard—made it plain: "The Opium Poppy Control Act, which was recently enacted, permits the licensing of opium poppy production only for the purpose of supplying the medical and scientific needs of the Nation for narcotic drugs. There is no immediate or presently prospective need for the growth of the opium poppy to supply medical and scientific needs, and, therefore, it is not now anticipated that any licenses will be issued."

Ike saw the problem plain as day, surprised that Harry Anslinger or someone else around him hadn't caught it. California poppy growers had already planted next year's crop, and Washington had granted them the right to harvest it as usual. But what would happen after that?

Ike turned away and went back to his cluttered desk, his mind already drifting toward the problems of his people in America at war. Six lynchings had been logged so far this year, most recently the Mississippi slaughter on Columbus Day of two Negro fourteen-year-olds, charged with attempted rape of a white girl. The mob had "overpowered" Quitman's city marshal and the boys had wound up dangling from a bridge favored by lynchers since the last World War, spanning the Chickasawhay River.

Worse yet was Arizona's "Phoenix Massacre" that left three dead, together with eleven wounded, on Thanksgiving Day. It started with a he-she confrontation at a small café. Because the man involved was from the all-black 364th Infantry Regiment, MPs and local cops rolled out together, one MP firing a shot that grazed another trooper from the 364th. Back at Camp Papago Park, more soldiers heard exaggerated stories of the incident and grabbed their rifles, heading into Phoenix for revenge. When it was over, two G.I.s and a civilian lay on morgue slabs, 180 others from the 364th briefly jailed, but only fifteen faced a court-martial on charges of "disobeying orders, mutiny, and inciting a riot." All were convicted, one sentenced to die, but FDR had commuted that verdict to fifty years, matching the others.

For safety's sake, the rest of the 364th had been transferred to Camp Van Dorn, near Centreville, Mississippi— and what could possibly go wrong there, in the armpit of Jim Crow?

Sawyer thanked his lucky stars again that son Payton was too young for the draft, or to enlist without permission from his parents. What he chose to do after the war would be his business, but the last thing Ike and wife Talitha needed at the moment was a boy in uniform, confronted by discrimination and mayhem at home, before he even made it to the meat grinder abroad.

*Just let him live, oh Lord,* Ike thought, and barely realized it sounded like a prayer,

————

*5116 KENMORE AVENUE, Chicago: December 29, 1942*

"I THOUGHT this kind of thing went out with Al Brady in Bangor," Devon Grant half-whispered.

"Not a chance," his father answered in the same low tone. "There'll always be more fugitives. Just stay alert and watch out for yourself."

The manhunt had distracted Aloysius Gantt from paperwork in Washington, chasing a lead from an informer named Whittaker Chambers, claiming that he knew a Commie spy named Alger Hiss, a Harvard-educated lawyer working for the Department of Agriculture. Gantt hadn't substantiated it before he got the order to join J. Edgar Hoover for his final "personal" arrest. His son's addition to the team had come as a surprise.

The great emergency: on October 9, frame-up victim Roger Touhy had a escaped from Joliet with cohort Basil Banghart and six other convicts serving terms that ranged from twenty years to life. Armed with a pair of .45s one inmate's younger brother smuggled in, they'd taken two guards hostage, scaled a prison wall, and fled back to the city they knew best, Chi-Town.

The breakout wasn't any kind of federal crime unless state lines were crossed, but Hoover had a brainstorm, claiming the fugitives had violated the Selective Service Act by "changing addresses" without notifying their draft board. Warrants in hand, G-men set out to track them down, but even focusing on Chicago didn't get it done. The rumor mill said Touhy wanted plastic surgery but it would cost $100,000. Keeping that in mind, Hoover accused Touhy and Banghart of a $20,000 robbery in a Chicago suburb, on December 18.

By then, agents had nabbed escapee Martilick Nelson in Minneapolis, but he wouldn't squeal on the others. Nonetheless, an incoming called them to another runner, William Stewart, in Milwaukee. There, they shadowed him until December 21, then spotted Banghart and another fugitive, Ed Darlak, in downtown Chicago. Fearing gunplay on the crowded street, they'd spent another week trailing their prey and lost them, but located two other escapees--Eugene Lanthorn and St. Clair McInerney—at their flat on Leland Avenue.

Hoover, with Gantt and son in tow, flew in for the arrest, which went down on December 28. Lanthorn and McInerney chose to shoot it out and died in a hail of lead, though Devon hadn't been compelled to fire a shot. Both corpses carried wads of cash, some thirteen grand, while McInerney's pockets also held an undertaker's address—creepy—and a snatch of verse that read:

> I wish I now were old enough
> To give some sound advice.
> To make each person weigh his thoughts
> And turn over twice.
> I wish my eyes had seen enough
> So I could make him see
> The way impressions in this life
> Can fool us easily.
> I wish my heart had held enough
> So it could not impart
> The worthiest philosophy
> To every human heart.

IT TOOK another day to trace Touhy, Banghart and Darlak to their hideaway, but here they were at 5:00 a.m., floodlights illuminating their first-floor apartment while a bullhorn demanded surrender. A harsh voice from inside snarled, "Let's fight!" but two others counseled sanity and Hoover had the chance to seize Touhy himself as he emerged with empty hands held high.

Holding a shotgun at the ready, Devon asked, "You think they'll have to face the draft board now?"

His father smiled but cautioned, "keep your voice down, eh? The Chief wouldn't appreciate your sense of humor."

"Right. To get along—"

"You go along," said Aloysius. "That's the Bureau's secret of success."

# CHAPTER 3

THE LATEST BULLETIN on Aloysius Gantt's desk told him that Justice had scrapped its sedition indictment of six months ago and started from scratch. The new counts included all twenty-eight defendants from July, plus six new additions: Frank Clark of Tacoma, once affiliated with the Silver Shirts, now western director of the National Gentile League; engineer George Deatherage, ex-Grand Commander of the Klan-like Knights of the White Camellia and founder of the American Nationalist Party, stripped of a navy contract as an "undesirable person" in 1942; Frank Fernenx, California member of the German American Bund, owner of a Nazi bookshop and several theaters that screened German films; Leslie Fly, née Paquita de Shishmareff, who'd once tried to buy the Klan outright for $75,000; Lois de Lafayette Washburn of Seattle, cofounder of the National Gentile League and the National Liberty Party; and the indictment's first publication, the weekly *New York Evening Enquirer,* a sounding board for Hitler founded by the original defendant William Griffin.

Gantt knew Griffin had suffered a heart attack soon after last July's indictments, whereupon his case had been dropped and his newspaper charged in his stead. Also listed in the filing, but not charged with any crime, were twelve more publications and thirteen pro-fascist organizations. That was a time-honored means of cautioning disreputable persons when no evidence existed for a trial, but in the end it meant nothing besides a shot at social ostracism.

And the rest?

Gantt didn't know if any of the counts would stick in court, but that wasn't his job. For now, Director Hoover had him poring over hefty files for anything the government could wield at trial. The effort gave Gantt time to think about his sons, one en route to a posting at the Bureau's L.A. field office for seasoning, the other roaming who knew where on duties for the OSS.

Real danger there for both of them, and Gantt knew there was little—make that *nothing*—he could do to help.

———

GUADALCANAL, *Solomon Islands: February 8, 1943*

THE JAPANESE HAD TAGGED Guadalcanal "Starvation Island" after seizing it in March of 1942, and building an airbase that threatened New Guinea and Australia. That wasn't any commentary on the wildlife of the Solomons—900 islands stretching over some 11,000 square miles in the south-western Pacific—but instead the rations they'd been issued, mostly rice, expected to subsist on it until war's end.

*Screw them,* Nolan O'Hara thought. He didn't give a damn about the enemy, hoping they'd starve before he had to finish killing them on this or some other island. Right now, he had a pressing problem of his own.

Keely was pregnant.

Nolan didn't understand it. They'd been careful, using condoms every time they got together, but it seemed at least one of the rubbers hadn't done its job. When Keely's letter caught up with him in Australia, two days prior to shipping out for the Canal, O'Hara had been stunned, elated, terrified and speechless, all at once. The doctors reckoned she was two months gone, on track for a delivery in mid-September. There'd been no facility for calling her directly, so he'd scribbled off a letter in response and trusted someone in the navy to deliver it sometime, somehow, as he was setting sail.

On top of unexpected baby news, Nolan had to consider all the dangers Keely faced at home. A Japanese submarine had shelled Santa Barbara while Tōjō's soldiers were seizing the Solomons, planting their flag on the Aleutians, sinking the carrier *Yorktown* during the Battle of Midway, overrunning New Guinea and sending another sub to shell Australia's Sydney harbor. Finally, in August, the 1st Marines had invaded Guadalcanal, teaching their enemies the real truth of starvation, stubbornly holding the airbase they'd renamed Henderson Field, while rival navies clashed and sank each other's warships in New Georgia Sound—nicknamed The Slot—which ran the full length of the Solomons.

O'Hara's outfit hadn't been called up to join the bloodshed until January, days after General Hajime Sugiyama and Admiral Osami Nagano informed Emperor Hirohito of their decision to withdraw from Guadalcanal. The evacuation, code-named Operation Ke, was scheduled for late January, by which time the Japanese had lost some 25,000 men to combat, disease and starvation. They were outnumbered two-to-one when U.S. Army soldiers started to replace the worn-out 1st Marines, but there were still enough to hold Mount Austen when O'Hara and the 2nd Division ran head-on into their last-ditch defenses.

Nolan had witnessed grim death for the first time in that engagement, and had killed at least nine Japanese soldiers that he was sure of, having watched them drop and die. Nine of 3,000 that would be, against 250 dead Americans, before somebody figured out that the surviving Japanese had been withdrawing to the island's west coast, boarding ships and sneaking off until the last of them were gone by February 7. Two days later, when General Alexander Patch declared Guadalcanal officially secure, it came down to the dirty work of mopping up holdouts who had been left behind by Operation Ke.

Nolan had seen the fresh G.I.s wielding their new M1 Garand rifles, the eight-shot semiautomatics that only a handful of marines had so far "liberated" from the army's stash, along with the improved M1A1 flamethrower—seven pounds lighter than the parent M1, with three times the range—and a one-man weapon christened the "bazooka" or "stovepipe," that fired 2.36-inch explosive rockets.

All the Corps could boast in terms of innovation so far was the Ka-Bar, formally, the USMC Mark 2 combat knife, slowly replacing the brass-knuckled Mark 1s issued since the First World War. Some hard-asses preferred the trench knives or packed both, while special outfits like Lieutenant Colonel Evan Carlson's crack commandos had been breaking in Marine Raider stilettos patterned on the British Fairbairn-Sykes fighting knife.

Like any of that mattered now, to Nolan. He would be a father in another seven months, God willing, and he didn't have a clue concerning when—or *if*—he'd ever see his wife and child.

———

*KASSERINE PASS, Tunisia: February 22, 1943*

PRIVATE DAVID JORDAN huddled in his one-man foxhole, trying not to give the Krauts a target as he peered down range. He'd still been training in the States when soldiers from the Big Red One had landed at Oran, Algeria, a month after his birthday, but he'd made it to the front with reinforcements as the outfit's numbers started getting whittled down. He had begun to see why troops from other units called the 1st the "Big Dead One," no compliment implied.

He'd made it for the tag end of a rough engagement at Medjez el Bab, a part of "Operation Torch," as Allied leaders called their fight for French North Africa, and now he was at Kasserine, a two-mile-wide gap in the Grand Dorsal chain of the Atlas Mountains, confronting *Generalfeldmarschall* Erwin Rommel's Afrika Korps Assault Group, two Panzer divisions, and the Italian Centauro Armored Division. All that with his M1 Garand, its sixteen-inch M1905 bayonet, and half a dozen Mk2 antipersonnel grenades, the famous "pineapples."

Today, it didn't feel like much.

Of course, he wasn't on his own. The 1st Division was a part of Major General Lloyd Fredendall's U.S. II Corps, supported by Major General Charles Keightley's British 6th Armored Division and Lieutenant General Kenneth Anderson's First Army, but even all that didn't feel like much.

*Rommel,* for Christ's sake, leading their opponents in the first major engagement between Axis forces and the Allies in North Africa. The Krauts had already kicked ass at Faid Pass, despite French reinforcements with 75-mm guns, and mauled the British 8th Army at Sidi Bou Zid, plowing through them as if they were nothing. Kasserine Pass was a fallback position, the literal last ditch, and Jordan had no reason to believe that he would make it out alive.

And here they came again, after two days of seesaw battle over turf that had no value other than a passage through the mountains between Feriana and Tebessa. American positions had been overrun and driven back on February 19, making a disorganized retreat to Djebel el Hamra at the pass's western exit. They'd hung on there through the twenty-first, launching a counterattack that captured some 400 prisoners aside from Germans and Italians slain. Jordan had shot a few of them himself, but there'd been no time in the midst of it for keeping score.

Now Panzers were advancing, infantry behind them, going hell-for-leather, all guns blazing. They ran into a U.S. artillery barrage and stalled until nightfall, when whispered orders coming down the line announced another pullout. Jordan hoped darkness would cover him as he crawled from his hole and started scuttling toward the rear.

The question that he had to ask himself: was he a coward, when it felt so good to run away?

———

Los Angeles FBI Field Office, *North Spring Street: March 12, 1943*

"Four things you have to think about out here," said Special Agent Randall Dukes. "The studios, the Mob, the Reds, and local law—not necessarily in order of importance. Watch your step with all of 'em, and Stafford will be happy."

Leland Stafford was L.A.'s Special Agent in Charge, too busy help Devon Gantt settle in beyond a terse greeting and handshake, assigning the scut work to Dukes.

"Doesn't sound that hard," Gantt said.

Dukes barked a laugh, replied, "You say that *now*."

"So, fill me in."

Gantt knew the basics, having studied up when he received the transfer west. The Bureau's office in L.A. had opened up in 1914, handling high-profile cases that had recently included teenage crackpot Russell Alexanderson—aka "The Leopard"—trying to extort $25,000 in uncut diamonds by mail from actress and pin-up girl Betty Grable. When not protecting Hollywood royalty, L.A.'s G-men watched for spies and helped round up enemy aliens for transport to desert camps scattered across the Great Southwest.

So far, he mostly liked the L.A. weather, and Camille had settled nicely in their small apartment in Van Nuys, although she missed her family and had been running up long-distance phone bills Gantt could ill afford on his G-man's starting salary.

*The things we do for love.*

"Okay, start with the studios," Dukes said. "They run this town and no one crosses them without a damned good reason. The Screen Actors Guild helps us watch out for

Reds who infiltrate the movie industry and try to foist their shit on John Q. Public. We've got an informant in the SAG, code-named 'T-10,' otherwise known as Ronald Reagan."

"The Gipper from *Knute Rockne, All American*? That guy?"

"The very same. He's a lieutenant in the army now, of course. Bad eyesight keeps him out of action, so he's over there in Burbank, running something they call the Provisional Task Force Show Unit, making propaganda films. He and his wife, Jane Wyman, will be glad to tell you anything they know about commies, but if you ask about the Mob, they clam up tight."

"Which mob is that?" Gantt asked.

"*The* Mob," Dukes answered back. "The Syndicate, you know?"

"Director Hoover says there's no such thing."

Dukes laughed again. "Oh, they exist, all right. You ever hear of Bugsy Siegel?"

"Sure. Who hasn't?"

"Well, he isn't just some cheap Manhattan thug. He's got this town sewed up as far as gambling, whores, whatever, with his pet gorilla Mickey Cohen helping him."

"Cohen?"

"A real palooka from Chicago, via Cleveland, where he threw in with the Dalitz syndicate. They sent him out in 1938 to front their action on the West Coast, while Siegel was working for New York."

"I read that Siegel's looking at a murder rap."

"My take on that: it's going nowhere, thanks to the D.A.'s office. Which brings me to the local law. Don't trust 'em. LAPD is as rotten with corruption as departments in Chicago, Saint Paul, and New York. Chief 'Two-Gun' Davis fired twenty percent of all his coppers for bad conduct— which did *not* include beating the hell out of Commies,

Negroes and union organizers—but Mayor Bowron found six hundred brothels going strong when he took office back in '39. Today, they've moved out to the suburbs, where Sheriff Biscailuz takes his cut and lets 'em slide. Same thing with gambling, dope and all the rest of it."

"While we do nothing?"

Dukes shrugged. "None of it's a federal crime. I'll tell you something on the QT, though. Chicago's outfit has been squeezing money from the studios for years now, threatening walkouts by the International Alliance of Theatrical Stage Employees. Justice has got indictments in the works— extortion, bribery, whatever—and they're just around the corner, coming any day now. Wait and see."

"Sounds interesting," Devon said. "What's up for us, meanwhile?"

"What else?" Dukes said, dropping a stack of warrants on Gantt's desk. "More fugitives. They love the sun and surf."

———

*H PAKANT, Northern Burma: June 9, 1943*

H PAKANT WAS a pesthole on the Uyu River, 217 miles north of Mandalay in the midst of inhospitable malaria-infested jungle, cut off from the world by monsoons between May and early October. It also boasted some of the world's richest jade mines, plus proximity to northeast India and China's Yunnan Province.

Colby Gantt, against all odds, found he was getting use to it—the snakes, spiders and scorpions, mosquitoes—and, of course, the Japs.

His task was winning over the indigenous Burmese to

service with the OSS against Imperial Japan. Where he was stationed, that included Karens, Shans, Chins and Kachins —the most warlike of the lot—who lived in isolated villages and knew the trackless jungles like New Yorkers knew their placid Central Park. Converting them into Allied guerrilla fighters was the goal for Wild Bill Donovan's Detachment 101, and others had the same idea.

One leader of the movement was a British colonel, Orde Wingate, a bearded advocate of unconventional guerrilla units who lived by the motto "Never ask favors but tell people if they care to help they can come along, that you yourself are going anyway." His zeal persuaded General Archibald Wavell, Commander-in-Chief of the Southeast Asian Theatre, to sanction creation of the "Chindits," a long range penetration group that took its name from a mythical Burmese lion, the *chinthe*. Gantt supplied whatever aid he could and tried to minimize the unit's high attrition rate in his reports to Washington.

Orde launched his first outing, dubbed "Operation Longcloth," on February 8, a grueling three-month slog across 1,000 miles of barely penetrable forest, cutting the railway line between Mandalay and Myitkyina, ambushing enemy patrols, returning in late April with 2,182 of his original 3,000 men, 600 hundred of those disabled by wounds or disease. Before they even made it back, Wingate was planning "Operation Thursday," set to go again in February 1944.

Elsewhere, Bill Donovan had finally convinced the Brits to share their ULTRA intercepts with his X-2 Division, led by attorney James Murphy, cracking Axis codes and running some double agents in Europe. By April, OSS had a base up and running in Istanbul, covering Turkey under ex-Chicago banker Lanning Macfarland. Czech engineer Alfred

Schwarz, code-named "Dogwood," finessed infiltration of anti-fascist groups in Germany, Austria, Hungary, and Romania. Other agents trained and supplied resistance movements in China, including Mao Zedong's Red Army through "Operation Dixie," and Hồ Chí Minh's Việt Minh— or League for the Independence of Vietnam—in occupied French Indochina.

Stateside, historian William Langer assembled 900 scholars for the Research and Analysis Branch, including historians, economists, political scientists, geographers, psychologists, anthropologists, and diplomats. International executive and lawyer Whitney Shepardson led the Secret Intelligence Branch, while a new Morale Operations Branch split from Special Operations to generate "black" propaganda against the Axis. After training in Nassau, the Maritime Unit advanced to sabotage missions in June, the same month X-2 transferred its headquarters to Algiers, infiltrating agents into France, Corsica, Italy and Sicily, Spain and Portugal.

Agents in the field required new tools—or toys, depending on your point of view. Those came from Research and Development, a collection of laboratories, workshops, and experts who turned out an arsenal of gear ranging from the extremely practical to farcical. In charge was Boston chemist Stanley Lovell, dubbed "Professor Moriarty," dreaming up no end of silenced pistols, limpet mines, and "BEANO" T-13 grenades (developed with the aid of Eastman Kodak Corporation), to allegedly explosive powder packed in Chinese flour bags and labeled "Aunt Jemima." Aside from killing tools, R&D produced tiny cameras, wiretap devices, electronic beacons, and portable radios including the "Joan-Eleanor" system, which allowed agents to speak securely with aircraft circling high overhead. To that, add countless I.D. cards, work passes, Axis ration cards and counterfeit currency, plus luggage, clothing, toiletries, and dental fillings matching those of foreign lands in microscopic detail.

One of R&D's flops was "Operation Campbell," a remote-controlled speedboat, disguised as a local fishing craft and guided by airplane, meant to crash and detonate against moored Axis ships. That one looked great on Lovell's drawing board but never worked at sea.

Colby slapped one more of the countless bloodthirsty mosquitoes that would plague him on this day, thinking about the States, deciding that he'd stick it out and see what happened next. Nietzsche had said, "Whatever does not kill me makes me stronger," and that was a sentiment Gantt shared.

He was alive and hanging in there, hoping good things really came to those who wait.

*GELA, Sicily: July 13, 1943*

YOU COULD'VE KNOCKED Dave Jordan over with a feather when a captain whom he'd never seen before addressed a group of noncoms and privates from the Big Red One, asking them all, "Who wants to join the Rangers?"

*What the hell?* thought Jordan. *After Kasserine?*

Tunis had fallen on May 7, followed by an Allied victory parade down Avenue Maréchal Galliéni to signal the end of fighting in North Africa. The surprise invitation came two days later, and despite his misgivings, Jordan had leapt at the chance for redemption.

What could happen next, except rejection by the unit or a sudden death?

He knew a bit about the 1st Ranger Battalion, starting with the fact that they'd covered his unit's retreat from Kasserine Pass. Beyond that, he'd heard as much as any other private from the Big Red One might know.

Major General Lucian Truscott had formed the Rangers in May 1942, modeled on Britain's Commandos but tagged with a name that sounded more American. Captain William Darby chose the first 600 members from a list of 1,500 volunteers, training them first in Northern Ireland, before getting down to dirty basics at the Commando Training Center in Scotland. Another 100 recruits washed out before the 1st Battalion went active in June, including one Ranger killed and several wounded by live fire training exercises. Their first taste of battle came at Dieppe on the French coast in August 1942, where three more Rangers died and several were captured. From there, it was on to Tunisia in February, where they'd killed fifty enemies, captured ten more, and earned the "Black Death" label from Italian troops at Sened Station. A month later, they'd captured 200 prisoners at Djbel Ank and given General Patton the opening he needed to wrap up Operation Torch.

Those successes convinced Washington to create two more Ranger battalions; the 3rd, activated at Nemours, Morocco, on May 21, and the 4th in Tunisia eight days later. What had happened to the 2nd? Jordan thought it might be training in the States but wasn't sure and frankly didn't give a damn.

Training of the new battalions under Major Roy Murray was every bit as tough as Jordan had surmised, and then some. Live fire with machine guns was a part of it, plus endless marching, scaling cliffs, mock landings from the sea, hand-to-hand combat using knives, garrotes, or nothing but their hands and feet. They killed and ate whatever local wildlife was available, to practice living off a hostile land, and learned to sit in darkness with their ears pressed to their grounded bayonet blades, listening for distant sounds.

All that to get them fit for Sicily and "Operation Husky" in July.

The landing beaches were divided: three U.S. divisions spearheaded by Rangers would storm the south coast at Licata and move northward toward Palermo, while four British Eighth Army divisions and Commandos hit the island's southeastern tip and advanced up the coast to Messina. Before dawn on July 9, charging ashore under floodlights, Rangers faced the Italian 18th Coastal Brigade and 429th Coastal Battalion, entrenched at Gela with barbed wire, machine-gun nests, artillery and pillboxes. Standing in reserve, ready to help, were 9,000 German soldiers of the Fallschirm-Panzer Division with seventeen Tiger tanks, seventy-five other armored vehicles, backed in turn by 213 Nazi warplanes waiting at various nearby airfields.

But it wasn't enough.

Bombers sank the USS *Maddox* offshore, but the Rangers pressed home their attack, capturing Gela by 8:00 a.m., disabling three artillery pieces and capturing 200 prisoners. Behind them, landmines crippled army trucks, six-wheeled "Duck" amphibious landing craft, and five navy bulldozers, stalling the Big Red One's attempt to help, but none of it stopped the Rangers. The Italian Livorno Division counter-attacked behind forty-five tanks, but Rangers stopped them cold, using captured artillery pieces to repel the assault. Next came Hitler's Hermann Göring Division and the 15th *Panzergrenadiers*, likewise broken on the Rangers' anvil and sent reeling backward.

Private Jordan, in the midst of it, lost track of how many defenders he had shot, had no idea which of them died or crawled away to lick their wounds, but as the sun set over Gela on July 10, he'd decided that he must not be a coward after all.

Next morning, bright and early, Nazi bombers sank the USS *Barnett*, while others struck the transport anchorage. At Gela, the Livorno Division returned for more punishment, this time with sixty German tanks, but they couldn't clear the beachhead. Rangers stopped them dead and captured 400 of the survivors. As day two burned down in the west, any remaining Axis tanks retreated into darkness, shell-shocked planners hoping maybe they could hold Messina.

By July 12, 90 percent of the Allied invasion force was ashore, and the Big Red One had seized Ponte Olivo airfield, welcoming its first U.S. bombers and fighters. Ranger heroes of the day resembled scarecrows in their tattered uniforms, shoes worn thin, most of their combat gear marked for salvage. Even so, their scouts had liberated ample wine from local stores to lift their spirits.

Waiting for new gear, Jordan and the rest were chafing at the bit, ready to go again.

———

*Harlem: August 3, 1943*

IKE SAWYER HESITATE on his stoop, scanning the street still littered with debris and kept his right hand within easy distance of his holstered .45. A squad car passed, the white cops glaring at him till Ike palmed his badge, then they moved on.

The riot, it appeared, had finally wound down from fury to exhaustion, and the ghetto residents who could afford it would be sleeping in this Tuesday morning after two wild days and nights. Street sweepers, Ike supposed, would earn some overtime.

The trouble had begun on Sunday night, when a policeman (white) tried to arrest a woman (black) for causing a disturbance in the Braddock Hotel's lobby, well known as a hooker hangout. Details differed, but a Negro soldier and his mother butted in, the soldier swinging at the cop, then trying to escape before a bullet from the cop's gun grazed his shoulder. Rumors spread like wildfire that a G.I. had been killed, inflaming some 3,000 residents who'd started throwing any object they could get their hands on at blue uniforms. Before the riot ended, six people (all black) were dead, 600 more (ditto) in jail, some 700 injured, with some 4,500 windows broken and an estimated 1,400 shops (mostly white-owned) looted. Newspaper estimates of damages ranged upward from $500,000 to $5 million.

Still, it could've been much worse.

Look at Detroit, for instance. Their riot had blazed for three days in June, requiring 6,000 federal troops to suppress it. Again, false rumors lit the fuse, leaving thirty-four dead (eight whites, the rest Negroes killed by cops and soldiers), with 433 injured (74 percent black), 1,800 jailed (85 percent black), and property damage pegged at $2 million. Mayor Edward Jeffries told reporters, "Negro hoodlums started it, but the conduct of the police department, by and large, was magnificent." Thurgood Marshall, executive director of the NAACP Legal Defense and Educational Fund, disagreed, comparing white cops to Hitler's Gestapo.

Five days before Detroit caught fire, false rumors of a black-on-white rape sparked a white riot in Beaumont, Texas, killing three people, leaving fifty-odd injured and 200-plus facing charges. A week before that, white servicemen and civilians rioted against Latinos in Los Angeles, targeting those who wore faddish "zoot suits," while police came after them, jailing the victims. Oakland suffered a similar Anglo outbreak, and state senator Jack Tenney— ironically, composer of the hit tune "Mexicali Rose"—led his California Senate Factfinding Subcommittee on Un-American Activities in a futile quest to "determine whether the present Zoot Suit Riots were sponsored by Nazi agencies attempting to spread disunity between the United States and Latin-American countries."

Before all that, in May, discord over interracial shipyard hiring had produced another all-white riot in Mobile, Alabama, leaving more than fifty Negro workers injured by 4,000 rampaging bigots. Meanwhile, the year's record for lynchings stood at three victims so far.

And yet, if the rumors Sawyer was investigating turned out to be factual, the greatest racial slaughter since the Civil War had taken place in Mississippi, three months before Harlem briefly lost its mind. The site was Camp Van Dorn, near Centreville, where Negro soldiers of the 364th Infantry Regiment had been unwisely relocated after last year's "Phoenix Massacre." Stranded in Jim Crow land, despised by local merchants and Wilkinson County's Sheriff, they had been subjected to daily humiliation prior to May 30, when said sheriff shot and killed Private William Walker for "resisting arrest." From there, word had it that other members of the 364th had armed themselves for a replay of Phoenix, before white MPs surrounded their barracks and sprayed them with automatic weapons, killing more than 1,200 soldiers.

Truth or bullshit? Ike was still checking, but the grapevine spoke of mass graves dug by bulldozers, a white community united in silence, and stray survivors of the slaughtered unit transferred to far-flung bases, a few to Alaska. In Centreville, even Mayor Omer Carroll was speaking of "up to fifty killed" in a wild night of violence.

Sawyer would keep on digging as his time allowed, but he knew going up against the army was a great way to get fired and blacklisted, no pun intended, so he'd definitely have to watch his step.

———

*LITTLE ITALY, Manhattan: August 29, 1943*

GREG JORDAN DIDN'T HAVE a clue his son had been in combat, much less overrun by German soldiers in North Africa. He *did* know that the failure to receive an army telegram reporting death or injury was good news of a sort, and all he could expect to learn except from newspapers or censored letters home—of which there had been none so far.

Meanwhile, the war was making money for his family and everybody else in *Cosa Nostra*. Washington had waited six days short of one full year since Pearl Harbor before it started rationing civilian use of gasoline. The problem wasn't gas per se—the government still had plenty of that— but *rubber* was in high demand for military use, and the production of synthetics hadn't gotten off the ground yet. FDR, on the advice of his "Brain Trust," had concluded that the best way to make auto tires last longer was to limit sales of gasoline, and so it came to pass, despite resistance in Congress.

Today, there were five classes of acknowledged drivers, two of which were limited on weekly purchases. Class A—your normal working stiffs—got three gallons per week, while Class B factory workers and traveling salesmen got eight. No limit was imposed on the remaining categories: Class C, police, essential war workers, doctors and mailmen; truckers in Class T; and Class X with its politicians and assorted other VIPs. Since January 1942, 7,500 rationing boards controlled by the Office of Price Administration were at work nationwide, each with three unpaid volunteer members. The War Production Board helped by banning civilian car sales, thus sticking dealers with 500,000 unsold vehicles. Dog food factories stopped canning scraps and sold dehydrated food packaged in cardboard, and so it went on down the line with everything from penicillin to food, women's hosiery and household appliances.

Hard times.

Civilians received their first ration books, for sugar, through public schools in May 1942, followed later that month by windshield stickers for Class A and B drivers seeking gasoline. Few were pleased with the new restrictions—but the Mob had a solution, for a reasonable price. First, it stole and resold ration stickers, cards and stamps, then set up printing presses to crank out counterfeits. The cash rolled in, and would until the limitations were removed by presidential order, after "the duration."

One mobster who didn't profit from the new gold rush was Lepke Buchalter. New York's Court of Appeals upheld his death sentence, with those of Lou Capone and Mendy Weiss, in October, setting their executions for early December. An appeal to the U.S. Supreme Court delayed that date, but the high panel proved indecisive. First, it declined to review the verdict in February, then changed its mind in March and scheduled arguments for May, *then* upheld the convictions on June 1. The next hitch, in July, came when Justice refused to deliver Lepke to Sing Sing for execution, first demanding a White House pardon from his federal narcotics sentence.

In the meantime, Irving Nitzberg finally walked out of prison a free man, thanks to a flawed indictment, while Kuppy Migden bargained his role in Irving Penn's slaying down to "attempted assault" and escaped with a slap on the wrist.

Madness.

Speaking of which, Chicago still remained the "god-damn crazy place" that Lucky Luciano had described twenty years earlier. On March 18, a federal grand jury had indicted eleven Outfit leaders—Frank Nitti, Phil D'Andrea, Paul Ricca, Charles Gioe, Louis Campagna, Frank Maritote, Ralph Pierce, Louis Kaufman, John Rosselli, and Nick Circella—for extorting over a million dollars from the International Alliance of Theatrical, Stage Employees & Motion Picture Operators. Turncoat union leaders George Browne and Willie Bioff were the government's star witnesses, but Circella slipped through the net when someone tied his witness-girlfriend, dice club hostess Estelle Cary, to a chair in her Chi-Town apartment and set her afire.

Frank Nitti also made an unexpected exit one day after the indictments, allegedly shooting himself twice—missing his head the first time, if you could believe it—at a railroad yard five blocks from home. Police, who'd tried to murder him on Tony Cermak's orders back in 1932, ruled Nitti's death a drunken suicide, prompted by "temporary insanity" and "severe claustrophobia" developed after he'd served eighteen months for tax evasion ten years earlier. The alternate version: witnesses reported seeing Frank enter an unmarked car with two detectives moments before his death. In either case, his passing was a boon to Paul Ricca, rising to become *capo crimine* with Tony Accardo as his *capo bastone*. If Ricca and the others went to prison, then Accardo —dubbed "Joe Batters" for his skill with baseball bats— would be the man in charge.

While that case was heating up, the Allies had invaded Sicily on July 9, helped along by Operation Underworld and *Don* Calogero Vizzini, of Villalba. On the day of the invasion, a U.S. Army plane had buzzed Vizzini's home, dropping a yellow silk handkerchief marked with an "L" for Luciano. Two days later, when General Patton's tanks entered Villalba, *Don* Vizzini climbed aboard the first in line and spent the next six days leading the victors around western Sicily, introducing them to helpful *mafiosi*. The American Military Government of Occupied Territories (AMGOT) was properly grateful, appointing Vizzini and *Don* Giuseppe Russo of Mussomeli as mayors of their respective hometowns, while Corleone's *Don* Michele Navarra was licensed to collect abandoned Axis vehicles.

The secret, as Luciano told visitors at Great Meadow: AMGOT coordinator Charles Poletti—now a colonel, New York's ex-lieutenant governor—was "one of our good friends."

By July 22, Patton had seized Palermo. Twenty-five days later, Messina was in Allied hands, ending both the Sicilian campaign and Operation Underworld. At ONI headquarters, the relevant files were shredded and burned.

Closer to home, things didn't go so well for Magistrate

Thomas Aurelio. Granted, on August 23 Democrats and Republicans had joined forces to nominate him for a seat on New York's Supreme Court, but one day later, he was caught on tape by D.A. Frank Hogan, who'd tapped Frank Costello's phone, hoping to solve the Carlo Tresca murder. Instead, the tap had snared Aurelio, as published on the front page of the *Times*.

*AURELIO*: Good morning, Francesco. How are you, and thanks for everything.

*Costello*: Congratulations. It went over perfect. When I tell you something's in the bag, you can rest assured. Well, we will have to get together, you, your Mrs. and myself, and have dinner some night soon.

*Aurelio*: That would be fine, but right now I want to assure you of my loyalty for all you have done. It's undying.

BOTH PARTIES instantly repudiated Aurelio's nomination, but Aurelio refused to step down and a proposed alternative candidate Matthew Levy squeaked by under the wire to take his place on the ballot for the American Labor Party.

Jordan could only smile at that. Unless all voters stayed home on November 3, Aurelio's election, as Costello said, was "in the bag."

But where in hell was David when the whole world was on fire?

———

*FBI HEADQUARTERS: September 9, 1943*

IT SEEMED to Aloysius Gantt that J. Edgar Hoover couldn't shake his bone-deep enmity for Larry Fly. The latest round had started in July, when Fly—now chairman of the FCC *and* the Board of War Communications, launched a year before—was charged by one of Hoover's pals in Congress, Edward "Goober" Cox of Georgia, with aiding the Pearl Harbor raid through his ban on warrantless wiretaps. Cox hated the New Deal and everyone attached to it. He also chaired a new Select Committee to Investigate the Federal Communications Commission, parading hostile witnesses while doggedly refusing Fly's request to testify in self-defense.

Denied that forum, Fly retaliated in the press and the *Harvard Law School Record*, declaring, "The challenge is to the bar. Has it the courage? If not, the bar may awaken too late to face the fact that our liberties have been permanently scarred. What is the bar going to do, or would you rather play golf?" Goober Cox, immune to libel charges in the halls of Congress, fired back calling the FCC "a nest of Reds" and "the nastiest nest of rats to be found in this entire country," personally branding Fly "the most dangerous man in Washington." The battle wound up in a draw, with Fly still managing the FCC and few minds changed on either side of the debate. Voters in Georgia loved their Goober and would doubtless keep on reelecting him as long as he drew breath.

Another congressional target—this time of the Dies Committee—was the Foreign Broadcast Monitoring Service, launched in February 1941 to screen and counter Axis propaganda. Martin Dies, as usual, was more concerned with Reds than fascists, accusing three top FBMS members of "un-American beliefs." Even Goober Cox couldn't swallow that load, noting that "Obviously, the U.S. could not conduct an intelligent program for counteracting enemy propaganda without a reasonably accurate knowledge of that propaganda. Monitoring of foreign broadcasts is the only way in which such knowledge can be obtained fully and promptly."

Good news for some interned "enemy aliens" had arrived with this morning's headlines, announcing Italy's surrender to the Allies. Most Italian American internees would soon be paroled, although awaiting their "exoneration" by a second hearing board. Mussolini had been jailed on orders from King Victor Emmanuel III, and there was talk around Bureau headquarters that Italy would soon switch sides as it had in 1915, declaring war against Hitler's Reich.

Gantt knew son Devon would be relatively safe from harm at the L.A. field office, barring confrontation with some desperate fugitive, but what of Colby? What was he involved in with the OSS, and how far had it taken him from home?

———

*Serpukhov, Moscow Oblast: September 26, 1943*

"Is it true they're eating people now, in Leningrad?" asked Darya Sokolva.

Leonid Babin replied, "They're eating anything that they can chew and hopefully digest."

"That's horrible."

"Indeed it is, *dorogoy*."

By December 1942 the NKVD had arrested 2,105 cannibals in Leningrad. They fell into two categories: *trupoyedstvo* (corpse-eating) and *lyudoyedstvo* (person-eating), the latter shot immediately as murderers, while the former were imprisoned. Murders for ration cards were more frequent, with 1,216 recorded in the first half of 1942 alone.

"I like this place," Darya told Babin, shifting gears.

His dacha stood on two acres of wooded land in Serpukhov, a town located sixty-two miles south of Moscow at the confluence of the Nara and Oka Rivers. It was a rustic getaway, but well appointed, with a parlor and two bedrooms, two wood-burning stoves, a modern kitchen and indoor plumbing, electrified by a generator housed in a tool shed nearby.

From this day to fruition of his scheme, the dacha would serve Babin as his love nest and makeshift maternity ward.

He had chosen Darya Sokolva carefully. She was nineteen, to Babin's fairly youthful fifty-four, and while she'd definitely "been around" in English parlance, an NKVD doctor who owed Babin multiple favors had certified her to be free of all diseases and presumably fertile. A thorough physical in that regard included close examination of her thyroid, breasts and hair growth, plus a pelvic exam for scarring from abortions (none), deformities (ditto), and incipient malignancy—the latter using a technique premiered that very year by gynecologists George Papanicolaou and Herbert Traut in their revolutionary text, *Diagnosis of Uterine Cancer by the Vaginal Smear*.

Darya was clean, healthy, and attractive enough to inspire Babin's ardor on cold Russian nights. What more did he need to produce a fine son, whom he'd raise to pursue his grand goal of revenge?

Darya's payoff for agreeing to Babin's unorthodox plan was threefold. First, he would allow her to survive, whereas summary execution would have been assured if she had listened and refused. The circle of acquaintances who knew

Babin's design was small and closely guarded, subject to elimination as the need arose.

Beyond continuing to breathe, Darya would have a life of relative luxury at Babin's dacha, eating the best food available, no longer working on her back except for him, while her police record was secretly expunged. Junior Lieutenant Zakhar Nikolaev, officer in charge of Darya's former domicile at the Coastal Monastery of Saint Sergius, had destroyed her file in front of Babin, fearing to displease the powerful Commissioner of State Security 3rd Class. He still might talk someday, of course, but Babin had him earmarked for elimination in the near future, before he changed his mind and started drafting blackmail plans.

Recent confusion at the NKVD's Lubyanka headquarters would make that easier. After separation from the NKVD back in 1934, the GUGB had been merged with it again in February 1941, then separated out once more in April 1943. Its present chief, Vsevolod Merkulov, could always use more officers, and if Junior Lieutenant Nikolaev vanished in the process, what was one more missing soldier in the greater scheme of things?

As for the master plan, Babin could not say how long it would take. Women were tricky things, might not conceive at once, even without the use of contraceptives—and if pregnant, of course, might produce a female child. Babin required a son who could be separated from his mother, trained from infancy to play the role Babin had scripted for him as a sleeper agent in America, worming his way into the FBI as cancer cells invade a human body. J. Edgar Hoover hired no women for his Bureau, so a daughter was superfluous, an obstacle to be removed and then replaced as soon as possible.

Nine months, if all went well; if not, perhaps another year or more.

Babin hoped he would not be forced to choose a second woman after Darya. He knew married couples who'd produce nothing but daughters, three or more, but he could not afford successive disappointments, much less ultimate defeat. Darya had already agreed to have a son removed, raised by the state, but how might she react if robbed of multiple offspring?

No. They must get it right the first time and be done with it.

Meanwhile, the war dragged on, with Leningrad still under siege, Nazis joined by the Spanish "Blue Division" during August 1942. Soon afterward, the Red Army had launched an eight-week Sinyavino Offensive that failed to lift the siege but thwarted Germany's offensive plan, dubbed "Operation Nordlicht." In January, "Operation Iskra" opened a land corridor along the coast of Lake Ladoga, permitting access to supplies, but "Operation Polyarnaya Zvezda" failed once more to lift the siege in February. By March, Berlin was leaking reports of the Katyn Forest massacre to blacken Stalin's reputation with the Allies.

News from Stalingrad was better. In November 1942, General Zhukov launched "Operation Uranus," aimed at encircling Germans inside the city, and while it succeeded, Hitler forbade retreat at all costs. One man's fanaticism in Berlin, however, could not turn the tide of battle. December witnessed "Operation Winter Storm," as the *Wehrmacht* tried and failed to relieve its soldiers trapped in Stalingrad. On January 21, Red Army forces overran the *Luftwaffe*'s last airbase in the region. Ten days later, despite Hitler's order, *Generalfeldmarschall* Paulus and his staff surrendered to newly promoted Marshal Zhukov, formally ending the battle. Some 10,000 German soldiers continued resistance in the ruins, living and hiding in sewers, but all were rooted out and killed or captured during early March.

Of nearly 91,000 *Wehrmacht* prisoners, only 5,000 would return to see their homes again—or what was left of them after incessant Allied bombing raids. An estimated 35,000 POWs were placed aboard transports to the east, of whom 17,000 died in transit from wounds, disease, forced labor, malnutrition, and the frigid cold.

By July, even Hitler could discern that he had failed, calling off the Kursk offensive too late for his men under fire. In August, "Operation Polkovodets Rumyantsev" liberated Kharkiv, in Ukraine. Italy dropped out of the war in September, but troops led by SS-*Obersturmbannführer* Otto Skorzeny rescued Mussolini from his mountaintop prison, installed by Hitler as head of the puppet "Italian Social Republic." Only yesterday, Red Army troops had liberated Smolensk on the Dnieper River, 220 miles southwest of Moscow.

Darya was checking out the dacha's kitchen, though it suddenly occurred to Babin that he didn't know if she could cook. No matter. He had not procured her to do housework or to please his palate.

Moving up behind her, Babin took one of her hands in his and drew her toward the nearer of the two bedrooms, saying, "We may as well begin, *da*?"

"Yes," she said, and followed after him.

---

*LITTLE ITALY, Manhattan: November 3, 1943*

THE VOTES WERE IN, and it appeared that chatting on a tapped phone line with Frank Costello hadn't hurt Thomas Aurelio at all. Greg Jordan had followed the effort to disbar Aurelio in October, including testimony from Costello —"That's just the way some Italians express things"—but referee Charles Sears found insufficient evidence to prove Aurelio knew Costello's reputation, and three days later, Aurelio buried Levy by a margin of 50,000 votes.

Another winner on November 2 had been Bill O'Dwyer, running unopposed for his old seat as Kings County's D.A. Granted, he was still in uniform and would be til war's end, presently wearing a brigadier general's stars as executive director of the War Refugee Board and a member of the newly-created Allied Control Commission for Italy. No one knew when he'd be back in Gotham to resume his duties, but the voters didn't seem to mind, as both the Democrats and GOP combined to back his reelection. Any stench that lingered from the Reles "suicide" or Albert Anastasia's sanitized police file clearly hadn't caught up with O'Dwyer yet.

In other news, *Don* Charles "Millionaire Charlie" Matranga had died in New Orleans from natural causes, four days before Gotham's election, elevating Sylvestro "Silver Dollar Sam" Carolla to serve as the Big Easy's *capo crimine* with Carlos Marcello as his underboss. Columnist Drew Pearson had exposed a plan by Louisiana congressman James Morrison to pass a special bill making Carolla a U.S. citizen immune to deportation, and while the bill didn't pass, Sam was still hanging onto his turf.

Lepke Buchalter, not so much. At last report, his execution—with subordinates Capone and Weiss—had been rescheduled for November 29.

These days, Greg Jordan worried less about his fellow mobsters, even his beloved brothers, than he did about son

David. Letters home were few and far between, with dates and places excised, nothing he could use to track Dave's progress in the army, but he knew enough to understand that all the censorship meant Dave was somewhere overseas and likely fighting for his life.

Thinking of France, so long ago, Jordan offered a silent prayer to long-forgotten saints that David would come through it somehow, with his mind and body both intact.

———

*TARAWA, Gilbert Islands: November 23, 1943*

IF GUADALCANAL WAS a steaming green morass, Tarawa was a sun-baked, white-hot chunk of Hell on Earth. Nolan O'Hara thought he might die here, but there was no quit in him, come what may.

The Gilberts are a chain of islands and atolls—ring-shaped coral reefs surrounding a lagoon, typically drowned volcanoes—some 2,400 miles southwest of Hawaii and 3,300 northwest of New Guinea. Japan had overrun the archipelago one day after Pearl Harbor and began constructing Tarawa's defense against amphibious assault. Tarawa's largest island, Betio, is a thin triangle roughly two miles long and a 800 yards across at its widest point. A long pier jutted from its northern shore, permitting peacetime cargo ships to anchor in the 193-square-mile lagoon.

But this wasn't peacetime.

Over eleven months, the Japanese had tunneled into Betio like termites into rotten wood. Their force included 2,609 combatants from the Imperial Japanese Navy and 2,217 construction workers, roughly 1,200 of the latter being

Korean forced labor. Aiming to stop attackers in the water or trap them on the beaches, the defenders had built 500 log-and-concrete pillboxes, installed forty artillery pieces in reinforced fire pits, and mounted fourteen coastal defense guns, including four eight-inch Vickers pieces purchased from Britain during the Russo-Japanese War of 1904-05. Additional support included fourteen Type 95 light tanks each bearing a 37-mm cannon and two 7.7-mm heavy machine guns. The garrison's commander, Rear Admiral Keiji Shibazaki, liked to say, "It would take a million men one hundred years to conquer Tarawa."

A million men weren't coming, although the invasion fleet was America's largest to date: seventeen aircraft carriers, twelve battleships, eight heavy cruisers, four light cruisers, sixty-six destroyers, and thirty-six transport ships bearing 35,000 troops. Vice Admiral Raymond Spruance commanded the fleet, with Major General Holland M. "Howlin' Mad" Smith in charge of the Fifth Amphibious Corps and Major General Julian Shoup leading the 2nd Marine Division.

Nolan O'Hara was a father now, his son born in September, while his unit rested and recuperated in New Zealand. They had named him Ryan, a decision made laborious by sluggish mail deliveries in the Pacific Theater. Now, Nolan wondered when he'd have his first glimpse of the boy —or if he ever would.

B-24 heavy bombers had opened "Operation Galvanic" on November 14, disrupting much of Tarawa's communication wire, laid down in shallow trenches. Naval gunfire silenced most of the rest, beginning at 6:10 a.m. on November 20 and continuing for three hours, destroying three of the island's four Vickers guns while minesweepers cleared the lagoon's shallows of lurking explosives.

The plan called for 6,500 marines to assault three beaches—Green, Red and Black—but it went awry immediately thanks to Mother Nature. Admiral Spruance had ignored advice that a neap tide would strand Higgins boat landing craft on the reef, leaving many attackers to swim ashore with their gear through withering fire or sink and drown in the lagoon. Nolan thanked his stars that he'd been crammed aboard a tracked "alligator" amphibious vehicle, taking hits as it crawled over the reef and churned toward shore, but at least providing some cover.

The rest was up to fate.

The moment that his alligator's ramp dropped on the beach, twin .50-caliber machine guns roaring overhead, Nolan was on his own. All plans for any kind of orderly assault were literally shot to Hell and gone. He ran, ducked, dodged and crawled through interlocking streams of fire, explosions wreaking havoc all around him, past the mangled bodies of fellow marines. Some of them screamed, while others were beyond making a sound.

It took forever for the first M3 light tanks to land, most of them hung up on the reef, but those that made it weighed in with their 37-mm cannons and three .30-caliber machine guns each. Marines on foot joined them in sealing off and detonating pillboxes, cleansing the wreckage with flamethrowers, or burying snipers alive in rifle pits the leathernecks called spider holes. It was a slogging, brutal business, Nolan numbed by killing, by the sights and sounds and stench of death.

As that first day ended, he had no concept of casualties, couldn't know that some 1,500 marines were dead already—or that Rear Admiral Shibazaki was a corpse as well, slain by a five-inch naval artillery shell that obliterated his command post and most of his staff.

By nightfall, robbed of their commander and communi-cations lines, Japanese units fought on in isolation, making up their own plans as they went along. Some of their marines swam out to shattered landing craft and the *Saida Maru,* a wrecked steamship whose hulk lay west of the main peer. They waited there, with rifles and machine guns, until daylight bared their targets and they started gunning down invaders from behind.

November 21 was worse than D-Day, many pillboxes still holding out, while small arms fire from the lagoon trans-formed the beach into a crossfire slaughter pit. Nolan teamed up with other orphan leathernecks from decimated units, some he recognized, most of them strangers til he met them under fire. They killed their way inland with rifles, hand grenades and flamethrowers, reducing one pillbox after another, some sprouting up to a dozen automatic weapons.

In the midst of that, some Japanese began crossing sand-bars to reach Bairiki, the next islet west of Betio, but the 6th Marine Regiment teamed with tanks and fighter planes to cut them off, reducing them to mincemeat shortly after 5:00 p.m. By sundown, the marines held all of western Betio, but there was still more killing to be done.

A blood-red sunrise hailed the advent of November 23 and more ongoing slaughter, herding Japanese across the southern coast of Betio and penning them into their last redoubt, east of an airfield. The defenders counterattacked at 7:30 p.m., building up to a 3:00 a.m. *banzai* charge that killed or wounded 173 marines, while losing 325 of their own to small arms and naval gunfire.

And so came morning on November 23, the final day of battle that the late Admiral Shibazaki had believed would last a century. Advancing toward another pillbox with marines who'd joined him since sunrise, Nolan had started to believe he might—just might—escape from Tarawa alive.

The hand grenade came out of nowhere, landing in their midst, closer to Nolan than some of the rest. He recognized it as a Type 97 with a complicated mode of operation: first screw down the firing pin, then pull a cord to bare the striker, hammer it against some solid object, and get rid of the grenade before its fuse ignited, three to five seconds later. Nolan reckoned he had one or two seconds before it blew, and flung himself on top of it instinctively.

Thinking, *Keely, Ryan, I'm so goddamned sorry that I never got to say goodbye.*

And nothing happened.

Nolan waited for the iffy fuse to run its course, finally guessed that he was lying on a dud. Rising to hands and knees, he scooped up the grenade and pitched it toward the nearest ruined pillbox and beyond.

"That was the bravest fuckin' thing I ever saw!"

Nolan glanced up and saw a young shavetail second lieutenant looming over him. He scrambled to his feet, answered, "more like the dumbest, Sir."

"Screw that noise, Private. You just saved this whole platoon."

"Sir, I—"

"You need to head back to the beach and get yourself checked out."

"But, Sir, I'm—"

"And then bring back all the ammo you can carry. That's an order!"

"Yessir."

Nolan turned away, other marines slapping him on his back, and started jogging toward the beach. *Alive,* he thought. *I'm still alive.*

Who could believe that shit?

He was passing a shell crater when a voice called out to him, "Hey, Mack! A little help?"

Nolan stopped short and peered into the crater, where another battle-soiled marine lay, both hands clutched against his bloody side. "You're hit," he said, and instantly felt stupid.

"Fuckin' sniper got me," said the casualty. "Can you help me outta here?"

"Sure thing." Nolan jumped down into the pit and read the smudged nametag on the marine's breast pocket. "Beckwith, is it?"

"*De La* Beckwith, that should be. The quartermaster said he couldn't fit it in. "My first name's Byron. Friends back home call me 'Delay'."

"Where's home?" asked Nolan, as he helped Beckwith stand up, right arm across O'Hara's shoulders, trying not to bump against his wounded side.

"Greenwood," Delay replied, wheezing with sudden pain. "In Mississippi."

"Well, let's see if we can get you back there, eh?"

They made it to the beach, hobbling like partners in some weird three-legged race, and Nolan gave his charge to the first corpsman they encountered, wished him well, and doubled back in the direction of an ammo dump they'd passed along the way.

Tarawa was secured at 1:30 that afternoon, Admiral Shibazaki's hundred years compressed into seventy-six blood-drenched hours. The 2nd Marine Division suffered 3,166 casualties, but the Japanese still had it worse. Of Tarawa's 3,636 defenders, only seventeen survived. Among 1,200 Korean slave laborers, 129 came through the massacre alive.

Nolan O'Hara knew it was a taste of things to come, but he was breathing and unscathed despite his mad attempt to save a bunch of leathernecks he didn't even know.

And if his luck held out, he'd live to see his wife and son someday.

———

*Nassau Yacht Club, Bahamas: December 5, 1943*

DECLAN O'HARA WATCHED the yacht *Playfair* churn southward on its way toward Cuba, thinking to himself, *Good Riddance. Now I can get back to work.*

His sojourn on Nassau—184 miles southeast of Miami, population 29,400—had distracted Declan from his duties with the SIS, but when Director Hoover issued orders to investigate a British VIP's murder, the only proper answer was, "Yes, Sir!"

Not that O'Hara didn't have enough to do already, traveling through South America on Bureau business. SIS Director Percy Foxworth had died in a plane crash near Paramaribo, Dutch Guiana, on January 15, along with Agent Harold Haberfeld and thirty-three others. Given the terrain, searchers could only find enough remains to fill a single casket. A liberty ship, the SS *P. E. Foxworth*, set sail in February, while Agent Jerome Doyle replaced Foxworth at SIS headquarters at Rockefeller Center.

Elsewhere in Latin America, Chile had severed diplomatic relations with the Axis five days after Foxworth's death, while Agent Robert Calhoun helped bag ten Nazi saboteurs in Venezuela a month later. Bolivia formally joined the Allies in April, though President Enrique

Peñaranda seemed to be on shaky ground with his own army. Colombia joined the Allies in November, around the same time Raymond Norweb, U.S. Ambassador to Peru, contacted Bureau headquarters to ask if a favored SIS agent's wife could visit him for Thanksgiving. JEdgar Hoover hit the roof, deeming it "rather presumptuous for the State Department or an Ambassador to inject himself into an administrative policy of this Bureau," and Adolf Berle ha backed him up. Request denied.

Just yesterday, Bolivia had formally declared war on the Axis powers, but warning signs of an impending coup against Peñaranda were increasing.

And in the meantime, Declan had been stuck with Harry Oakes.

Not literally, since the American-born British Canadian gold mine owner, entrepreneur, investor and philanthropist, 1st Baronet of Nassau, had been murdered at his mansion on July 7, shot and set afire in his bed during a raging thunderstorm. None of his family was present, but a houseguest found the corpse next morning and summoned police. For reasons yet unclear, the Axis-friendly Duke of Windsor— formerly King Edward VIII, until he'd abdicated to wed an American divorcée—called Miami PD, which dispatched Captains James Barker and Eddie Melchen to help British cops solve the crime, and it went downhill from there.

Dominating the investigation, Barker and Melchen had arrested Oakes's son-in-law, Count Alfred de Marigny, a French Mauritian playboy who'd claimed Sir Harry's eighteen-year-old daughter as his third wife in 1942, without informing her parents. Pile on suspicion that Marigny wed and dumped his first two wives to profit from their fortunes, and he didn't make a bad suspect, except...

Defense attorneys Godfrey Higgs and Raymond

Schindler soon saw glaring problems with the prosecution's case, including Captain Barker's faking evidence, lying to claim a fingerprint Marigny left on a water glass at police headquarters was found at the Oakes murder scene. Jurors acquitted Marigny, but his reputation in Nassau couldn't be salvaged. The Duke of Windsor branded him "an unscrupulous adventurer with an evil reputation for immoral conduct with young girls," and the same court that acquitted him recommended deportation. Now Marigny was off to Havana, taking his bride and her fortune to another island in the sun.

Meanwhile, Declan had picked up rumors that Meyer Lansky was behind the Oakes killing, his motive based on gambling. Meyer had reportedly finessed the deal with the Duke of Windsor and Bahamian Finance Minister Stafford Sands—"coincidentally" the jury foreman at Marigny's trial —but Harry Oakes opposed the scheme and had been rallying his wealthy friends to block it. Two of Lansky's goons allegedly made their last pitch to Oakes on the night he died, then fled the island under cover of the storm.

In any case, no further charges were anticipated, much less against Lansky, and O'Hara would be glad to resume his assignment with the SIS.

After all, hadn't his chief proclaimed the Syndicate didn't exist?

———

*HPAKANT, Burma: December 15, 1943*

COLBY GANTT WAS GETTING sick of the rain-drenched jungle, leeches and the rest of it, but he had orders and the Southeast Asian Theater of Operations would remain a major scene of action until Tokyo surrendered or its people were annihilated.

At the moment, Colby didn't care which happened first.

China remained a major problem for the OSS, since Admiral Miles and General Dai Li had organized the Sino-American Cooperative Organization to ramrod all clandestine and guerrilla warfare projects in China. SACO was hopelessly corrupt, geared more toward crushing Chiang's domestic enemies than beating back the Japanese, relegating OSS officers to delivering supplies that Dai Li promptly looted for himself. Bill Donovan *had* managed to create Detachment 202 at Chungking, relieving Miles of his command and permitting the OSS to operate without navy interference, but Dai Li remained a problem till Donovan informed him that the OSS would do its job in China whether he like it or not. An unexpected ally—General Claire Chennault of "Flying Tigers" fame, now chief of U.S. air power in China—required current intelligence on bombing targets, satisfied by creation of a new OSS "Air and Ground Forces Resources Technical Staff" to supply it.

Elsewhere in Asia, the Chindits continued their long-range raiding in Burma, while a similar unit, code-named GALAHAD, was activated in India, managed from Kandy in Ceylon by OSS Detachment 404, created in November. Former French Indochina remained up for grabs, and Frenchmen were trained in North Africa, then sent to infiltrate their former colony from China, but they managed little in the face of native anticolonial fervor. An October memo from OSS headquarters urged a new approach, namely to "use the Annamites to immobilize large numbers of Japanese troops by conducting systematic guerrilla warfare in the difficult jungle country" and to "convince the

Annamites that this war, if won by the Allies, will gain them their independence." Rebel leader Hồ Chí Minh seemed amenable, but Gantt foresaw trouble if Washington betrayed his Việt Minh fighters somewhere down the road.

So far, some of the greatest OSS accomplishments had come from occupied Europe, where German diplomat Fritz Kolbe had turned against his Nazi masters in August, first offering his service as a double agent to the Brits, then turning to the OSS when London spurned him. Allen Dulles had been handling Kolbe, gleaning vital information including Hitler's expectations for the coming D-Day invasion, Nazi V-1 and V-2 rocket programs, their revolutionary Messerschmitt Me 262 jet fighter, exposure of an Axis spy working inside the British embassy in Ankara, even Japanese plans for defense of Southeast Asia.

While Kolbe tunneled from within the Reich, OSS detachments had accompanied the U.S. Fifth Army at Salerno and Anzio, while other agents parachuted into Rome and Naples, behind enemy lines. In Yugoslavia, operatives from OSS/Bari and OSS/Cairo aided both Josip Tito's National Liberation Army and Draža Mihailović's Chetnik Detachments of the Yugoslav Army. OSS/Cairo and OSS/Brindisi shared duties in Greece, sailing six-man caïque fishing boats from Alexandria to Cyprus before infiltrating the Greek islands. Three-man "Jedburgh" teams—one Yank, one Brit, and one Frenchman—had parachuted into France beginning in September, laying groundwork for the mass invasion code-named "Operation Overlord" in June of 1944.

For all that, Colby's favorite European operation was carried out by OSS agents in Berne who'd monitored "neutral" Switzerland's shipments of ore to Swedish-owned ball bearing plants at Erkner and Schweinfurt, marking the factories as targets for U.S. Eighth Air Force raids in August and October.

Stateside, the OSS had acquired a new training facility as Washington's once-posh Congressional Country Club edged toward foreclosure, unable to keep up its rent. Bill Donovan got it for a song, plus a promise to restore its 400 acres of manicured lawns, Olympic swimming pool, golf course, tennis courts, palatial clubhouse and surrounding wooded acreage at war's end.

And the OSS continued enlisting recruits from all walks of American life. "Jumping Joe" Savoldi, ex-professional wrestler and running back for Notre Dame, won accolades for his various exploits—parachuting as "Giuseppe DeLeo" into North Africa, Italy, and France; personally guarding Wild Bill Donovan during his meeting with General Patton at Palermo. Chef Julia Child signed on after the Women's Army Corps and the U.S. Navy's WAVES deemed her "too tall," becoming a top-secret researcher in Donovan's office, then moving closer to the Asian front on Ceylon. Historian Arthur Schlesinger Jr. joined up after failing his military medical examination, spending every spare moment on a book, *The Age of Jackson*, that won a Pulitzer Prize. Zionist Arthur Goldberg tried the army, then served as chief of the OSS Labor Desk until Donovan moved him to the Secret Intelligence Branch, organizing anti-Nazi unionists across Europe.

A real standout was U.S. Navy Lieutenant Jack Taylor, a California orthodontist turned gung-ho commando, starting with the OSS Maritime Unit, commanding fourteen coastal missions in Greece and the Balkans, later parachuting into Austria and being captured, caged at Mauthausen–Gusen concentration camp. Actor Sterling Hayden, aka "Lieutenant Hamilton," transported supplies from Italy to Yugoslav partisans and parachuted into occupied Croatia, earning a Silver Star for his rescue of downed Allied pilots. Even bitterness engendered by Japanese internment didn't stop the OSS from recruiting soldiers from the all-Nisei 442nd Infantry Regiment to interrogate prisoners, translate documents, monitor radio communications, and conduct covert operations behind enemy lines.

And as the war progressed, OSS units proliferated: OSS/Oujda in eastern Morocco, organized in September 1943; OSS/Bastia, Corsica, in October; the Service de Renseignement (SR), merged with Charles De Gaulle's Central Bureau of Intelligence and Operations in November; and the Special Projects Office, created in December as a catchall for any "special assignments and missions" was directly supervised by Bill Donovan. Some of their designs fell through—like the plan to hide mustard gas capsules in floral arrangements, thereby blinding officers at German High Command Headquarters—but they had greater success collecting details on Nazi secret weapons, including bunker-busting Röchling shells, *Wunderwaffe* V-weapons, "Fritz X" radio-guided bombs, sonic cannons, Goliath tracked mines, even a futuristic "sun gun" designed to focus destructive heat from outer space that never made it off the drawing board.

Spying was the future, Colby realized, and he meant to be part of it.

If only he could make it through the present global war alive.

————

*FEDERAL BUREAU of Narcotics Field Office, Manhattan: Christmas Eve, 1943*

IKE SAWYER HAD his shopping done ahead of time this year, but still couldn't escape certain last-minute paperwork before he made it home.

Out west, California's "Poppy Rebellion" was finally dying down, starting with a January meeting that included two FBN spokesmen, the state Chief of Narcotics Enforcement, an attorney for the California Farm Bureau Federation, the Chairman of the Committee of California Poppy Growers, and sixteen growers (excluding nine who held permits to harvest opium poppies in 1943). In July, California's narco chief wrote to Harry Anslinger, saying, "You may be assured that there will be no further permits issued by this department for the growing of poppies in California, at least until the matter is entirely clarified by your department."

In early December, California Attorney General Robert Kenney logged a court ruling that "obliged" him to issue poppy-growing permits, but he'd solved that problem by attaching a proviso to each license, warning that a federal license was also required to legitimize cultivation. A few planters forged ahead with new crops, but between the threats and inclement weather, it came to nothing.

While California fizzled out, Mob news was making headlines in Chicago, and Ike followed every bit of it. On December 22, federal jurors had convicted Outfit leaders Ricca, Campagna, D'Andrea, Gioe, Pierce and Rosselli of extorting money from the IATSE, their judge imposing sentences that ranged from seven to ten years, plus uniform $10,000 fines. It sounded good to Ike, but he was also picking up rumbles from Washington, about backroom negotiations with Attorney General Tom Clark, seeking intercession for reduction of the sentences, or at the very least, transfers to lockups easier to stomach than Atlanta's federal pen. Bagmen-turned-rats Bioff and Browne had both received wrist-slaps, and were due for parole sometime next year.

So many fronts to watch, and none that Sawyer could affect by any humble efforts of his own.

*To hell with it,* he thought at last. *It's Christmastime.*

He packed his briefcase and went home.

# CHAPTER 4

DAVID JORDAN THOUGHT he was about to die, and there was nothing he could do but stand his ground—or rather, burrow into it and fight until somebody came along and finished him. He'd been a month approaching this moment and wished he had it back to live over again.

On New Year's Day, the Rangers had begun intensive training for their next fight at Pozzuoli, in Catania, captured by the Allies in October 1943. All three battalions would be spearheading "Operation Shingle," the U.S.'s amphibious assault on Anzio, beginning at midnight on January 22, combined in what was now christened the 6615th Ranger Force.

It had started off like clockwork, landing from British ships with the U.S. 3rd Infantry Division south of Nettuno and approaching Anzio's pier in landing craft. Colonel Darby's 1st and 3rd Battalions landed without opposition, followed by the 4th, and held the beach by dawn despite a belated counterattack by surprised *Wehrmacht* troops under *Luftwaffe Generalfeldmarschall* Albert Kesselring, Hitler's commander of the Italian Theater.

But it went downhill from there.

The Anzio battleground was a basin of reclaimed marshland, faced by enemy-occupied high ground. From there, Kesselring's artillery sank the British destroyer HMS *Janus*, while his troops shelled the beachhead and stopped drainage pumps to flood the basin with saltwater, stalling the American advance. By January 25, the invaders faced eight German divisions with three more en route. Kesselring ordered an all-out attack for January 28, then pushed it back to February 2.

While the *Generalfeldmarschall* waffled, a British reconnaissance unit relieved Darby's Rangers, sending them back to regroup at San Antonio. After a day in bivouac, they'd pushed off at 1:30 a.m. on January 29, the 1st and 3rd Battalions marching through deep drainage ditches, moving silently past German sentries who never glimpsed or heard them. Their target: Cisterna di Littoria on the Appian Way, four miles outside the endangered beachhead, to sever strategic Highway 7 between Rome and Brindisi.

It had sounded good in briefings, but it didn't work.

The 4th Battalion's goal was Isola Bella, but they'd run into determined resistance from Nazi-occupied farmhouses, gun emplacements, and a roadblock reinforced by half a dozen medium tanks. They'd missed connecting with the 1st and 3rd Battalions, the latter ambushed by a German tank along its route of march, with commanding Major Alvah Miller killed. Rangers demolished the first tank with a "sticky bomb," but then emerged from hiding into a full-scale ambush including snipers, machine guns, more tanks, mortars and howitzers—in fact, the whole crack Hermann Göring Panzer Division and the 4th Parachute Division.

Deprived of choices, the Rangers fought and died where they stood, some sacrificing themselves with more sticky bombs, 1st Battalion's Major Jack Dobson critically wounded near sunrise. By 8:30 a.m. the two battalions were surrounded, outnumbered ten to one and taking heavy casualties. Dave Jordan's 4th Battalion pushed onward to help, but hit a steel wall at the hamlet of Femina Morta —"Dead Woman," if you could believe it—where Colonel Darby's command post was also surrounded. Darby, anguished, heard the last radio message from a 1st Battalion sergeant: "Some of the fellows are giving up. Colonel, we're awfully sorry. They can't help it, cause we're running out of ammunition, but I ain't surrendering. They're coming into the building now!" Another voice took over then, shouting, "They're closing in, but they won't get us cheap!"

From the 1st and 3rd Battalions, only six Rangers out of 767 escaped back to Femina Morta, where the remnants of the 4th Battalion waited to receive them. Dave Jordan was amazed to find himself unscathed, aside from minor cuts and bruises, when pursuing *Wehrmacht* troops and Panzer tanks hove into view, pursuing the spent handful of survivors from Cisterna.

Up into the firing line he went once more, crouched in a shell crater and dropping German infantrymen one by one, leaving the tanks for other Rangers with bazookas or the few remaining sticky bombs that now required a human sacrifice to plant them on the armored body of a tank and rip the handle free, igniting a five-second fuse to detonate the charge of jellied nitroglycerine. They worked all right, but no one Jordan saw run forward with one of the fat grenades in hand survived incoming small arms fire.

And still the dwindling force of Rangers held their ground, supported by remnants of the 83rd Chemical Mortar Battalion and the 509th Parachute Infantry. Jordan fired blindly through the drifting battle smoke and rain of soil thrown skyward by explosions, deafened by the gunfire, Panzers clanking, men on both sides screaming as they died.

It was the time, he guessed, when fragments of his short life should be flashing through his mind, but all that he could manage was the robotic loading and reloading of his M1 rifle, emptying each eight-round clip as fast as he could squeeze the semiautomatic weapon's trigger, pausing once to fix its bayonet in case the Germans got that close when he was still alive.

And then his universe exploded, turning upside down. Jordan was airborne, no idea what happened to his rifle, landing hard inside a world of pain. Most of it radiated from his left leg, and he peered down toward it, blinking warm blood from his eyes to see the whole limb twisted in a crazy "Z" shape that reminded him of half a swastika.

He started shouting for a corpsman, anybody who could help him, but had no idea if anyone could hear.

Hell, with the way his ears were ringing, Jordan couldn't even hear himself.

———

*Manhattan: March 6, 1944*

THE WORLD'S slowest telegram reached Gregory Jordan at home, four days in transit from the War Department if its date could be believed. He thanked whatever gods might still exist that Angelina was out shopping when it came,

Gemma in class at Horace Mann, in Riverdale, her senior year with Easter break still one full month away.

Greg needed time to process what he read, part of his mind recalling that his parents would've wept over a telegram like this concerning him, more than a quarter-century ago. It read:

WE REGRET TO INFORM YOU YOUR SON PRIVATE DAVID JORDAN WAS ON TWO FEBRUARY WOUNDED IN ACTION IN ITALY PERIOD YOU WILL BE ADVISED AS REPORTS OF CONDITION ARE RECEIVED PERIOD PRIVATE JORDAN MAY WRITE PERSONALLY AS ABLE STOP:
ULIO THE ADJUTANT GENERAL

BEFORE HE HAD to share the news, Greg made a call down-town and learned the "ULIO" wasn't a coded term, but rather the surname of Adjutant General James Alexander Ulio, chief administrative officer of the U.S. Army.

As if that helped. As if the general had even seen the telegram that bore his name.

As Greg expected, there were bitter tears when Angelina came home from her shopping, cursing him for "letting" Dave enlist. Gemma had taken it a little better, coming home from school, but now both Jordan women were shut up in separate bedrooms, nothing but the muffled sounds of weeping audible behind closed doors.

Wounded in action—"WIA" in army parlance—and what did *that* mean? The good news: David was alive and likely to remain that way if he had made it off the battlefield, into the hands of army medics, surgeons, nurses, or whomever.

And the great unknown: how *badly* was he injured. Jordan was aware of other telegrams that said a serviceman was "slightly wounded." Leaving off the adjective in David's case could mean he was an amputee or paralyzed, even a hopeless vegetable, or—

"Stop it, damn you!" Jordan said aloud. He didn't know a thing about his son's condition yet, and fretting over it in ignorance was pointless. Until someone told him otherwise, hope still remained. It could be worse.

Take Louis Lepke for example.

After more extended wrangling over custody between the state and feds, including harsh recriminations between Governor Dewey and Attorney General Biddle, Lep had been ensconced at Sing Sing's death house with Lou Capone and Mendy Weiss. Kings County denied a new trial in late January, while Bill O'Dwyer—still on military leave— offered and then withdrew a plea for executive clemency six days later. New defense counsel filed another writ of certiorari with the Supreme Court in Washington on March 4, but it came too late, as Lep, Capone and Weiss kept their date with Old Sparky that same afternoon.

Not merely wounded, much less "slightly." They were fried, Buchalter and Weiss buried close to each other at Mount Hebron Cemetery in Flushing, Queens.

Who else was yet to follow them?

*Not Davey,* Jordan thought. *Please, God.*

But would his prayer, a blasphemy, fall on deaf ears? Or was there anyone to hear it after all?

Disgusted with himself, Greg went to pour himself a triple hit of twenty-year-old Highland single malt and see if that might help.

*Camp Edwards, Massachusetts: May 25, 1944*

DAVE JORDAN HAD BEEN on a roller-coaster ride since he was blown up at Cisterna sixteen weeks ago. It wasn't always fast —far from it—but he still had trouble grasping that he'd been transported close to 7,000 miles between that day and this, still without knowing what ultimately lay in store for him.

Against all odds, a corpsman had discovered him before he'd bled to death among the other Rangers and their gray-clad German enemies, carrying Jordan piggyback until they met a litter team who'd taken up the burden and trans-ported him back to the nearest beach, where a landing craft had carried David to a hospital ship offshore. From Anzio, where other Yanks were still fighting and dying for a foothold, he'd been ferried back to England, undergoing emergency surgery en route, then more of the same at the 25th General Hospital near Stockbridge, England. The 25th, as he'd learned, was a military offshoot of Cincinnati General Hospital, shipped over aboard the *Queen Mary* in December 1943.

It was there, between operations and vague assurances from doctors that he "might well" walk again, that Jordan had learned his fellow Rangers' fate. By Colonel Darby's count, a mere eighty-seven of the original Rangers were still alive, the shattered 1st, 3rd and 4th Battalions disbanded. Some survivors were dispersed Stateside as instructors, others folded into the 1st Special Service Force, an elite American-Canadian commando outfit under the command of the U.S. Fifth Army. Back home, fresh trainees with the

2nd and 5th Ranger Battalions were working overtime in preparation for the ultimate invasion of Fortress Europe sometime that summer, code-named "Operation Overlord." Colonel Darby had been shifted to command the 179th Infantry Regiment, part of the 45th "Thunderbirds" Infantry Division still fighting at Anzio, suitably decorated with the Distinguished Service Cross, the Silver Star, the Legion of Merit, the Purple Heart with two clusters, the Croix de Guerre, the Soviet Order of Kutuzov (third degree), and the British Distinguished Service Order.

But David Jordan's war, clearly, was done.

On March 30 he'd left England aboard the hospital ship USAHS *Shamrock*, formerly the USS *Mercy* in World War I, then the passenger liner SS *Havana* until she struck a reef in 1937, next the SS *Yucatan* until she sank in New York Harbor three years later, refloated as the SS *Agwileon* in 1941, finally reclaimed by the navy after Pearl Harbor to resume her original function as the *Shamrock*. It wasn't an encouraging record, but the ship seemed solid enough to Jordan; 129 feet long, carrying 602 patients and a crew of 318 across the Atlantic, making twenty-one miles per hour on a journey of 5,000 miles from England to Charleston, South Carolina.

Call it ten days with luck, and fortune had smiled on the unarmed vessel, placing them in port on time.

From Charleston, arriving on April 8, he was carried aboard a hospital train for a thousand mile trip to New England, spending twenty hours rocking on the rails to reach Camp Edwards on Cape Cod, with its army convalescent hospital. Built for the National Guard in 1931, Edwards had been leased by the army nine years later to support one of its hospitals in the "ZI"—Zone of the Interior. On the side, it trained nurses prior to transit overseas.

Jordan had kept track of the news from Europe while he

traveled, and more was coming through to him right now, as the radio on his ward wrapped up Bing Crosby singing his new hit, "I Love You." The Armed Forces Radio Service took over from there, informing listeners that Allied forces had finally broken out of Anzio and were pushing on toward Rome. Monte Cassino, southeast of the Italian capital, had stalled advancing Yanks and Brits through four assaults, until bombers demolished the peak's ancient monastery. More bombers were pounding Germany and occupied France nonstop in preparation for D-Day next month.

A shadow fell across Dave's bed and he glanced up to see his father standing there alone, eyeing his son's left leg in traction and encased in plaster from his toes to his thigh. "Looks painful," he observed, a small catch in his voice.

"Hey, Dad. It could be worse."

"What's the prognosis?"

"Doctors say I'll walk again, sometime. They're undecided on how badly I'll be limping."

"Jesus, Dave."

"At least we both have Purple Hearts, eh?"

"And a Bronze Star came with yours, I hear."

"Apparently, they give awards for living now."

There was an awkward pause before his father said, "We got your letter, obviously. It was...nice."

"I do my best. Mom couldn't make it?"

"She's hates hospitals, you know. And Gemma has her senior finals coming up at Horace Mann."

So they were sticking to small talk.

David replied, "The prep school, right. She's not tired of the Bronx yet?"

"Not the part she sees of it, commuting back and forth."

"Has she decided where she's going next?"

His father frowned at that. "She's been accepted to

Columbia, a couple other schools, but I don't know. She met a guy. Name's Paulo Ricca."

"It'll happen. Am I hearing disapproval?"

"Not in principle. He seems all right. Studied business administration at CCNY for two years and he runs a Brooklyn print shop, looking to expand when he can swing it."

"So, an *older* guy."

"Three years, less than your mom and I."

"That's not so bad."

"I guess. At least he's not...you know."

Dave knew. "Connected," he filled in.

"Right." His father shifted gears again. "No clue when you'll be getting out of here?"

"I'm still in plaster for a few more weeks. When it comes off, the steel pins stay. They're warning me cold weather may be aggravating for a while. Of course, I have to start PT and learn to walk again before they turn me loose. Nobody wants to guess how long that takes. The medics say it's up to me, how hard I work at it."

"You never were a shirker."

"Yeah. Look what it got me."

"Is there anything you need?"

"Besides two legs that work? I think they've got it covered here."

"Any idea what you'll be doing when they cut you loose?"

"College first, then law school, if I find one that's accepting gimps."

His father scowled at that. "I know a few with open slots for *heroes*. Congress just passed something called the G.I. Bill, waiting for FDR to sign it now.

"I heard. Serviceman's Readjustment Act."

"So, pick your college, and whatever the new law won't cover—"

"I can work, like everybody else," Dave said.

"Right. Sure. And when it's time for law school, we can set up interviews and—"

"*I* can set up interviews. Dad, this isn't your problem."

"It would be my pleasure," sounding like he meant it.

"We can talk about it later, when I'm on two legs."

"Okay. Sounds good. I guess I'd better let you get some rest."

"You're heading back?"

"Business, you know. I'll try and talk your mother into coming next time."

"Don't push too hard, okay? I should be home before you know it."

"And it can't be soon enough."

They shook hands like two grownups, then his father took Dave by surprise, stooping to kiss him lightly on the forehead, near the bandage covering a scalp wound. When he turned to go, Dave wanted to call after him, but he'd run out of things to say.

*Hell of a thing,* he thought, and tried his best to focus on the radio.

———

BANZAI CLIFF, *Saipan, Mariana Islands: July 9, 1944*

LANCE CORPORAL NOLAN O'HARA WATCHED, almost entranced, as hundreds of defeated Japanese soldiers and panicked civilians stood in line to kill themselves, rather than being taken captive by Americans whom, they'd been told, would torture them to death before devouring tender women and children. Nearby, at another precipice dubbed "Suicide Cliff" by marines, identical scenes were unfolding in tandem.

"They must be fuckin' nuts," somebody said, behind O'Hara.

"So?" another voice responded. "Fuck 'em all. Who wants to feed 'em, anyway?"

Rumor had it that Emperor Hirohito himself had ordered mass *seppuku* on Saipan, fearing that members of the island's lower caste civilian population might surrender, thereby subverting Japan's "fighting spirit" at home. General Tōjō had reportedly delayed the order briefly, then broadcast it as required by his divine master. The bloody carnival was underway before U.S. marines could reach the island's northern cliffs, and after four grim weeks of battle they were in no mood to intervene.

Saipan had been a long time coming. First, Howlin' Mad Smith's Amphibious Corps had secured the Marshall Islands in January and February, seizing Majuro, Kwjalein and Eniwetok, while the navy bombarded the Kuril Islands, northernmost outposts of the Japanese homeland, and raided the enemy naval base at Truk in the Carolines. At the end of February, U.S. forces had captured the Admiralty Islands, isolating Rabaul on New Britain. Yanks were battling for Bougainville in the Solomons and had landed on northern New Guinea. On April 14, code-breakers had deciphered the itinerary of Marshal Admiral Isoroku Yamamoto—commander of Japan's Combined Fleet, architect of the Pearl Harbor raid—and mounted "Operation Vengeance," dispatching fighters from Guadalcanal to kill him four days later, as he flew over the Solomons. Saipan's invasion fleet had sailed from Pearl on July 5, a week before aircraft carriers began raining fire and steel on the Marianas.

Saipan is the archipelago's second largest island, forty-five square miles in area, located five miles northeast of Tinian and 120 miles north of Guam. Its western approach offers sandy beaches with an offshore reef creating a spacious lagoon; on the east, another reef obstructs the approach to rocky cliffs. Saipan's highest point is Mount Tapochau at 1,560 feet, while its lowlands are chiefly lime-stone forest teeming with wildlife. Typhoon season runs from June through December.

Historically, Japan had captured Saipan in 1914 and received formal control from the League of Nations four years later, turning it into one of the Empire's most impor-tant Pacific settlements. Immigration in the 1920s included Japanese, Koreans and Okinawans who established large sugar plantations. In December 1941 it was the launching pad for invasions of Guam, the East Indies and Southeast Asia. By 1943 Saipan's population included 29,348 Japanese settlers plus 3,926 Chamorro and Caroline Islanders.

Sailing against them came the 2nd and 4th Marine Divi-sions under Major Generals Thomas Watson and Harry Schmidt respectively, with the U.S. Army's 27th Infantry Division under Major General Ralph Smith—no relation to his Howlin' Mad namesake. A squad of Navajo "code talkers" was also on hand, using their native dialect to keep the Japanese from eavesdropping on Allied radio chatter.

Bombardment of Saipan by fifteen battleships and eleven cruisers began on June 13, pouring 165,000 high-explosive rounds inland before 8,000 marines stormed the western beaches two days later. Japanese defensive fire sank twenty alligators before they reached land, but by nightfall marines held a beachhead six miles wide and a half-mile deep.

General Smith's G.I.s hung back, landing a day later, joining marines on their drive toward the Ås Lito airfield. Lieutenant General Saito Yoshitsugu had abandoned Ås Lito on June 18, thereby dooming all hope of resupply and reinforcement. As the Yanks fought on, their nicknames for the island's major features indicated the severity of battle: "Death Valley," "Hell's Pocket," and "Purple Heart Ridge." Rooting out defenders with flamethrowers and grenades, stalking snipers house-to-house in Garapan, the island's largest village, leathernecks and army "dogfaces" took heavy casualties but killed defenders out of all proportion to the size of their invading force.

And as usual, the Japanese seemed glad to help their adversaries' cause by human sacrifice. Their largest *banzai* charge to date, conducted at dawn on July 7, hurled 4,300 defenders toward inevitable bloody death. Three thousand able-bodied men led the attack behind a dozen carrying a huge red flag. Behind those came the rest, wounded and bandaged, some hobbling on crutches, barely armed. General Saito had demanded it, saying, "there is no longer any distinction between civilians and troops. It would be better for them to join in the attack with bamboo spears than be captured."

So they'd attacked, and nearly all of them had died.

By 4:15 p.m. on July 9, Vice Admiral Richmond Turner had declared Saipan officially secured, although Captain Sakae Ōba and forty-six other survivors of the final *banzai* charge faded into the forest, fighting as guerrillas until they were hunted down and slain or driven to the northern cliffs in bleak despair. Others took the easy way out. Vice Admiral Chūichi Nagumo shot himself on July 6, along with General Saito, Major General Keiji Igeta and Major Tirashi Hirakushi.

Now the final nightmare was in progress, as Saipan's survivors did their utmost to obey their emperor and die as an example to the folks back home. O'Hara watched as half a dozen women and their children jumped into oblivion, holding hands like cutouts in a daisy chain. None of them screamed, just vanished into space, plummeting toward the rocks and sea below. Nolan was numb from watching it but couldn't turn his eyes away.

Next came a tattered soldier, two stars on his collar tabs identifying him as a *gunsō* or sergeant. Smiling as he stood before his enemies at the cliff's edge, he bowed from the waist, then palmed and primed a hand grenade just like the one O'Hara had survived on Tarawa. He tapped its striker on his mushroom helmet, pressed the fragmentation bomb against his ear, and waited.

Nothing.

Glaring in frustration at his frag grenade, the sergeant tried again, and with the same result. Fierce tears were streaming down his cheeks when some marine or other called out, "Fuck this noise" and shot him. As the sergeant staggered backward, ten or twelve more rifles spoke, blasting him into space and out of sight.

*Christ, let it end,* O'Hara thought, but nobody on high was listening. The stark parade of death went on an on, sometimes to hoots and clapping from the leathernecks, more often simply watched in silence.

It came down now to toting up the dead. Of 71,000 invaders, 3,426 were killed or missing, and 10,464 wounded —including a twenty-year-old private first class named Lee Marvin, who'd met O'Hara over lukewarm chow and talked about his goal of becoming an actor someday. The defenders had it worse: of 32,000 combatants, 24,000 had died fighting, while 5,000 committed suicide, along with 1,000 civilians.

It was too much for O'Hara's mind to process, but he knew one thing: whatever followed Saipan, he wouldn't be going home to wife and son until the war was over or he caught what battlefield survivors called a "million-dollar wound" disabling him from further action.

Wounded, dead, or fighting for another blighted island somewhere down the line, battling his way toward what could only be a massacre if the invasion forces ever reached Japan.

Some choice. But it was all O'Hara had.

———

*MANHATTAN: August 28, 1944*

DAVID'S second letter from Camp Edwards sounded wistful, with a tinge of hope that hadn't been apparent when Greg Jordan saw his son in May. He was out of traction, with his cast removed, but scar tissue and long disuse had atrophied the muscles in his wounded leg, so he was learning how to walk again from scratch, with the assistance of a nurse whom he described as "blonde and cute."

The army censors kept hands off this letter, now that Dave was home and they saw no risk to Camp Edwards from the Axis overseas. If it came down to fighting Nazis on Cape Cod, Greg reckoned they would all be well and truly screwed.

At home, the frost was thawing slowly. Gemma, now a graduate and clearly torn between Columbia and Paulo Ricca's charm, had felt the chill between her parents since

Dave joined the army and was getting tired of it, sniping at each of them in turn when she could get away with it, as if she hoped uniting them against her would help things return to normal.

Greg and Angelina had made love once since their son enlisted—fiercely, almost desperately—after they'd received the telegram that he was wounded but alive. She'd wept and cursed herself for staying home when Greg went up to Massachusetts, but he thought she'd mellowed out since then and stopped blaming herself.

But when would she stop blaming him?

It almost came as a relief these days, when Jordan could distract himself with *Cosa Nostra* business. Another of Lepke Buchalter's Brooklyn Troop, Jack Drucker, had dodged the chair with a second-degree murder conviction in the 1937 hit on Walter Sage, receiving life at Dannemora on May 5, but Vito Genovese was the *mafioso* making most of Gotham's headlines lately.

It began with one-eyed Ernie Rupolo, assigned to kill Carl Sparacino back in 1943 for knocking over protected craps games, and while he'd tried his best, Sparacino survived three shots to the face and squealed to police. Convicted of attempted murder in April 1944, Rupolo turned informer on his own account, blowing the whistle on *Don* Vito's role in the 1937 slaying of Ferdinand Boccia. Coincidentally, U.S. Army Central Intelligence Division Agent Orange Dickey had begun investigating Vito's black market business in Italy, arresting two Canadian soldiers who'd stolen army trucks for Genovese. In July, Boccia murder accomplice Peter LaTempa had also turned stool pigeon and was lodged at Brooklyn's Civil Prison in protective custody. One month later, a Gotham grand jury indicted Vito for Boccia's murder, along with sidekicks Peter DeFeo, Gus

Frasca, Michele Miranda, and George "Blah Blah" Smurra. It looked like dark days ahead for *Don* Vito, arrested by Dickey in Naples, but first Dickey would have to clear a path through reams of paperwork obstructing extradition to the States.

Gurrah Shapiro didn't have the luxury of red tape coming to his rescue. Convicted of extortion and conspiracy in May, he had received a term of fifteen years to life. Three months earlier, he'd sent a note to Lepke at Sing Sing. It read: "I told you so."

The biggest joke in town, meanwhile, was Frank Costello. On June 14 he'd accidentally left $27,200 in the backseat of a New York taxi, whose driver dutifully turned it in to the city's Lost Property Bureau on Broome Street. When Frank turned up to retrieve it, he found that Mayor La Guardia and Police Commissioner Valentine had beat him to the punch, putting a hold on the unexplained cash. While headlines had a chuckle at "Forgetful Frank," Costello took the loss to heart, slapping NYPD with a lawsuit in New York's Supreme Court that could drag on for a year or more.

Strange times. In Greg's opinion, Frank would've been wiser to absorb the loss and stay out of the papers following the hubbub over Judge Aurelio, but no one had solicited his view. And Jordan had enough to deal with as it was, at home.

It rankled, seeing nephew Dominic around the neighborhood, living it up, while David had been shot to hell by Nazis, but he kept that to himself, never allowing any hint of animosity to show when he saw Dom or met his father, Jordan's brother Carlo, at the *ristorante*. Everyone had troubles on the home front, these days, and Greg was a master of concealing what he felt inside.

No ulcers from it yet, thank God, and that was something of a miracle itself.

———

THE CUTE BLONDE nurse's name was Claire Thurman. Dave Jordan thought she smiled too much for someone who spent nine hours a day nursing the almost-walking wounded back to something that resembled health, but she had likely been instructed on the finer points of bedside manner by her various superiors.

Whatever, she was good at keeping after him until Jordan could move by fits and starts, initially supported by a set of gymnastic parallel bars—ironically, as Dave now knew, invented in the 19th century by some Kraut in Berlin. From there, as he grew stronger and regained a measure of mobility, fighting the jolts of pain from his left leg, he'd graduated to the use of crutches, then a pair of canes with rubber tips to stop them skidding out from under him. Through all of it, Nurse Claire was at his side, encouraging him whether he did well or poorly, softly shushing him when Dave began cursing his luck with every malediction he'd picked up at school or overseas.

She'd heard it all by now, no doubt, and Jordan knew he'd be a sap if he allowed himself to think she ever spared a moment's thought for him once she had clocked out for the evening.

Stupid—and verging on pathetic, if he ever thought she'd give a sweet goddamn about a crip.

When not struggling to walk again, Dave listened to the

radio and kept up with its bulletins of war against the Reich. Allied troops had captured Rome on June 4, followed shortly by D-Day at Normandy, 155,000 invaders storming Hitler's Fortress Europe and smashing through his proud Atlantic Wall in history's largest amphibious military operation. Paris welcomed Allied liberators on August 25, after General Dietrich von Choltitz ignored Berlin's order to leave the City of Lights "a heap of burning ruins." Belgium still lay ahead, then Germany itself, and why did Jordan feel a pang of guilt at missing out on more chances to die?

Whenever possible, he focused on the future: college with the G.I. Bill, then law school if he found a decent place to take him. Call it seven years of study yet to go—and then, what?

He could always join his father, but unlike his cousin Dominic, he didn't want to be "mobbed up" in any way. That left a host of firms where he could start as an associate, if one of them accepted him, and work ten-hour days until he'd clawed his way onto a partner track, or he could hang his shingle out and try to do it on his own in a society already overburdened with attorneys.

Either that, or move away—perhaps somewhere out west, and break new ground where no one knew that "Jordan" was a tricked-up alias for "Giordano."

It was all too much to think about, when Dave still couldn't walk between the beds in his hospital ward without a helping hand. Get past that hurdle, if he could, and maybe there'd be time enough to seek a future in a world no longer fighting for its life.

———

*Pavuvu, Russell Islands: September 23, 1944*

BY MOST ACCOUNTS, Pavuvu was that most elusive dream of seafarers, a bona fide tropical paradise. The Russells consisted of two small islands—Pavuvu the larger at fifty square miles—and several islets of volcanic origin, located thirty miles northwest of Guadalcanal, but without the Canal's steaming jungle and pestilent swamps. Coconut plantations had predominated until 1941, when the native Lavukal people abandoned them in the face of Japanese invasion, then returned during U.S. occupation of the Solomons in 1943.

For Nolan O'Hara and the rest of the 2nd Marine Division, rest and recuperation on Pavuvu was a hazy, lazy time of card games, beer rations, and desultory preparation for their next mission, as yet to be determined. They'd avoided going straight back to the meat grinder on Tinian and Guam, but cheered Hideki Tōjō's resignation as Prime Minister of Japan on July 22, heaving a collective sigh of relief when the 1st Marines were ordered to assault Peleliu in the Palau Islands on September 15. They were still battling there, and might be for a month of Sundays in the face of stubborn Japanese resistance on "Bloody Nose Ridge."

Pavuvu, by contrast, was like a little slice of J. M. Barrie's Neverland in *Peter Pan*—or would've been, except for the Mad Ghoul.

The Ghoul had started as a rumor: some gyrene awoke screaming one night, claiming a tall, dark prowler with a knife had crept into his tent and tried to hack through the mosquito netting. True or false? The netting *had* been cut— or simply torn somehow—but no one else had seen the grim intruder.

Not until the second time.

Okay, no one had seen him then, either, but he had stabbed a sleeping leatherneck once in the shoulder, maybe with a Ka-Bar or a trench knife, who could say? It wasn't self-inflicted, since no bloody knife was found, and guards were doubled around camp, armed both with lightweight M1 carbines and for backup, not-so-lightweight .45s.

Nobody dozed on guard after the stabbing, fearful that they might wake to a plunging blade or not wake up at all. Nolan O'Hara took his turn, one night a week, and while he hadn't glimpsed the Mad Ghoul yet, that didn't stop the stalker hunting as he pleased. In two week's time he'd knifed two more marines: one in his tent, as with the first; the other, walking back from the latrines, had grappled with the Ghoul but lost him, while sustaining gashes on both hands and arms.

Now it was Nolan's turn on guard duty again, and he would've been lying if he'd said he wasn't pretty goddamned nervous. On a whim, he'd staked out the company's latrines, since they had been the scene of the most recent incident, checking his carbine's safety—set for "off"—and making sure its thirty-round "banana" clip was set firmly in place.

The weapon's .30-caliber cartridge was smaller than the Garand's thirty-aught-six, firing a 110-grain bullet to the larger rifle's 165 grains, and its 300-yard range fell short of the Garand's 500 yards, but Nolan figured that a slug traveling 1,900 feet per second packed enough wallop to drop a man at any decent range.

In fact, he'd seen it do so personally, both on Tarawa and on Saipan.

As for his backup .45, no man could stand before it if he wasn't wearing armor.

Nolan, nerves aside, reckoned his odds of stumbling on

the Ghoul were slim, say one out of the 20,000 leathernecks currently stationed on Pavuvu. He'd discounted native islanders, although one of them might have suffered a psychotic break and run amok, but if he'd had to bet, O'Hara would've said the Mad Ghoul must be a shell-shocked marine.

After an hour smelling piss and shit with quicklime spread to help a bit, he was prepared to try some other spot for lurking in the dark. Just as he pushed off from the palm tree he'd been leaning on, however, something rustled in the nearby undergrowth, and Nolan saw a man-shaped shadow edging into view. The not-so-funny party: he wasn't coming from the main encampment, but *approaching* it by way of the latrine, slinking along, taking his time.

And had that glint of errant moonlight been reflected from a blade in his right hand?

O'Hara raised his carbine, calling out the standard "Halt! Who goes there? Let me hear the password!"

On Pavuvu, they weren't bothering with "L"-laced pass-words such as lollypop or Lilliputian, meant to trip up Asian tongues. Tonight's password, well known throughout the camp, was "Broadway."

Simple, right? Except the man standing in front of Nolan didn't answer him in words. Rather, he snarled like some kind of wild animal and rushed forward, his right arm rising, and there was no doubt about the object in his hand being a knife.

"Stop, or I'll fire!" Nolan commanded.

Nothing from the Ghoul except another raspy growl.

*Fuck it,* O'Hara thought, and squeezed off half a dozen rapid shots from thirty feet. He saw his charging adversary stagger, seem to trip over his own feet, then sprawl headlong on the ground, knife tumbling from the fingers of his outflung hand.

O'Hara bellowed for the sergeant of the guard and kept it up until that individual arrived, panting from his mad dash to the latrine. Together, they approached the fallen prowler, rolled him over at gunpoint, and saw the gleam of captain's bars on his fatigue lapels.

"Fuck me!" the sergeant snapped. "You bagged a fuckin' officer!"

"I bagged the fuckin' Ghoul," Nolan replied. "And there's his knife to prove it."

"I need some brass to handle this," the sergeant said. "You stay right here. I think the bastard's dead, but if he moves, make goddamned sure of it. We don't need him claiming he came to take a shit and you got trigger-happy."

Nolan swallowed hard and watched the sergeant sprinting back toward camp, hoping he'd saved the day instead of stepping into line for a court-martial that could get him hanged.

———

*Los Angeles: October 14, 1944*

THE PUSHBUTTON RADIO in Devon Gantt's 1941 Chevrolet Deluxe sedan was playing Bing Crosby's new hit song, "San Fernando Valley," as Gantt neared the Bureau's L.A. field office. Crosby had lifted it from a Gene Autry movie with cowboys and rustlers, turning it into a love song about California.

> I'm packing my grip
> I'm leaving today.
> I'm taking a trip
> California way.
> I'm gonna settle down and never more roam,
> And make the San Fernando Valley
>     my home.

IF YOU BELIEVED THE SONG, the Golden State had miraculous curative powers for body and soul.

> I'll forget my sins
> I'll be making new friends
> Where the West begins
> And the sunset ends
> 'Cause I've decided where yours truly
>     should be
> And it's the San Fernando Valley for me.

GANTT WISHED him luck with that, along with all the suckers who believed it. Of course, Bing had *his* mansion and a growing family in L.A. already, star of stage and forty-plus Hollywood films since he'd first hit the silver screen in 1930. Lord help any wanderers who thought they'd put down roots in California and mirror his success.

That said, the region's population *was* growing swiftly: 1.5 million citywide and 2.8 million for L.A. County in the last census, while boosters loved to talk about "Greater Los Angeles," a sprawling area of 34,000 square miles that included Ventura County to the west, Orange County to the southeast, and the "Inland Empire" of San Bernardino and Riverside Counties to the east. This very year, the Pacific Electric Railway's streetcars—"red cars" in popular parlance, with no political connotations—had carried 109 million riders over more than 1,150 miles of track spanning a four-county district.

Not that the fabled Land of Milk and Honey was a paradise for all of its inhabitants. If you were Japanese these days, it meant removal to a desert concentration camp while "native sons" bought up your property for five cents on the dollar and Bureau of Internal Revenue collector Harold Berliner—dig the irony, hepcats—filed $188,274 in tax liens against your race, claiming, "These people not only tried to cheat their adopted country over a period of years, but did not hesitate to try to defraud their own race by withholding Social Security taxes."

There was poison in the hearts of many Californians, and now *real* poison in the air over Greater L.A. In July, Los Angeles had suffered through its first foul smog—a slangy contraction of "smoke" and "fog"—a choking, eye-watering haze that cut urban visibility down to three city blocks and sparked fears of Japanese chemical warfare.

And constantly, behind the thin veneer of sun and surf, lay crime. Major crimes had increased over last year in all categories except auto theft—another jolt of irony in a city on wheels—with murders increased nearly 30 percent in twelve months.

It helped sell papers, naturally, if the murder victim was a VIP like twenty-year-old socialite and oil heiress Georgette Bauerdorf, found awash in the overflowing bathtub of her West Hollywood apartment by a maid on October 12. On the last day of her life, Georgette had lunched and shopped with her father's secretary, then visited the Hollywood

Canteen on Cahuenga Boulevard that night, heading for home around 11:15 p.m. The maid found her next morning, raped and badly beaten, strangled with a wad of gauze shoved down her throat.

Nothing for G-men to investigate, but Devon Gantt had always loved a mystery.

L.A. County sheriff's officers discovered that the automatic nightlight outside Bauerdorf's apartment door was partially unscrewed to render it inoperable, but fingerprints on the bulb led them nowhere. A robbery motive was iffy: deputies found Bauerdorf's jewelry, a large roll of two-dollar bills, and sterling silver worth thousands untouched in her flat, but $100 was missing from her purse, along with sister Connie's borrowed Oldsmobile, found abandoned and out of gas on East 25th Street, with a fresh dent in one fender.

A neighbor of Bauerdorf's had awakened to screams around 2:30 a.m., including a female voice crying, "stop, stop, you're killing me!" but he'd chalked it up as a family spat and went back to sleep. Deputies recovered Georgette's date book, bearing names of several servicemen, but they all had solid alibis, including a "swarthy" soldier who'd repeatedly cut in on nearly all of Bauerdorf's dance partners at the Hollywood Canteen the night she died. A coroner's jury stated the obvious—Georgette had been murdered—and proposed a "thorough investigation" to solve the crime, but it was going nowhere fast. In fact, detectives claimed the apartment revealed "no signs of a struggle," despite clear evidence of rape and Bauerdorf's many defensive wounds, including multiple bruises, smashed knuckles on her right hand, and a handprint on one thigh clearly visible "even to the fingernail marks piercing the skin."

*I'd love to solve that for them,* Gantt thought, as he pulled into the Bureau's parking lot, but there was no angle for him to get involved.

Neither could he meddle with the local Syndicate, whose existence J. Edgar Hoover denied. That might be news to Bugsy Siegel, arrested for bookmaking on May 25 at the Sunset Tower Hotel suite of crony Allen Smiley. Also present but spared from arrest was George Raft, who'd moved to Hollywood at Owney Madden's urging in 1927 and had made forty-odd films since then. Raft and fellow actor Mack Gray had testified for Siegel at trial, as character witnesses, but they needn't have bothered. Bugsy and Smiley pled guilty to reduced charges of illicit betting on horse races and paid fines of $250 each.

Meanwhile, Smiley had moved a few doors down the Sunset Strip to new digs at the Sunset Plaza Apartments, where he'd engaged in August's "Battle of the Balcony" with neighbor-bandleader Tommy Dorsey and action movie star Jon Hall.

As sheriff's deputies reported it, Dorsey and actress-wife Patricia Dane had been out drinking with friends, celebrating Dane's twenty-sixth birthday, before coming home for the proverbial "nightcap party." Tommy—the "Sentimental Gentleman of Swing" and pushing forty—had a short fuse where Patricia was concerned, and he'd slugged Hall with a bottle for giving her a goodbye hug at their front door. Hall fought back like the cowboy star he was, and they wound up on Dorsey's second-story balcony, Tommy trying to give Jon the heave-ho while Hall choked him, shouting, "If I go, I'm taking you with me!"

That was when Patricia summoned next-door neighbor Smiley to assist her hubby in the brawl. Before it ended, someone slashed Hall's face, neck, and upper body, slitting one nostril open and requiring fifty stitches. Before lawmen arrived, a dozen tipsy witnesses all came down with a shared case of amnesia, and while Hall refused to press charges, prosecutors still slapped Smiley and both Dorseys with counts of felonious assault. The only witness willing to relate what she had seen, Jane Churchill, turned up with a broken knee after associates of Smiley and The Bug had warned her not to talk—a "traffic accident," as she explained it, just before her mind went blank. The case was dropped in time for Smiley and Siegel to pay their gambling fines and get back to their lives as slightly soiled celebrities.

In other local news, the Los Angeles River delivered its annual flooding; the San Bernardino Freeway opened, speeding transit from L.A. to the Inland Empire; and a heart attack killed real estate mogul and *Los Angeles Times* publisher Harry Chandler at age eighty, passing the newspaper, 1.5 million acres of land, and thirty-five lucrative corporations down to his son Norman.

*It's nice to be rich,* Devon thought, as he locked up his Chevy, entered the office, and found Agent Randall Dukes already sorting through overnight memos piled up on his desk.

*Then again,* Gantt amended, *it isn't half bad being me.*

———

U.S. EMBASSY, *Havana: October 15, 1944*

AGENT DECLAN O'HARA thumbed through last week's issue of *Time* magazine—Yugoslavian resistance leader Marshal Josip Tito on the cover, painted by Russian artist Boris Chaliapin—while he waited for his meeting with U.S. Ambassador Extraordinary and Plenipotentiary Spruille

Braden. He'd been forced to look up Braden's title, learning that the only difference between an "extraordinary" ambassador and an "ordinary" one was that the former's post was permanent, while the latter served only for a specific purpose.

Not that anything seemed permanent in South America these days. Braden had been Washington's ambassador to Colombia from February 1939 to March 1942, appointed to replace prickly George Messersmith two weeks after Pearl Harbor, but only arriving in Cuba five months later. Still, tardy or not, Braden—formerly a copper miner in his native Montana, then Chile—might be an improvement over Messersmith, who'd made a personal crusade of meddling needlessly in SIS affairs.

Things had been going well so far this year, for the SIS overall. Argentina had severed relations with the Axis powers in January, while Chilean police helped Bureau agents silence German radio transmitter PQZ at Antofagasta, deporting spy ring leader Guiflermo Hellemann for interrogation in the States. In Argentina, Declan himself oversaw the destruction of the *Abwehr* radio HDZ, which transmitted messages to Nazi receiving stations in Europe and was instrumental in breaking Germany's "ENIGMA" code. The Brazilian Expeditionary Force had sent its first troops to Italy in July, joining General Willis Crittenberger's U.S. IV Corps. In Venezuela, as assistant legal attaché, Agent Robert Calhoun had directed raids against fascists and diamond smugglers until his recall to the New York City field office earlier this month.

But it was Cuba that concerned headquarters most, these days. Under President Batista, the SIS had established a close, efficient liaison with the Cuban National Police, granting the Bureau better coverage than it enjoyed in any other Latin American nation. Alas, Batista had left office five days earlier, replaced by President Ramón Grau, while the Cuban government experienced a sweeping turnover in administration of its executive, military and police branches. Most Bureau-friendly officials were forced into exile, including the old "Palace Clique" led by Chief of Police Jose Carreno, Sub-Secretary of Defense Luis Collado, and Army Chief of Staff General Genovevo Perez.

As spelled out in a recent SIS memo: "Revolutionary groups have served notice on Grau that they consider this clique is responsible for blocking the 'true revolution' in Cuba, and if not eliminated, the revolutionaries will be forced to take things in their own hands."

President Grau had defeated handpicked Batista's successor Carlos Saladrigas Zayas in June, and while SIS agents continued to work when they could with Cuba's *Servicio de Investigaciónes de Actividades Enemigas*—the Investigation Service of Enemy Activities—Grau was not about to risk further violence from ABC radicals. At the same time, however, the new president was still grappling with his predecessor. As noted by Ambassador Braden in July: "It is becoming increasingly apparent that President Batista intends to discomfit the incoming Administration in every way possible, particularly financially. A systematic raid on the Treasury is in full swing with the result that Dr. Grau will probably find empty coffers when he takes office on October 10. It is blatant that President Batista desires that Dr. Grau San Martin should assume obligations which in fitness and equity should be a matter of settlement by the present Administration."

*Fitness and equity?* Declan suppressed a smirk. When had those terms ever applied to Cuba?

That thought, in turn, brought him back to Aloysius

Gantt's Havana visit eleven years earlier, glimpsed by Mob lawyer and their mutual former classmate Greg Jordan in close conversation with a Cuban military officer, on the eve of Attorney General designate Thomas Walsh's sudden death en route from Havana to Washington, D.C. O'Hara still hadn't decided what to make of that, but there was something...

"The ambassador will see you now," Braden's receptionist announced, and Declan laid his magazine aside, stood up and smoothed the wrinkles from his gray linen suit, pushing thoughts of Gantt from his mind as he moved to face the dragon in his den.

———

*MYITKYINA, Burma: November 19, 1944*

MYITKYINA HAD BEEN an important trading town between Burma and China since ancient times, invaded for the first time in 1892 when Baptist minister George Geis arrived and built himself a mansion that he modestly christened the Geis Memorial Church. The Japanese showed up a half-century later, seizing the town and a nearby airfield, making it a major scene of conflict for the next two years.

Now Colby Gantt stood in the heart of town, rain pouring down and eighty-five degrees regardless, while life at last began returning to a semblance of normality for Myitkyina's Kachin, Shan, and Bamar peoples, No one passing by appeared to notice him, despite his military garb, poncho, and Thompson submachine gun slung over his shoulder.

Japanese planes from Myitkyina's airfield had harassed

the Allies mercilessly, interdicting travel on the Ledo Road and Burma Road, major supply lines to the Chinese troops in Burma and beyond. General Stillwell, back in April, had devised a plan to fix that, mounting a three-pronged attack by 3,000 soldiers including Merrill's Marauders, Orde Wingate's Chindits—minus their founder since he'd died in a March plane crash over India—and two Chinese divisions trained by U.S. Army instructors. They'd captured the airfield on April 18, then foolishly left the Chinese to take Myitkyina itself. They'd botched it horribly, inflicting heavy casualties upon themselves from "friendly fire," even delivering supplies by accident to Japanese defenders, before Stillwell pulled them back and tried again with round-eyed leaders, finally securing the town on August 3. Colby had joined others from OSS Detachment 101 in harrying the Japanese retreat, making sure that only tattered and dispirited survivors reached their base at Bhamo on the Ayeyarwady River.

After Myitkyina, the Japanese had suffered a string of losses throughout the Burma-China-India Theater, including failure to capture Imphal, central India, after a four-month campaign that inflicted severe losses on the Imperial Army. When Lieutenant General Albert Wedemeyer replaced Stillwell in October, he proved himself an ally of the OSS and cooperated with its agents rather than obstructing them.

By then, the OSS had nearly 13,000 agents operating worldwide, including some 4,500 women. Despite continuing hostility from Chiang Kai-shek and General Dai Li in China, they established an espionage training school near Chunking on 200 acres nicknamed "Happy Valley," staffed by Lieutenant Dan Heagy and six radiomen. From there, agents infiltrated Siam and French Indochina, creating a

600-man guerrilla army, providing the Tenth Air Force with 80 percent of its bombing targets, and rescuing 400 Allied airmen who'd been shot down.

In North Africa, OSS/Algiers was constantly in motion, shifting first to Chrea, Algeria, in January, then to Caserta, Italy, in July, still running operations throughout Algeria, Morocco and Tunisia. July also saw OSS/Cairo renamed the 2791st Provisional Operations and Training Unit, though its designated tasks remained unchanged.

In Europe, OSS/London continued parachuting "Jedburgh" and "Sussex" teams into France, wreaking havoc on Nazi forces ahead of Allied invaders who'd landed on D-Day. X-2 also diversified, creating Special Counter-Intelligence teams to translate and decode captured German documents; an Intelligence Insurance Unit using established insurance firms to collect information on Axis industrial targets; and an Art Looting Investigation Unit, staffed by art historians who compiled a list of dealers trafficking in treasures stolen by the Reich.

Which brought Colby's thoughts round to Operation SAFEHAVEN, launched in May and based in Switzerland, often hampered by hostile U.S. Ambassador Leland Harrison and his staff. To duck that pressure, much of the operation was run from Portugal and Spain, but obstruction still persisted from Ambassador Carleton Hayes in Madrid, who deemed spying on "friendly" nations "un-American" and reported identified U.S. intelligence agents to Spanish police. Even at home, conflict persisted, with the State Department and Treasury squabbling over which should claim recovered Nazi loot, both largely shunning intercession by FDR's Foreign Economic Administration, created in September 1943.

Without a diplomatic hook, the OSS sought other ways

of tracking Nazi loot from occupied Europe into "neutral" nations and abroad. By August 1944, its agents knew that the German legation in Stockholm was selling diamonds looted from the Dutch State Bank; that Swiss National Bank had sold 256 bars of looted gold for 14.8 million francs to the Turkish Central Bank, subsequently sold back from Turkey to the German Reichsbank, which in turn sold it for 13.8 million francs to Lisbon's Banco de Portugal; that another million francs worth of gold went to the Basel-based Bank for International Settlements; and that Stockholm's Enskilda Bank had received more than $4.5 million from Germany's Reichsbank, acting as intermediary for the Nazi purchase of German bonds and securities held in New York. One beneficiary of such backdoor deals was New York's Union Banking Corporation—seized in 1942 under the U.S. Trading with the Enemy Act—whose board of directors included ex-Yale cheerleader Prescott Bush, patriarch of a clan with clear-cut political ambitions.

SAFEHAVEN's goals went beyond tracking Nazi thieves, however, including ambitious plans to block German economic penetration outside the Reich's borders, to ensure that Nazi assets were available for postwar reparations to Hitler's victims, and to prevent the escape of German leaders already marked as defendants for war crimes prosecution, should they survive the conflict.

One place where Colby thought Bill Donovan had dropped the ball—or was prevented from engaging by his D.C. masters—lay in failure to support July's plot to assassinate *Der Führer* at his "Wolf's Lair" at Rastenburg, East Prussia. Colonel Claus von Stauffenberg led the plot to kill Hitler with a bomb in his bunker, but the blast that killed four and wounded thirteen had spared the primary target. Sweeping Gestapo reprisals followed, with 7,000 suspects arrested and

4,980 executed. A lucky break for the Allies cast suspicion on Field Marshal Erwin Rommel, who'd committed suicide in October, trading his life for an honored soldier's funeral and amnesty for his loved ones.

Agents were more successful elsewhere in Europe. OSS/Brandisi remained the center of aerial and maritime operations throughout the Mediterranean, while operatives from OSS/Bucharest preceded the Soviet invasion of Romania, linking up with partisans in Transylvania, Hungary, Slovakia and Ukraine. OSS/Sofia operated under cover of an Air Crew Rescue Unit, then withdrew when the Red Army occupied Bulgaria. OSS/Paris was a relative late bloomer, established in August after liberation of the French capital, while all but two agents in Czechoslovakia were lost to torture and death at Mauthausen. In Belgium and Holland, the OSS established active units in Brussels and Eindhoven by September.

Even in the Reich's cold heart, Germany and Austria, agents did their best. Fourteen "Joan-Eleanor" teams penetrated Stuttgart, Berlin, Munster, Regensburg, Munich, Landshut, Leipzig, Plauen, Straubing and Bregenz, though many of their radios suffered damage in transit. In Austria, despite partisan collaboration, 50 percent of the agents sent from England and France were captured, along with nearly all of those initially dispatched from Italy. Even then, survivors managed to coordinate resistance actions in Innsbruck, Klagenfurt and Linz. "Operation Halyard" airlifted supplies to partisan forces in Serbia, while in the far-off Pacific, agents based on Guam operated a Joint Intelligence Center including photographic missions and some maritime sabotage.

New OSS recruits in 1944 included Hollywood actor-turned-director John Ford, involved in 131 films since 1913, present at Omaha Beach on D-Day, though most of his footage would never be broadcast Stateside. Soldier-physician René Veuve had joined the OSS while fighting with Free French Forces, serving under the codename *Joyeuse* ("joyful"), after Charlemagne's sword. Bruce Sundlun, sole survivor of his thirteenth bombing mission over Germany, escaped to Switzerland and worked under Allen Dulles in Bern.

And there were also traitors to be dealt with. Saul Padover, a London-based political analyst for the Federal Communications Commission, sold out OSS-friendly Mayor Franz Oppenhoff in Aachen, leading to Oppenhoff's murder by the Gestapo, then skedaddled for the States and employment with *PM*, a short-lived leftist newspaper in New York City. By May 1944, the OSS itself revealed that Czech engineer Alfred Schwartz's "Dogwood" information chain was badly compromised and had to be shut down.

Despite such gaffes, Washington recognized Bill Donovan's contributions to the war effort, promoting him to major general in November 1944. That didn't mean U.S. diplomats—much less Director Hoover at the FBI—supported Wild Bill's postwar plan to run a larger, more sophisticated version of the OSS after the war. In fact, if anything, success further solidified the obstacles erected in his path.

*No good deed goes unpunished,* Colby thought, and made his mind up not to be among the operatives who were winnowed out when peace or its facsimile arrived.

Before he had to think about that, though, he still needed to make it through the war alive and whole.

———

*THE LUBYANKA BUILDING, Moscow: November 27, 1944*

ANOTHER THANKSGIVING GONE by in America, and Leonid Babin still had nothing to give thanks for at home. Despite his own best efforts—and what he viewed as a suitable response from Darya Sokolva—she still wasn't pregnant after fourteen months of coupling at his dacha in Serpukhov.

Hounded by frustration, Babin had submitted to another semen test that seemed to verify his potency, for all the good that did. Plotting her fertile days on a wall calendar, Babin had hoped they would succeed within a month or two, but now more than a year had passed and he was on the verge of losing hope.

Where might he find another subject for his personal experiment?

The Coastal Monastery of Saint Sergius would normally have been his first choice, but he'd burned that bridge already, by eliminating Junior Lieutenant Zakhar Nikolaev. Nikolaev's replacement, Senior Lieutenant Ujarak Zima, was older than his predecessor and presumably a wiser man, although he knew nothing of Babin's deal with Nikolaev. Even if Babin attempted to deceive him—say, for instance, that he simply longed for clean, young company to keep him warm at night—Zima might balk at the destruction of a new girl's file or keep a copy for himself, to use at need.

And as for killing him, how many Coastal Monastery officers could die or disappear before a whiff of something rotten reached Lavrentiy Beria?

Too risky. Vengeance against J. Edgar Hoover's agency in the United States meant nothing if Babin was executed first, or packed off to the Gulag while his scheme collapsed in ruins.

He would give Darya a bit more time to prove herself, but if she wasn't carrying his child by war's end, Babin would need a new plan, starting out from scratch.

And from *Izvestia*'s headlines, exaggerated as some of the more excitable might be, Babin imagined Hitler's Reich would be collapsing within six or seven months from now, at the outside.

Red Army troops had cracked the epic siege of Leningrad on January 27, after 872 days of bombing and strafing, starvation and cannibalism. Retreating *Wehrmacht* troops had looted and destroyed Saint Petersburg's historical Palaces of the Tsars, plus many other homes and landmarks, absconding with stolen art treasures, but after Operation Barbarossa it all sounded like the tantrum of an angry child.

While that was going on, Red troops encircled two *Wehrmacht* corps south of Kiev, reentered Poland, and pushed westward toward the Baltic countries. Count Ciano, Italy's Foreign Minister and Mussolini's son-in-law, learned that family ties couldn't save him when he was seized and shot by *Il Duce*'s revived Fascist movement. Red Army units were momentarily blocked from Estonia, several units annihilated at Lake Peipus in February, while the Leningrad Front launched the first of four Narva Offensives, lasting from February through July. By May, Soviet forces had overrun the Crimea and captured Odessa in the Ukraine.

Preoccupied Soviet troops were missing from D-Day in June, but they compensated with "Operation Bagration," a massive thrust to reclaim Byelorussia. By July they held Minsk and Vilnius, in Lithuania. Near month's end, Red soldiers liberated the starving scarecrows of Majdanek

Concentration Camp and executed their SS jailers. August found Russian troops in control of Romania and nearing the East Prussian border. Bulgaria fell in September, while more troops entered Hungary, Yugoslavia and Latvia. At October's Moscow Conference, Stalin and Winston Churchill had carved out their respective spheres of Balkan postwar influence.

By November, even Hitler himself could glimpse the premature end of his "Thousand-Year Reich." Deserting his Wolf's Lair at Rastenburg, he fled to Berlin and established his final headquarters underground, in a fortified bunker. Six days later, Heinrich Himmler ordered demolition of the gas chambers at Auschwitz-Birkenau, hoping to bury all incriminating evidence.

As if the Nazi bastards could escape their just desserts.

Granted, some potential war crime defendants had already fled via "ratlines" through Spain and Portugal to South America, aided with fraudulent passports and other documents provided by their allies in the Catholic Church. ODESSA—the Organization of Former SS Members—was already taking shape to shield some of the worst offenders in their flight abroad or to the cover of new, fabricated lives in Germany itself. *Die Spinne* ("The Spider") served a similar function, an alternate network for fugitives led by Otto Skorzeny's "Fascist International." Catching them all might prove impossible, and Babin left that task to others, likely Jews, who craved a personal revenge.

His needs lay elsewhere, first with Darya in Serpukhov, then at the very bastion of his enemies in Washington, D.C.

And he would not give up until his luck and life ran out.

---

*FBI Headquarters: December 20, 1944*

It seemed strange to Aloysius Gantt: the longer that his country was at in war, the more chaotic things seemed on the home front. He'd hoped that they would level out, get better organized, but such didn't appear to be the case.

Casting his mind back to the First World War, a quarter-century ago, it didn't seem to Gantt that things had been so strange, the hectic "slacker" raids aside. Of course, *that* war had only lasted nineteen months—at least, for the United States—versus three years and going strong this time around.

For instance, Gantt couldn't recall any naturalized Americans losing their citizenship during World War I, but FDR had signed a Denaturalization Act on July 1, revoking the citizenship of anyone who renounced it in writing. So far, about 5,000 Japanese interned at California's Tule Lake had done exactly that.

And speaking of Japan, inquiries into the Pearl Harbor raid were piling up. In February the Navy Department had ordered Admiral Thomas Hart, former commander of the Asiatic Fleet, to conduct a one-man investigation with all possible haste, to prevent witnesses or crucial documents being lost in the fog of war. Hart was not empowered to assess blame or make recommendations, so he took four months to issue his 565-page report, containing testimony and correspondence from forty naval officers. New information: zero.

Next up was the Army Pearl Harbor Board, created simultaneously with the launch of Hart's inquiry. Led by Lieutenant George Grunert, deputy commander of the Eastern Defense Command, the three-man panel also included Major General Henry Russell, mobilized from the National Guard, and Major General Walter Frank, commander of the Air Service Command at Ohio's Patterson Field. After grilling 151 witnesses in three months, the board censured General George Marshall, Army Chief of Staff, and General Leonard Gerow, from the War Plans Division, for failing to brief General Walter Short at Pearl on last-minute "MAGIC" intercepts of Japanese correspondence. Unlike Short, neither Marshall nor Gerow were relieved of their commands.

A third investigation, by a Naval Court of Inquiry, convened one day after the army's board, ordered "to give its opinion as to whether any offenses have been committed or serious blame incurred on the part of any person or persons in the naval service, and in case its opinion be that offenses have been committed or serious blame incurred, specifically recommend what further proceedings should be had." That panel—composed of retired Admirals Orin Murfin, Edward Kalbfus and Adolphus Andrews—exonerated Admiral Kimmel and blamed the army for "deficiencies in personnel and material" on Oahu, also scolding Admiral Stark for lack of "sound judgment" in withholding critical data from Kimmel. In closing, the court urged that "no further proceedings be had in the matter."

A solo civilian was next to weigh in. John Flynn—a lawyer-journalist, anti-Semitic FDR basher, and cofounder of the America First Committee—smelled conspiracy at Pearl and blew the perceived whistle in September, with a booklet titled *The Truth About Pearl Harbor*. He concluded that the Roosevelt administration had provoked Japan, then concealed warnings of the impending attack from Pearl's commanders to hasten war with the Axis. Like all who'd come before and those who followed him, Flynn was entirely ignorant of Dušan Popov's warning, spurned by J.Edgar Hoover four months prior to the attack.

The Supreme Court got involved in Pearl's aftermath with *Korematsu v. United States,* argued in October and decided only yesterday. The case challenged Executive Order 9066 as unconstitutional, but six justices rubber-stamped forcible removal of Japanese Americans from the West Coast. Justice Owen Roberts was among the three dissenters, likely influenced by his work on the first Pearl Harbor inquiry.

Despite the navy's October call for a halt to investigations, two more one-man examinations of the raid were already in progress. One, launched in September, had Colonel Carter Clarke from the Military Intelligence Division probing "the manner in which certain Top Secret communications were handled" pursuant to oral instructions from General Marshall. The other tasked Major Henry Clausen—a former assistant U.S. attorney from San Francisco an "a civilian at heart" when he signed on "for the duration"—to supplement the Army Board's investigation "until all the facts are made as clear as possible, and until the testimony of every witness in possession of material facts can be obtained." Neither report was expected till sometime next year.

On a positive note, at least for Director Hoover, nemesis Larry Fly left the FCC in August to practice law in New York. His replacement was Paul Aldermandt Porter, a lawyer-politician who'd been chief of publicity for the Democratic National Committee in this year's election campaign.

As for the Great Sedition Trial, Justice had scrapped its second indictment and tried a third time in January 1944. That time around, defendants included twenty-two from the prior indictments, plus Garland Alderman from Michigan, national secretary of the National Workers League; Lonnie Dennis, a weird spokesman for fascism and guest of Hitler at 1936 Nuremberg Party Congress, once billed as "The Mulatto Boy Evangelist," whose father was a white Georgia attorney, his mother Dad's "high yellow" mistress; Ernest Elmhurst, né Hermann Fleischkopf, head of the Pan-Aryan Alliance and another visitor to Nazi Germany; August Klapprott from the German American Bund; another Bundist, Gerhard Kunze, who'd succeeded Fritz Kuhn as top man in 1939, then fled to Mexico, already serving fifteen years for violating the 1917 Espionage Act; New Yorker Joseph McWilliams, founder of the Christian Mobilizers and the American Destiny Party; Michigan die maker Eugene Sage, co-founder of the Black Legion and the National Workers' League, briefly charged with conspiracy after Detroit's 1942 Sojourner Truth riots; and Peter von Stahrenberg, a Gotham mechanic and head of the American National Socialist Party, who'd proudly declared, "My religion is National Socialism. That's the only religion I believe in. Christianity is the bunk."

Notably missing from the list when trial convened on April 17 were top Klan leaders, any Italian American leaders of groups such as the Fascist League of North America, and the far right's most prominent spokesmen: Father Charles Coughlin and Reverend Gerald Lyman Kenneth Smith, ex-crony of the late "Kingfish" Huey Long. G-men had investigated Smith three times without finding any evidence of subversion amidst his anti-Semitic ravings, membership in the Silver Shirts, or his America First Party, which ran him as its hopeless long-shot presidential candidate in 1944.

Twenty-four attorneys defended the accused, all but three of them unpaid court appointees, while several defendants chose to grandstand as their own counsel. The proceedings before Judge Edward Eicher soon degenerated into farce, lawyers and non-lawyers competing with objections and 500 motions for a mistrial, all denied. Eicher fined seven lawyers for contempt and expelled two from his courtroom, while the American Civil Liberties Union watched and did nothing, despite inclusion of a California executive committee member, Ellis Jones, among the thirty-three defendants.

That show might still be going on if Eicher hadn't died from a heart attack on November 29, replaced on the bench by FDR appointee Bolitha Laws. Judge Laws asked prosecutor Oetje Rogge if he wanted to start a new trial, then recognized the government's dearth of evidence and gave the defendants what they'd sought all along: a mistrial, declared on the third anniversary of Pearl Harbor.

Gantt didn't know if the circus would start up afresh in the new year, but he was inclined to doubt it. After three indictments and seven months of courtroom chaos that had driven one judge to his grave, perhaps it would be best to let the whole thing go.

There was a *real* war to be won yet, and Gantt had a son stuck in the middle of it, somewhere overseas. The same was true of his old classmate, Declan O'Hara, though Declan's foreign posting with the SIS had driven yet another wedge between them, and O'Hara's son Nolan was off in the Pacific, fighting Japanese on islands most Americans had never heard of prior to 1942.

As for Aloysius Gantt, despite the load of work that came his way at Bureau headquarters, couldn't help observing J. Edgar Hoover with Clyde Tolson, thinking that the world at war was leaving him behind.

———

*Camp Edwards, Massachusetts: December 26, 1944*

"Your parents didn't make it after all?" Claire Thurman asked, frowning a bit.

Dave Jordan tried to shrug but didn't like the way it made him feel while he was leaning on two canes. "My mother has a thing about hospitals," he replied. "I don't know how that started, somebody she lost, I guess. My old man has a busy practice in New York."

"A lawyer, right?"

And she'd been listening when Jordan rambled on during their PT sessions.

"Right," he said, and left it there. No getting into family below the surface. "And they've got my sister's wedding coming up next month."

"I guess she's passing on Columbia for now?"

So, *really* listening. "Nobody's saying it, at least to me, but I suspect she's settling for the stock domestic life."

"Well, I suppose it's her decision."

"Sure, just not what either of my parents had in mind for her. Slaving in the kitchen and *bambini*. You know how it is with us *italiani,* eh?"

"Weddings are nice," Claire said, trying to change their conversation's tenor. "Have you met the groom?"

"Not yet. I got a wedding invitation, but who knows if I'll be there?"

"What day next month?"

"The nineteenth. That's a Saturday."

"Three weeks and change." Claire hesitated. Said, "You've made great progress, David, but you'd better take that up with Doctor Addison."

"Old Smiley." Meaning that the forty-something medic never dropped his poker face.

"He's focused on results," Claire said, defending her taciturn boss. "What's best for you, in this case, so you don't come back to us."

"Believe me," Jordan told her, "once I'm out of here, I'm gone."

Was that the smallest wince of disappointment on her face, or his imagination working overtime? She covered it, saying, "Home's better, absolutely."

Covering? Dave brushed that off, thinking, *Yeah, right. She'll miss me like she'd miss a hundred other gimps.*

His mind jumped to the news he'd been pursuing via radio. Ten days ago, the *Wehrmacht* had launched an assault in the vast, forested Ardennes region, hoping to recapture Antwerp. One day later, SS troops had slaughtered eighty-four captive G.I.s at Malmedy, while Nazi regulars surrounded the important crossroads at Bastogne. So had begun the Battle of the Bulge, immortalizing General Anthony McAuliffe three days prior to Christmas, when he'd answered "Nuts!" to Field Marshal Walter Model's surrender demand. The siege had broken just that morning, prompting cheers on Jordan's ward—and likely raging from *Der Führer* in Berlin.

Between announcements from the front, Jordan kept up when he was able with the bulletins that might affect his family. Albert Anastasia had been discharged from the army in November, when they finally decided he was overage at forty-three. Ten days later, CID Agent Dickey had received the FBI's file on Vito Genovese, formally arresting him the day after Thanksgiving. Acting Brooklyn D.A. Thomas Hughes had issued an arrest warrant on murder charges in early December, but if Jordan knew the U.S. Army, red tape could stall *Don* Vito's extradition for months.

At least his dad wouldn't be handling that case. He had enough shady work as it was, with Dave's uncles Primo and Carlo, without getting sucked into another family's travails.

*And maybe,* Jordan thought, *it wouldn't be so bad to miss his sister's January wedding, after all.*

———

*FEDERAL BUREAU of Narcotics Manhattan Field Office: December 26, 1944*

ANOTHER CHRISTMAS LAY behind Ike Sawyer, leaving him to wonder where the time had gone. Talitha had turned forty in July, but she still seemed as young and beautiful as when he'd met her at the Cotton Club, during Prohibition.

Well, *nearly* as young and beautiful. Bearing four children in the past seventeen years and losing one of them, plus all the other knocks that life in Harlem had delivered, left no one unscathed. Still, Ike saw her through loving eyes that didn't notice the odd wrinkle here and there, whether it came from laughter or from tears.

Son Payton had turned fifteen and enrolled at Benjamin Franklin High School, opened in 1942 on East 116th Street, overlooking the Harlem River. Keisha was eleven, midway through sixth grade at Patrick Henry Elementary on East 103rd Street, while six-year-old Frederick was at the same school, in first grade.

Their first-born, Tillman, would have been looking forward to his high school graduation now, if the goddamned diphtheria hadn't reached out to strangle him when he was only three.

Ike tore his mind away from family and focused on the latest news from California, where twenty-three farmers with federal permits had planted 1,310 acres of opium poppies by February. Come spring, when persuasion to plow the crop under had failed, Harry Anslinger moved to seize and destroy the poppies, but growers took their case to federal court, challenging the Opium Control Act's constitutionality. In August, a three-judge statutory emergency court upheld the law unanimously, and the disappointed growers scrubbed their plans for a Supreme Court appeal.

Scratch the Golden State's final "poppy rebellion."

Politics was all the rage this year, beginning on July 11, when FDR announced his plan to seek an unprecedented fourth White House term. By then, Republicans had gathered for their national convention at Chicago Stadium, nominating Governor Dewey with Ohio Governor John Bricker as his running mate.

The Democrats also reserved Chicago Stadium, rallying on July 19. Roosevelt was nominated as expected, but he hit a snag on the vice-presidential balloting. The president desired to keep incumbent Henry Wallace, put party conservatives deemed him "too progressive" and far too friendly with labor, throwing their weight behind Missouri Senator Harry Truman—widely known as "the senator from Pendergast" for his vast indebtedness to Kansas City's mobbed-up boss, dating from 1922. Doubtless aware that he would lose that fight, Roosevelt skipped the convention entirely and visited General MacArthur in the South Pacific to talk strategy, simultaneously ducking any personal appearance that might cue the delegates to his declining health.

The GOP predictably went crazy in its run-up to Election Day, lambasting FDR as a would-be dictator, citing all the presidents before him who'd refused to seek a third term, much less four. For all the heat they generated, though, nothing could overcome the tide of Allied victories abroad that carried Roosevelt to triumph on November 7, with 25,612,916 votes to Dewey's 22,017,929—translated to 432 votes versus 99 in the crucial Electoral College. Nationally, Republicans had carried twelve states to FDR's thirty-six.

More Negroes should've voted that November, since the Supreme Court's April decision in *Smith v. Allwright* deemed southern "white primaries" illegal, but racism was stubborn, shifting gears to impose poll taxes black's couldn't afford and hamstring them with "literacy" tests conducted by white registrars.

An oddity from Dixie was the sudden fall of North Carolina's Robert Reynolds—longtime fan of Hitler and a Silver Shirts associate—who once told his Senate colleagues, "The dictators are doing what is best for their people. I say it is high time we found out how they are doing it, and why they are progressing so rapidly. Hitler has solved the unemployment problem. There is no unemployment in Italy. Hitler and Mussolini have a date with destiny. It is foolish to oppose them, so why not play ball with them?" In 1939 he'd formed his own group called The Vindicators, but that wouldn't fly in 1944. In his place, the Democratic Party nominated former governor Clyde Hoey—pronounced "Hooey," if you could believe it—and Reynolds stepped aside.

More good news of a sort arrived in April, when the Bureau of Internal Revenue slapped Klan headquarters with a $685,000 lien for back taxes owed from its gold rush days in the 1920s. Georgia revoked the Klan's charter, so Imperial Wizard Colescott sold the order's assets and retired to Florida, glumly telling reporters, "Maybe the government can make something out of the Klan. I never could." In his absence, Grand Dragon Samuel Green—an Atlanta obstetrician—held the Georgia remnants together *sans* charter, doubtless scheming toward some future resurrection.

Meanwhile, there was racial violence everywhere Ike looked. There'd been two lynchings in the South: a fifteen-year-old Negro boy in Florida who'd sent a "love note" to one of his white slayers' daughters in January, and sexagenarian Isaac Simmons, a Mississippi minister who'd hired a lawyer to defend his debt-free farm from white land thieves in March. One of the six killers faced trial, naturally acquitted by his fellow crackers.

In a January replay of last year's riots, two people were stabbed in a brawl at a Mexican nightclub in Oakland, prompting white cops and navy shore police club and jail any Latino caught wearing a zoot suit, sometimes shaving their heads for good measure. Elsewhere in California, a munitions explosion at the Port Chicago Naval Magazine killed 320 persons and wounded another 390, mostly Negro stevedores and sailors. When survivors refused to work under deadly conditions, fifty were convicted of mutiny and jailed for fifteen years each.

August brought mayhem to Seattle's Fort Lawton, where three tipsy Negro soldiers—scheduled to ship out next morning—scuffled with Italian prisoners of war, then called for reinforcements from their barracks when they got the worst of it. One POW died, sending forty-three black soldiers to a court-martial that jailed twenty-eight for terms of six months to twenty-five years at hard labor.

Even the vast Pacific's captured islands weren't secure. On Guam, over Christmas, a fight over native Chamorro women left one Negro marine dead, shot by white marines.

The resultant melee saw forty-three marines—all black—imprisoned for rioting and attempted murder.

Ike often wondered if his homeland or the world at large would ever change, and nothing he saw in the headlines made him hopeful. All a working man could do these days, it seemed, was feed his family and try to keep them safe from harm in a society that ranked them second best when it considered them at all.

———

*TENLEYTOWN, Northwest Washington, D.C.: December 31, 1944*

ALOYSIUS GANTT SWITCHED off his radio and walked back to his wing chair, where a tumbler of Jameson Gold Reserve sat waiting for him on an end table. Gwen had turned in early, saying that she didn't feel like ringing in the New Year with their sons both far from home, and Gantt saw no point in debating it.

He had his Irish whiskey and the latest news to keep him warm.

The *Abwehr* hadn't given up its plan to infiltrate America with Operation Pistorius. That scheme's successor, "Operation Magpie" had been cooking in Berlin for months, staking its hopes on agents Erich Gimpel and William Colepaugh. Gimpel had begun his spy career in the Thirties, tracking ship movements while posing as a radioman for Peruvian miners. Deported to the States after Pearl Harbor, he'd been interned in Texas, then shipped home to Germany, where the *Abwehr* snapped him up. Colepaugh was a native Connecticuter and graduate of MIT whose Hitler worship got him in hot water with the Bureau and his draft board. Working his way to the Reich aboard a Swedish freighter, he'd convinced SS Major Otto Skorzeny that he'd make a perfect spy against his homeland. Gimpel welcomed him, convinced that Operation Magpie would require a Yank well versed in modern songs and dances, baseball stats and gossip out of Hollywood.

The pair had sailed together on a U-boat, in September, landing two months later in a snowstorm at Bar Harbor, Maine. They carried ample cash in their baggage, Colepaugh having convinced Skorzeny that a minimum of $15,000 was required to last a year in the U.S.—this at a time when the average family income was $2,250—and if they ran short of currency, they also had diamonds to sell. Reaching Boston by 7:00 a.m., they'd briefly rented digs, then moved on to New York.

At sea, meanwhile, the sub that had delivered them sank a Canadian freighter, prompting Boston G-men to investigate the possibility of spies coming ashore. They'd found two locals who had glimpsed a pair of strangers slogging through the snow but passed them by without a second thought. Where were the strangers now?

Colepaugh, for his part, had abandoned his mission to live a playboy's dream in Gotham, dining at fine restaurants, boozing and chasing anything in skirts, spending an estimated $2,700 on sybaritic pleasures in one month. When he got tired and semi-sober, he'd approached an old school chum, confessed his errand for *Der Führer*, and sat waiting for the Bureau to arrest him. Four days later, on December 30, they'd bagged Gimpel as well, at a 7th Avenue newsstand where he purchased Peruvian papers each morning.

It was another bust for Germany, just when their luck had turned against them on all fronts. Gantt regretted being left out of the action, all the glory going to Boston SAC

Virgil Peterson, but at least it was a solid win to finish off the year.

And what was 1945 holding in store for him, for sons Devon at the L.A. field office and Colby overseas, working for Wild Bill Donovan's OSS? Gantt didn't have a clue, but he was looking forward to a drop-in at headquarters in the morning, his first step toward finding out.

# CHAPTER 5

THE WAR WAS OVER—HALF of it, at least, and that would be Dave Jordan's half, the European Theater. Over for some, that was, the dead and those who'd passed through physically unscathed.

And when would Jordan's war end? He could only wait and see.

The last four months and change had been a roller-coaster ride. Allied troops broke out of the Bulge in January and declared it their win. February saw Belgium swept clean of Nazis, Dresden in flames, 9,000 bombers pounding Germany and some hitting Prague by mistake. While V-2s kept falling on London, Allied pilots targeted their launch sites near The Hague and killed 511 Dutch citizens, again by mistake. G.I.s crossed the Rhine at Remagen and captured Cologne, then Mainz. April's "Operation Grapeshot" swept the *Wehrmacht* out of northern Italy, unimpeded by the sudden death of FDR and Harry Truman's succession. Heinrich Himmler offered a secret truce through the Red Cross but it was rejected, while *Der Führer* put a price tag on his head. In Italy, a group of partisans lynched Mussolini, his girlfriend, and other members of his puppet government, prompting a general cease-fire. At month's end, Hitler snuffed himself and new bride Eva Braun, after appointing Josef Goebbels as Reich Chancellor and Grand Admiral Karl Döntiz as Reich President.

The end came swiftly after that. Rather than surrender, Goebbels and his wife killed their six children, then themselves, on May 1. Three days later, Dönitz ordered all U-boats to halt operations, then joined *Wehrmacht* Chief of Staff Alfred Jodl in unconditional surrender on May 7. Today, Tuesday the eighth, was Victory in Europe Day.

There had been cheering in the ward when that news broke, but most of those present knew they still had a long road back to whatever might pass for health and home.

And now, as if on cue, here came Doctor Smiley, aka Captain Trace Addison, M.D. He looked no worse than usual: a slender, sallow man in white whose frown suggested he'd just finished sucking on a lemon, maybe two or three.

Jordan decided to feign cheerfulness, greeting the medic with, "Good morning, Sir. What's the good word?"

Addison blinked once, like a lizard, and replied, "I guess you heard, the war's over in Europe."

"Yessir. I was thinking of good news for *me*, Sir."

Addison brandished a clipboard but didn't consult it as he answered, "Nurse Thurman tells me your PT's going well."

"I think so, Sir."

"Good, good. A few more weeks of that, and when you're down to one cane, we can likely get you back to Jersey."

Jordan forced a smile, not touching Addison's faulty geography. "A few more weeks, Sir?"

"Three to four, I'd say. Unless we hit some kind of setback."

*We,* Dave thought. *As if your leg got shot to hell.*

Instead of spitting that at Dr. Addison, he kept his smile in place and managed, "Yes, Sir. Thank you, Sir."

"Don't mention it," said Addison and moved off down the ward.

———

*SERPUKHOV, Moscow Oblast: August 10, 1945*

"I'M PLEASED to say it's definite, Commissioner. The lady is...with child."

*At fucking last,* Leonid Babin thought. But said, "There is no doubt?"

"None, sir." Dr. Lazar Serbsky, Major of State Security, looked vaguely injured by the question, but he dared not voice it. "There can be no doubt at all."

"How long?" Babin demanded.

"From my observations and the lady's recollection of her last *menstruatsiya*, I would say six weeks, very near the end of June."

*Yes!* Babin had been with Darya the same day Italy surrendered to the Allies, which had been June 29.

"Then we expect the birth...?"

"Normal gestation is thirty-six weeks," Dr. Serbsky replied. "Late March, next year."

With any luck, Babin surmised, the *ebanatyi* war would

be over by then, a fading memory, and he could start his own.

"Thank you, Major," Babin said, stressing Serbsky's rank to keep their NKVD pecking order foremost in the doctor's mind. "I need not mention that this must, of course, remain—"

"Between the two of us, Commissioner," the doctor finished for him. "Absolutely. Without question."

"Excellent," Babin replied, already wondering when he could rid himself of Serbsky. As an afterthought, he asked, "And how would you assess the lady's mood?"

"It's often difficult to say with young mothers," said Serbsky, frowning as he chose his words with care. "I would say she appeared to be...relieved."

"As are we all. What complications should I watch for?"

Serbsky seemed about to shrug, then stiffened and suppressed it. "There will a certain fluctuating moodiness at times. That's only natural for an expectant mother, most particularly with a first child. Bad signs would be any major cramping prior to a week or so before the scheduled birth, and also bleeding. In the case of either symptom, summon help at once, Sir, any hour of the day or night."

"I'll summon *you*, Major."

"Of course, Commissioner. I am at your disposal."

"Very well, then. Have a safe trip back to Moscow."

Meaning, *Stay alive and fit until I'm done with you.*

He saw the doctor off and locked the dacha's door behind him, shutting out the world. Before he went to visit Darya in the bedroom and congratulate her on their mutual success, Babin paused to consider how the Third Reich had collapsed in such dramatic fashion after New Year's Day.

Red Army troops had penetrated East Prussia in January, then seized Lithuania and captured Warsaw, installing a friendly regime to rule Poland. Crossing the Oder River on the last day of that month, they'd come within fifty miles of Berlin. February's Yalta Conference with Stalin, FDR and Churchill had begun discussing postwar spheres of influence in Europe, while the *Wehrmacht* fought to keep its hold on Hungary. Red soldiers took Vienna in April and pressed into Berlin's suburbs while the Brits and the Americans marked time, having agreed to hand Stalin the German capital. Hitler had lost his mind when SS General Felix Steiner ignored orders to sacrifice his undermanned brigades against Russia's combined Byelorussian and Ukrainian Fronts, deposing Himmler and Göring before his escape through the trapdoor of suicide. Occupied Berlin had overnight become a Saturnalia of bloodlust and revenge: as many as 100,000 German women raped, some up to sixty times and more. Himmler, captured by Brits in May, had killed himself with cyanide, but no one missed him while the NKVD transported some 1.6 million Germans to Russia for "reparations" in the form of dead-end forced labor. By June, Berlin and the nation it once ruled had been divided into four Allied zones of occupation: one each for America, Britain, France and the USSR. On August 8, Moscow belatedly declared war on Japan, than marched into Manchuria an hour later.

But from all that death would come new life: a child whom, if it proved to be a boy, would be molded from infancy into a tool of Leonid Babin's revenge upon the FBI, so long delayed.

Wearing a smile he actually felt for once, Babin moved toward the dacha's bedroom and the woman with that life growing inside her, crucial for the coming thirty weeks or so to Babin's cherished dream.

———

*CAMP EDWARDS: September 7, 1945*

"THREE OR FOUR WEEKS" had turned into four months, but David Jordan hadn't found a way to rush the final diagnosis that would set him free. If he were honest with himself, he had severe misgivings about going home to New York City, worried that it might not feel so much like home, or that the strife between his parents—Mom's anguish, Dad's guilt—would prove to be a burden that he couldn't bear.

Not that their letters to the hospital, much less his father's awkward monthly visits, even hinted at discord between them. Dave knew his family too well for any blunt confessions to be necessary, and his sister's notes provided all the clues that he required. He'd missed her January wedding, but she'd nagged groom Paulo Ricca into visiting Camp Edwards on their honeymoon, and what a thrill that must've been for him.

Hey, welcome to the family. Mobsters, and now a gimp who might come hobbling over for a Sunday dinner now and then, assuming that the army ever let him go.

Dave wondered if they'd make it, lugging all that Giordano baggage with them into their new life, but that was out of his control.

For now, he had to think about his own place in the world—and that world, or at least half of it, still remained at war.

Granted, the Japanese were reeling now, beyond a doubt. The morning after Independence Day, General MacArthur had pronounced the Philippines entirely liberated. Five days later, U.S. Navy planes had raided Tokyo for the first time, followed by bombers over Kure that had sunk the battle-ships *Haruna* and *Ise*. A Japanese I-boat took down the USS *Indianapolis*, killing 300 seamen outright and dumping the other 896 into shark-infested waters, but not before it had dropped off an atomic bomb nicknamed "Little Boy" on Tinian, in the Marianas. One day after that, July 31, American planes had plastered Kobe and Nagoya with incendiary bombs.

Whatever happened in Japan from that point on, Dave had to think about New York and what came next for him. He pictured Cousin Dominic, who spent the war in Little Italy, protected from conscription by his juvie record and a bribed psychiatrist's purported diagnosis that he suffered from "schizotypal personality disorder"—apparently a catchall category that included paranoia, nervousness in social situations, transient psychosis, and "unconventional beliefs" that could mean damned near anything from voodoo to proclaiming that the Earth was flat.

Dave wasn't sure that he could face Dom now, but reck-oned he could fake it well enough for family occasions and the odd night out in Gotham. More important to him at the moment was the G.I. Bill and getting into college, hope-fully Columbia, and sticking with it through law school. He had the brains for it, no doubt. At least his head hadn't been scrambled by the blast that left him with a lifelong limp.

And what about a family, his mom was bound to ask, meaning his own, a wife and kids. There had been no one special when he'd left for boot camp at eighteen, and other than a prostitute he'd fumbled with before the Big Red One shipped out, somehow avoiding clap in the process, there'd been no woman in his life while he was overseas.

As for Nurse Claire, as Dom might say, *fuhgeddaboudit*.

She wasn't for him, and Jordan wondered whether he was right for anyone.

He wasn't impotent—the shrapnel that had maimed him missed the family jewels, if only by an inch or two—but Dave hated the thought of stripping down and showing off his gruesome scars. A hooker could be paid to act as if she didn't mind, but if he cared about the woman, hoped to have her in his life full-time—well, what kind of bizarre, pathetic life would that turn out to be for both of them?

*Fuck it,* he thought. *Or rather,* don't.

No grandkids for his parents, then, unless they came from Gemma, and Dave found that thought didn't depress him. Two world wars had scarred his family so far, and who'd be dumb enough to bet that there would never be another, maybe this time facing off against the Reds instead of teaming up with them?

Grabbing the single cane he used these days, Jordan stood up with no more than the usual amount of pain from his left leg and started off for six or seven circuits of the ward, each step bringing him closer to New York.

———

*OKINAWA, Ryuku Islands: September 7, 1945*

"FLOATING RESERVE," a private first class said. "The fuck is that?"

"It means we stay on shipboard till they change their minds and send us in," Nolan O'Hara answered back.

He'd been promoted to full corporal since Saipan and could've simply told the Pfc. to can it, but O'Hara wasn't thrilled by the assignment either. Not that he was looking forward to another beachhead, far from it, but floating out at sea while others did the heavy lifting felt like an insult.

At least there'd been no repercussions from him shooting Captain X, back on Pavuvu. No one in authority had told him who the Mad Ghoul was, officially, and that was buried in a secret file somewhere, with closure for the captain's family embodied in a lying telegram that claimed he'd died while on a "training exercise," preparing for his next campaign.

Since then, in January, more B-29s had plastered Tokyo, MacArthur's troops had kept his pledge about returning to the Philippines—even if Dugout Doug was forced to film his private landing half a dozen times to get it perfect for the newsreels—while the 4th and 5th Marine Divisions seized a black corral speck in the Volcano Islands known as Iwo Jima, translated as "Sulfur Island."

Which placed Okinawa next in line.

"Okie," as the marines had started calling it before they ever glimpsed it, was the largest of the six major Ryuku Islands, stretching in an arc from Taiwan to the southern-most Japanese island, Fukuoka. It lay 340 miles from Japan, measuring seventy miles long and seven wide, honey-combed with caves and jam-packed with 76,000 Japanese defenders, plus 39,000 drafted Ryukuan natives. Word had it that the Japanese had even forced some 1,800 middle school boys to "volunteer" for their own special "Iron and Blood Imperial Corps" as a desperate last-ditch resort, while high school girls were drafted into a "Lily Corps" nursing unit.

Bastards.

But civilians placed at risk by savages wouldn't dissuade Admiral Spruance Turner's Fifth Fleet from invading Okinawa on schedule, set for April Fool's Day.

In fact, the battle had begun five days earlier, soldiers of the 77th Infantry Division stormed the Kerama Islands, fifteen miles west of Okie, securing them by March 31, while marines grabbed Keise Shim, four miles west of Naha, the Okinawan capital, to mount and man "Long Tom" artillery. Each 155-mm gun could hurl a 100-pound shell fourteen miles, with an estimated "accuracy life" of 1,500 rounds.

"Operation Iceberg" had begun on schedule, the Pacific Theater's largest amphibious assault to date. The invading Tenth Army included the 1st, 2nd and 6th Marine Divisions, plus four army divisions—a total of 88,000 marines and 102,000 G.I.s, plus 9,000 service troops.

But Nolan hadn't hit the beach on D-Day, being posted with the rest of the 2nd Marines in a "demonstration group" off the southeastern Minatoga beaches to preoccupy defenders while the landings went ahead elsewhere. It worked, all right, but then the 2nd went back into floating reserve—just in time to meet "Operation Ten-Go," Tokyo's plan to sink the Fifth Fleet with warships and *kamikaze* suicide pilots. Japan's largest battleship, the *Yamato*, would lead the assault and ideally beach herself on Okinawa to continue the battle from shore, if Admiral Seiichi Itō made it that far.

And Ten-Go had plenty of targets off Okie: nine battleships, seventeen aircraft carriers, twenty-three cruisers, fourteen destroyers, and six light carriers, with thousands of seamen and marines aboard. Call it a turkey shoot, and you'd be near the mark.

Except these turkeys could shoot back.

Japanese retaliation had begun with submarines, sinking one U.S. destroyer and one minesweeper in late March, plus a sub depth-charged by Japanese destroyers. The first *kamikazes* from Kyushu struck on April 2, damaging another destroyer, then returned four days later, blasting nine more ships. By April 30, thirteen more were sunk or badly damaged.

And O'Hara felt as if he had a bullseye on his back.

The *kamikaze* pilots and their backup from the "Thunder God Corps," bolted into rocket-powered Yokosuka MXY-7 Navy Suicide Attacker *Ohka*—nicknamed *Baka* ("fool") bombs, diving with 2,600 pounds of explosives at 620 miles per hour—had come out expecting to die, and every man afloat around Okie was happy to oblige before they struck, if possible. That meant massed fire from every gun in the Fifth Fleet, including marines who cut loose with their M1s, BARs, Thompsons and newly issued M2 selective-fire carbines, even Colt automatics, while screaming every curse they knew at the unfriendly sky.

Defensive fire worked to a point, downing 1,100 Japanese aircraft by April 30, but it couldn't drop all the attackers. They came in swarms, some 1,500 in mass attacks from Kyushu, 185 individual sorties from the same airfields, and 250 sorties from Formosa, where the enemy had concealed 700 planes from U.S. spotters. Land-based *Shin'yō* ("sea quake") suicide motorboats roared out from Okie to join the fandango, each bearing 660 pounds of explosives. Before the bitter end, thirty-six Allied ships went down, with another 368 damaged, costing the U.S. Navy 4,907 dead and 4,574 wounded. On the other side, Tokyo lost 1,430 aircraft and sixteen combat ships—including *Yamato,* intercepted by 300 planes while only 180 miles southwest of Kyushu, sunk with Admiral Ito and 3,055 of his 3,332 crewmen.

The battle ashore was equally bloody, despite the 2nd Marine Division's successful feint. Northern Okinawa was officially secured by April 21, but the island's southern half required more time and grueling effort, hampered by a late May monsoon that turned hills and roads into a morass reeking from corpses. Many men who slid down muddy hillsides wound up with their pockets full of maggots from the rotting dead.

The 2nd Marines finally went ashore on June 1 and waded into their share of the gruesome action, Nolan cursing every step along the way as Admiral Minoru Ōta and some 4,000 sailors crowded into caves at the Okinawa Naval Base on Oroku Peninsula. Ōta sent off a farewell telegram to his superiors on June 12, then shot himself a day later, while Generals Mitsuru Ushijima and Isamu Chō chose ritual *seppuku* on June 22. Colonel Hiromichi Yahara asked permission to join them in death, but Ushijima refused, saying, "If you die there will be no one left who knows the truth about the battle of Okinawa. Bear the temporary shame but endure it. This is an order from your army commander."

So Yahara lived, while many others died. On August 15, Admiral Matome Ugaki joined a futile *kamikaze* attack on Iheya Jima, fourteen miles northwest of Okinawa. The final death tally included 2,938 American marines, 4,675 G.I.s and 4,907 seamen, plus 82 Brits, versus 77,166 Imperial Japanese soldiers, 149,193 Okinawan civilians 82 Koreans, and 34 Taiwanese. Roughly half of the Iron and Blood Imperial Corps children died, including some goaded into suicide bomb attacks on American tanks. Another 55,162 Americans were wounded, while 7,401 Japanese regulars and 3,400 Okinawan conscripts surrendered.

Thousands of civilians killed themselves, à la Saipan, after the Japanese warned them Americans would rape and torture them. Why not, when soldiers of Imperial Japan had executed 1,000 native "spies" who spoke no Japanese and raped hundreds of native women as the battle turned against them in June? Would not *gaijin* invaders be even more dangerous?

All that death, and three casualties stood out in American minds Stateside: on April 18, a sniper on Iheya Jima killed Ernie Pyle, beloved war correspondent for the for the Scripps-Howard newspaper chain. One month later, artillery fire slew army Lieutenant General Simon Bolivar Buckner Jr., and another sniper struck the following day, picking off Brigadier General Claudius Easley.

Regarding Japanese threats of American rape, Marine Corps spokesmen from Okie to Washington insisted that they knew of no rapes by U.S. personnel on the island, but Nolan could have enlightened them on one case, at least.

Operation Iceberg had included some 2,000 Negro marines, comprising the 1st and 3rd Ammunition Companies and the 5th, 37th and 38th Depot Companies. Nearly all were ashore by April 4, and nearly all performed their duties honorably.

All but three, that is, from 37th Depot.

Native inhabitants of Katsuyama village, near Nagao in the northern part of Okinawa, got to know them well and hate the sight of them: three nineteen-year-old leathernecks who turned up periodically, led girls and women off into the brush, and took turns raping them. It had become almost a daily ritual until the locals noted that their tormentors arrived unarmed, laughing, and when the villagers surrounded them at last, bare hands served poorly as defensive weapons. All three had been slain, their corpses hidden in a grotto henceforth called *Kuronbō Gama*, translated as "Cave of the Dark-Skinned Boys." Missing from base, the three were listed first as AWOL, then as possible deserters, finally chalked off as "missing in action."

Which, Nolan supposed, was a vague kind of truth.

He'd heard the scuttlebutt, the same as everybody else, but didn't think it was his duty to report the hearsay claims of crimes committed and avenged. He wanted to put Okinawa in his rear-view mirror and forget about it, if he could.

The Corps' planners were already preparing for the battle that could end all battles—on the teeming islands of Japan itself, with 72 million people pledged to die fighting for their emperor.

———

*Rangoon, Burma: September 23, 1945*

THE BURMESE CAPITAL'S name translated into English as "End of Strife," and while he packed for his return to the U.S., Colby Gantt wondered if that might be an omen. Would the Second World War's end bring peace on Earth at last?

The truth be told, he hoped not.

Where would that leave him?

The Strand Hotel on Strand Road—where else?—had been part of a posh Far Eastern chain for whites only until the Japanese had quartered soldiers there in 1941, then transferred ownership to Tokyo's Imperial Hotel in '42. New management, including Burmese for the first time in the hotel's history, had kept it up as best they could, but it would need a major overhaul if they were going to recapture glory days of old.

Not that it mattered, since he'd likely never set foot in the place again.

Gantt's war had galloped toward its end since January,

with American bombers based near Calcutta raining hell on Bangkok, Formosa and Singapore. Japanese troops fled across the Irrawady River with Lieutenant General William Slim's Burmese and Indian forces in hot pursuit, liberating Mandalay and Rangoon, while Aussie soldiers seized Brunei and began reclaiming Borneo.

In mid July Washington deactivated OSS Department 101, reporting that its complement of 689 Americans had trained 10,000 native guerrillas, inflicted an equal number of Japanese casualties, took down 51 bridges, derailed nine trains, and rescued 232 stranded U.S. airmen.

Which didn't mean hostilities were at an end. On August 9, the day an A-bomb wiped out Nagasaki, OSS Major Paul Cyr led Chinese guerrillas on "Mission Hound," blowing a railroad bridge across the Yellow River near Kaifeng in Henan Province. That same day, fighting between Chiang's Nationalists and Mao's Communists burst into the open, a sign of things to come.

But Colby, packing up his single battered suitcase, worried more about Indochina. In March, amidst rumors of an American invasion, Vichy Governor-General Jean Decoux proclaimed an "independent" Empire of Vietnam, led by puppet Emperor Bảo Đại while Prime Minister Trần Trọng Kim formed a short-lived Vietnamese government of sorts. Two months later, ostensibly to hasten victory, European Allies had divided it along the 16th parallel, sending Chinese Nationalists to disarm Japanese in the northern half, while Brits took the south. At the same conference, France pled for and was granted a return of all its prewar colonies.

Việt Minh leader Hồ Chí Minh despised that plan, using a copy of America's Declaration of Independence furnished by the OSS to draft his own Proclamation of Independence for Vietnam on September 2. Six weeks later, he'd sent a letter to President Truman, protesting restoration of French rule in Indochina, but Truman blithely ignored him. Hô had followed up over the next six weeks with four letters and a telegram to Secretary of State James Byrnes, who likewise gave him the silent treatment. Colby had seen copies of those missives, marked their almost pleading tone as Hô expressed his "great respect and admiration" for America, and couldn't fully understand why Washington would slam the door on him without the courtesy of a reply.

In the midst of that one-way correspondence, Major General Douglas Gracey's 20th Indian Division reached Saigon, disarmed the Japanese, and rearmed 1,400 French soldiers liberated from nearby internment camps. Two days later, a cadre of Việt Minh guerrillas attacked the French colonial administration, killing 150 European civilians. October saw Britain's recognition of French rule in Vietnam's southern zone, while Chinese Nationalist troops ran amok in the north, raping, killing and looting.

Colby imagined he could hear a time bomb counting down in Indochina, hoping he would be stateside before it blew.

One home front case that he regretted missing was the *Amerasia* raid and all that followed after. *Amerasia* was a leftist journal of Far Eastern affairs, founded in 1937 by Frederick Field and Philip Jaffe—a naturalized American born in Russia and friend of the CPUSA Chairman Earl Browder. In January 1945 OSS analyst Kenneth Wells noted an article lifted nearly verbatim from one of his own reports on Thailand, filed in 1944. Agents burglarized *Amerasia*'s New York office on March 11, finding hundreds of classified government documents and alerting the State Department. State, in turn, requested an FBI probe, which produced a second burglary and installation of illegal wiretaps.

The Bureau finally identified the government leakers as State Department employees Emanuel Larsen and John Service, plus Lieutenant Andrew Roth with the Office of Naval Intelligence. On June 6, G-men raided *Amerasia*'s office—this time with a warrant—and seized 1,700 classified military documents. They arrested Jaffe, Larsen, Roth, Service, *Amerasia* editor Kate Mitchell, and freelance reporter Mark Gayn on charges of unauthorized possession and transmittal of government documents.

And at that point, everything went off the rails. The defendants had reached out to Washington fixer Thomas "Tommy the Cork" Corcoran, who in turn "went right up to the top of the damn thing"—in this case, Attorney General Tom Clark, who'd persuaded a federal grand jury not to indict John Service. Jaffe, Roth and Larsen *were* indicted, but their lawyers got a tip that G-men had burglarized Jaffe's home and the case fizzled out. Jaffe pled guilty and paid a $2,500 fine; Larsen anted up $500 for a "no contest" plea; and Roth's charges were dismissed outright.

*Such bullshit*, Colby thought, and Clark was in the thick of it. Admitted to the Texas bar in 1922, he'd partnered with his dad for five years, then served as civil district attorney for Dallas County, where he'd earned his reputation as "a fixer's fixer." Representative Lyndon Johnson had invited Clark to Washington in 1937, where he'd drifted through Justice at the Bureau of War Risk Litigation, the Antitrust Division, Alien Enemy Control, the War Frauds Unit, and finally the Criminal Division, two years before he succeeded Francis Biddle as attorney general.

How many shady deals along the way? Gantt didn't like

to think about it, but it was the way things worked in government, from Podunk Hollow to the nation's capital.

Now the OSS he'd served was being scrapped, chopped up, and scattered to the winds. President Truman had just signed Executive Order 9621, terminating the Service on October 1. The State Department absorbed Research and Analysis, renaming it the Interim Research and Intelligence Service under U.S. Army Colonel Alfred McCormack. The War Department took over Secret Intelligence and X-2, merged as a new Strategic Services Unit under ex-OSS Deputy Director for Intelligence Brigadier General John Magruder. SAFEHAVEN's funding dried up without recovering a dime of Nazi loot, but anyone who cared to run it down in future would have ample leads to stolen billions, sitting in the vaults of neutral nations and the West. As for Wild Bill Donovan, he was officially retired and on his way to Nuremberg, prepared to aid in prosecuting Nazi war crimes.

Colby wasn't sure what lay in store for him when he got home, but he'd heard rumbles of a new Central Intelligence Group in the making, which intrigued him. Wherever he wound up next, the OSS had taught him to prepare for action without limits in a world that seemed immutable to lasting peace.

*Los Angeles FBI Field Office: October 6, 1945*

CAMILLE WAS MIFFED at Devon Gantt for spending Saturday morning at work, but what choice did he have? Hollywood's

"Bloody Friday" had left at least forty persons injured and an uncertain number in jail.

Granted, a local riot wasn't federal business, but with Reds lurking behind the scenery and the Mob-connected IATSE involved, SAC Leland Stafford wanted all hands on deck.

A six-month strike by 10,500 set decorators from the Conference of Studio Unions had lit the fuse in March, bringing pickets to all major movie studios and delaying production on several films, including David Selznick's epic Western *Duel in the Sun* and the biopic *Night and Day*, starring Cary Grant as Cole Porter. Sadly for the strikers, while Disney, Monogram and certain independents quickly signed new contracts, industry giants Columbia, Fox, MGM, Paramount, RKO, Universal, and Warner had 130 films gathering dust on their shelves, prepared to sit it out for the duration.

Enter the IATSE, allegedly cleansed of Syndicate influence three years earlier. Its leaders threatened fines and expulsion for any members who backed the rival CSU, but many still refused to cross the picket lines. By October, the strikers' cash and patience was exhausted. At least 300 gathered outside Warner Brothers on the fifth, met with high-pressure fire hoses wielded by studio security men. Scabs who tried to enter suffered beatings, while their cars were overturned and torched. LAPD sent officers to reinforce outnumbered Burbank cops as the mob swelled to 1,000 or more, the belligerents fighting it out with chains, hammers, nightsticks and teargas.

No one knew if it was over yet, and while the CSU's commanders deemed the fight a victory, it smelled to Devon like a Pyrrhic one. Bureau informer Ronald Reagan's SAG voted to cross the picket lines, while Red influence at the

CSU was being placed under a microscope and AFL President William Green challenged the rebel union's on-set jurisdiction.

When he had time, Devon also followed events in Las Vegas, 270 miles northwest of L.A. and technically none of his business, covered by a Bureau resident agency overseen from Salt Lake City. Nonetheless, Gantt tracked developments in the Nevada desert, gleaning any information that might come his way.

The key was Bugsy Siegel, with his mistress Virginia Hill, an Alabama farm girl who'd never worn a pair of shoes until she lit out for Chicago at age seventeen, whose mobbed-up lovers included Chi-Town gambler Joe Epstein, New York's Joe Adonis—and, of course, The Bug. They'd rented digs in Vegas earlier this year, after Siegel fell in love with legal gambling and persuaded pal Meyer Lansky to finance his dream.

But where to build the ultimate resort? Downtown's "Glitter Gulch"—aka Fremont Street—was already crowded "sawdust joints," all within walking distance of low-rent hotels and the town's first stoplight. Lansky and Siegel spent $600,000 there, for the El Cortez, but Siegel had his eye on something bigger, better, and removed from downtown's hurly-burly by a comfortable seven miles.

What he came up with was a forty-acre spread on Highway 91, purchased by pioneer Charles Squires for $350 in 1905, sold for $7,500 in 1944, now held by Billy Wilkerson, publisher of *The Hollywood Reporter* and owner of three hot nightspots on L.A.'s Sunset Strip. He planned to build a grand resort one mile south of the Hotel Last Frontier, opened in 1941, but found himself $400,000 short and went in search of new investors.

He hit on Lansky and The Bug, a friend of Billy's from

the 1930s, when he'd patronized Wilkerson's L.A. nightclubs. The partners bought into Billy's unfinished Flamingo, approved his choice of Del Webb as construction manager, then muscled Wilkerson into a truly silent, one-third partner's role. Building proceeded, rife with cost overruns, employee thefts, and unforeseen disasters like a concrete fracture that had drained the swimming pool. When Siegel flew into psychotic rages, Webb was rightly worried—until Benny told the quaking contractor, "Don't worry. We only kill each other."

Not entirely true, but construction move forward, Lansky and his New York partners fuming as the cost rose from the early $1.5 million estimate, climbing toward $5 million and beyond.

Devon knew trouble could be brewing there, and while he couldn't take a sanctioned interest in Las Vegas, he intended to collect each scrap of information he could find and keep it all on file, against a future rainy day.

Hell, even in the desert, on those rare occasions when it rains, it pours.

————

*FEDERAL BUREAU of Narcotics Manhattan Field Office: November 30, 1945*

IKE SAWYER SIFTED memos on his desk and knew—no great surprise—that peace between the Allies and the former Axis wouldn't change his job a bit, unless pursuit of drug dealers became more difficult and time consuming.

Out in California, state legislators had amended their Pharmacy Law to cover "hypnotic drugs," listing nineteen in all, plus "any compounds or mixtures thereof" that the mind could devise. Administration fell to the State Board of Pharmacy, which defined professional standards and could yank a druggist's license for abusing them, without imposing prison time.

The "hypnotic" drug that worried Ike most was amphetamine, discovered by American chemist Gordon Alles in 1929 while seeking a decongestant and asthma bronchodilator to replace the stimulant ephedrine. Alles patented his find in 1932, while the Philadelphia firm Smith, Kline & French grabbed a parallel patent for its Benzedrine Inhaler, containing 325 milligrams of oily amphetamine base. Refined into tablets and prescribed for depression, annual sales of Benzedrine topped $500,000 by 1941, when war came along and turned addiction to revamped "Dexedrine" tablets into a worldwide epidemic with no end in sight.

All sides made free use of Benzedrine during the war, handed out to U.S. pilots and stocked in soldiers' emergency kits, likewise picked up by the Brits, Germans and Japanese. Nazis called their version "Pervitin," doled out to *Luftwaffe* pilots as "Stuka-Tablets" or "Herman-Göring-Pills," and to Panzer crews as "Tank Chocolates," but their impact proved so troubling that the *Wehrmacht* cut back its usage, one report noting that "A soldier going to battle on Pervitin usually found himself unable to perform effectively for the next day or two. Suffering from a drug hangover and looking more like a zombie than a great warrior, he had to recover from the side effects." Some soldiers turned violent against their commanders, and the pills were also taking flack for certain "unauthorized" war crimes. Hitler himself had received daily amphetamine injections from personal physician Theodor Morell, from 1942 until the day he killed himself.

Even so, the amphetamine trade was too profitable for corporations to resist. In 1943, SKF filed patent infringement lawsuits against New Jersey's Clark & Clark for marketing Benzedrine look-alike tablets and colorful diet pills mixing amphetamine with metabolism-boosting thyroid hormone. Meanwhile, psychiatrists Russell Monroe and Hyman Drell, stationed at a military prison in 1945, reported 25 percent of inmates eating the contents of Benzedrine Inhalers for the "kick" it provided.

On the gloomy U.S. racial front, ex-Senator Robert Reynolds had announced formation of the American Nationalist Party in January, with close ties to Gerald L. K. Smith. Active in four major cities by spring, it counted Christian Mobilizer boss Joe McWilliams among its major fundraisers until reporters blew the whistle in July and it tanked in October.

In February, an Alabama grand jury considered the case of six white men who'd raped black victim Recy Taylor at gunpoint five months earlier. She'd identified the kidnap car and its driver named his cohorts, one of whom confessed, but Sheriff George Gamble refused to arrest them and grand jurors refused to indict after Gamble called Taylor "nothing but a whore." Racists celebrated their triumph by threatening her family and firebombing her home.

A week before V-J Day, Mississippi lynchers murdered "biggity" Negro veteran Eugene Bell for rejecting a job in a white planter's fields. Amite County Sheriff Wiley Smith told Bell's survivors, "it's bad, but I regret there's nothing I can do. If I try to arrest them, a mob would form and kill all of your family." And, doubtless, vote Smith out of office at the next election.

Over in Georgia, Dr. Green had officially revived the Klan with an October cross-burning, campaigning for the reelection of two-time governor Eugene Talmadge and stretching out the order's tentacles into surrounding states. In Washington, the War Department thought itself magnanimous for permitting white soldiers to bring home Austrian war brides—unless, of course, said soldiers were black, whereupon they would be instantly discharged.

*Maybe next year there'll be a change,* Ike thought, and knew it wouldn't do a goddamned bit of good to keep his fingers crossed.

———

CORRIENTES PROVINCE, *Argentina: December 4, 1945*

THE JUNGLE CRASH site was a bloody mess. Declan O'Hara and his search team from the Argentine Federal Police had nearly missed it in the rough country twenty-three miles south of Pellegrini, a village nestled near the Paraguayan border. All the same, they'd been obliged to look.

O'Hara's main interest among the U.S. Army C-47's fourteen dead was Bureau Special Agent Jeremiah Delworth, "legal attaché" for the SIS in Asunción, Paraguay, lost while traveling 1,300 miles south to Montevideo, on the Uruguayan coast. The rest included five lieutenants, three sergeants, two corporals and three crewmen, ostensibly engaged in a "geodetic mission." O'Hara had to look it up, learning that geodesy dealt with measuring the Earth and its specific parts—which sounded like the weakest cover story that he'd ever heard.

Before the crash, things had been running smoothly for

the SIS in South America. Ecuador and Paraguay had both declared war against Germany on February 2, followed by Uruguay and Venezuela on the fifteenth, and Argentina on March 27. Only Japan remained of the Axis when Chile weighed in on April 11, trailed by Brazil on July 6, but tardy concessions were better than nothing.

Cuba remained the only trouble spot on Declan's crisis map. In February, guided by SIS agents, Cuban National Police had caught Canadian national Thomas Manion with forged travel papers and two military uniforms he hadn't earned, wanted in New Jersey for impersonating officers. That was a win, sending Manion to prison for sixteen months, but the SIS had lost a friend in April, Cuban Palace Secret Police Chief Enrique Enriquez, when drive-by shooters machine-gunned him en route to lunch in Havana with the Service's legal attaché. With Nazis thin on the ground in Cuba, J. Edgar Hoover marked the island as "a center of extensive communist activities," boasting in D.C. that SIS investigation of Reds "has been very productive and of great value to the Bureau."

Maybe. But just try asking Chief Enriquez—or his widow—if the island's revolutionary movement had been neutralized.

Now Declan stood among the mangled, burned remains of fourteen men, remembering the plane crash that had killed SIS Director Percy Foxworth nearly three years earlier. This time, extraction had been deemed impossible, or at the very least a waste of time. The grim alternative: cremation at the crash site.

Overhead, a pale green parachute blossomed, descending slowly with a wooden pallet slung beneath it, bearing cans of gasoline. The Cuban cops were joking now, excited by the prospect of a cookout, and O'Hara turned away from them, thinking, *Just get it over with, and let me get the hell away from here.*

His home in Washington had never seemed so far away.

———

ALOYSIUS GANTT SUPPOSED he had to give the Japanese credit for their stubborn ingenuity, even while facing ultimate defeat. In February they'd devised a scheme for using *fūsen bakudan* ("balloon bombs") as the world's first-ever intercontinental weapon.

Lofted from the eastern coast of Honshu, some 9,300 unmanned balloons bearing incendiary bombs had followed the Pacific jet stream westward, toward targets in Canada and the United States. Most had been shot down or detonated with a minimum of damage over rural areas. In March, they'd scored one lucky hit on the Manhattan Project's Hanford Site, along Washington State's Columbia River, but while power was short-circuited, the project engineers restored it soon. So far, the campaign's only casualties had been five members of a church in southern Oregon, burned while picnicking atop Gearhart Mountain. If the *fūsen bakudan* worried atomic scientists, they hid it well, conducting their first A-bomb test in New Mexico on July 16.

In Washington, meanwhile, repetitive inquires still continued into the Pearl Harbor raid. Colonel Clarke completed his in early August, his 225-page report conveniently finding "no written evidence" that anyone in authority had been forewarned of Japanese code intercepts via MAGIC. Major Clausen's probe wrapped up a month later, covering 695 printed pages with nothing much except concerns about the future of cryptography.

Next came Admiral Henry Hewitt, ordered by Secretary of the Navy Forrestal in May to conduct "further investigation of facts pertinent to the Japanese attack." Hewitt spent two months reviewing prior inquiries and outdid his predecessors by releasing 1,342 pages of nothing new at all.

Still dissatisfied, Congress had created a ten-man joint committee in November, chaired by Kentucky Senator Alben Barkley, to "make a full and complete investigation of the facts relating to the events and circumstances leading up to or following the attack." Whether they were serious, or members simply craved to see their names in headlines, Gantt couldn't have said for sure, but they were not expected to complete their epic work before next spring. So far, as to the August 1941 warning from Dušan Popov, not a word had surfaced in the public record.

Harry Truman had assumed office as president in April, after FDR collapsed and died at his "Little White House" in Warm Springs, Georgia. Kept in the dark about most things, including the Manhattan Project, Truman cautiously began cleaning house in June, dismissing Attorney General Francis Biddle so awkwardly that when he was done, Biddle threw an arm around Truman, saying, "See, Harry, that wasn't so bad." Biddle moved on to serve as one of eight Allied judges at the Nuremberg Trials. His replacement at Justice: Tom Clark, described in *Life* magazine as "a good prosecutor and good lawyer, but most of all a thorough politician."

At Nuremberg, Supreme Court Justice Robert Jackson opened for the prosecution with a speech consuming several hours on November 21, before the trial's twenty-four defendants lined up to claim they were "only following orders." Verdicts were not expected for a year or more, but two Nazi spies in the States—Erich Gimpel and William Colepaugh—had already been convicted and sentenced to hang in February, their punishment later commuted to life imprisonment by President Truman.

Overall, between January 1940 and May 1945 the Bureau had investigated 19,299 alleged cases of home front sabotage. Evidence supported 2,282 of those claims, but they all came down acts of spite, malicious mischief, of sheer negligence. No Axis agents stood accused of any proven sabotage during the war.

The strangest case to date, in Gantt's view, was the trial of expatriate American poet Ezra Pound, born in 1885, living abroad since he was twenty-three. Enamored of fascism, he'd accepted pay from Mussolini's government for making hundreds of radio propaganda broadcasts lambasting his homeland, Jews, and FDR. Arrested by Italy's U.S. conquerors in April, Pound was extradited to the States for trial on treason charges before Chief Justice Bolitha Laws of Washington's district court. Deemed by Laws as mentally unfit for trial, Pound landed in the psych ward at St. Elizabeths Hospital, whose previous patients included presidential assassin Charles Guiteau and army surgeon William Minor, accused murderer and a leading contributor to the *Oxford English Dictionary.*

Pound would presumably go free one day, once he was suitably forgotten by another generation. In the meantime, dark suspicion kept swirling around Alger Hiss, lately secretary-general of the United Nations Charter Conference in San Francisco. In September, a Ukrainian defector from the Soviet embassy in Ottawa, had accused an "assistant to an assistant" to U.S. Secretary of State Stettinius of spying for Russia, but the informer didn't know the agent's name. J. Edgar Hoover jumped to the conclusion that it must be Hiss,

encouraged in December when confessed Soviet spy Elizabeth Bentley named "Eugene Hiss" as a secret Russian
courier. The name was wrong, but Hoover had no problem
tapping Hiss's phones illegally and launching an investigation of his wife Priscilla.

Would it come to anything? Gantt didn't know, but if the
Chief wanted another sacrifice, it was his role to serve as an
inquisitor. What happened to the evidence he found, if any,
would be up to Hoover and his boss, Tom Clark.

————

LITTLE ITALY, *Manhattan: December 20, 1945*

GREG JORDAN WASN'T LOOKING FORWARD to another Christmas, even if this one would be the first of five to call for cele-
bration in the postwar world.

His mother, Francesca, had set the tone by passing in
October at age seventy-six, startling her three surviving sons
with the fact that she outlived their father by more than six
years. Greg reckoned that missing her husband Fausto had
as much to do with it as age.

Primo, her eldest, wasn't doing well himself at fifty-
seven, smoking like a chimney for as long as Jordan could
remember, coughing like a coal miner who'd spent his
whole life underground and stubbornly refusing to consult
a doctor.

Brother Carlo and his wife Caprice, both in their early
fifties now, getting by all right despite their sons: the elder,
Dominic, had just turned twenty-one like David, but
without going go war, while brother Angelo, nineteen, was
following Dom's bad example on the streets.

Speaking of Dave, Greg hoped he might be home sometime in spring of next year, but he'd miss the holidays and
sister Gemma's January wedding. That was coming none too
soon, as Greg had learned in anxious whispers from his
wife. Gemma had been afraid to face him, but she'd told her
mother she was carrying fiancé Paulo Ricca's child, due to
arrive in August. There went Columbia and all her other
dreams for good, and Greg had briefly mulled a plan for
making Paulo disappear, then put it out of mind. If Gemma
brought her kid into the world without a father, he and
Angelina would most likely wind up raising him or her.

And what a crazy world it was to raise a baby in.

Better for some than others, sure, including Vito
Genovese. In Italy, Agent Dickey with the army's CID had
learned of Vito's Gotham indictment in January, eight days
before key witness Peter LaTempa croaked at Brooklyn Civil
Prison. He'd been taking medicine for gallstones but had
somehow managed to ingest poison instead—enough, the
medical examiner declared, "to kill eight horses"—or one
stoolpigeon. Assistant D.A. Edward Heffernan decided it
was suicide. Dickey and Vito boarded the SS *James Lykes* in
May and reached Manhattan on June 1, with Vito arraigned
the next day. He pled not guilty of course, and more months
of stalling began.

"Operation Underworld," by contrast, seemed to be
winding up. On V-E Day, Charley Luciano's attorney petitioned Governor Dewey for executive clemency, asserting
that his client had rendered critical war aid. Dewey, who'd
put Luciano away in the first place, promised to "take it
under advisement."

And then, there was Bill O'Dwyer. He'd left the army as a
brigadier general, when President Truman abolished the
War Refugee Board in September, and scurried back home

for a whirlwind mayoral campaign. Three days before the vote, Brooklyn D.A. George Beldock vowed to pursue Albert Anastasia's murder of Peter Panto in 1939, but Tammany and Gotham's voters didn't seem to care. On November 6 O'Dwyer triumphed over GOP rival Jonah Goldstein and five third-party hopefuls, coasting to victory with 57 percent of all ballots cast. His victory speech assured New Yorkers, "It is our high purpose to devote our whole time, our whole energy, to do good work."

Ten days later, a grand jury convened to reinvestigate the Panto hit. Just this morning, it had returned a presentment —far from an indictment, bearing no threat of reprisal— charging O'Dwyer with "laxity" for his failure to jail Anastasia. If the new mayor gave a damn, he didn't bother showing it, and the Mad Hatter must be laughing up his sleeve.

It was another near miss, with a bullet dodged by all concerned.

Jordan couldn't help wondering what lay waiting for his family and their associates in the new year ahead. Who would survive, and what would be left of them if they did?

———

*Naval Base San Diego: December 20, 1945*

It took two bolts from heaven, finally, to end the war. The first was "Little Boy," dropped over Hiroshima, on Honshu, from the B-29 Superfortress *Enola Gay,* flattening 70 percent of the industrial city's buildings and directly killing 70,000 people, some with their shadows burned into concrete like petrified ghosts. Three days later, Superfortress *Bockscar* dropped "Fat Man" over Nagasaki on Kyushu, another industrial center, blitzing 80 percent of its buildings and killing 35,000 inhabitants outright.

That was the end of Imperial Japan, threatened with an abortive military coup on August 14, a ceasefire ordered two days later by Emperor Hirohito. Three weeks later, General MacArthur accepted the ex-Empire's unconditional surrender aboard the battleship *Missouri* in Tokyo Bay.

From there, all that remained was for Americans to occupy the prostrate nation and impose the will of Washington, while Moscow set about "liberating" Manchuria. Instead of a last, cataclysmic battle with at least one million U.S. casualties, Major General Harry Schmidt's V Amphibious Corp, including the 2nd and 5th Marine Divisions, met no resistance whatsoever when they occupied the Sasebo-Nagasaki area on September 4. Nolan O'Hara viewed the devastation with a grim detachment that surprised him, then decided that it shouldn't have, after the things he'd seen and done in four brutal island campaigns.

In fact, whatever sympathy he felt for his defeated former enemies focused on children he encountered, many of them scarred, all of them traumatized. And even then, a small voice in his mind still swore they had it coming for the sins of their fathers.

Far more deserving of his sympathy were 20,000 Allied prisoners of war, immediately freed to wander wherever they chose after the Japanese surrender. That wasn't the military plan, but freedom caught those walking scarecrows by surprise, some craving payback, many of them simply in a daze, and some collapsing where they stood. It took three weeks to round them up and transport them offshore to hospital ships headed back to the States, Britain, or Holland, with vague schemes for salvaging their shattered lives.

As for the Japanese, now subjects of America till further notice, they reacted in diverse, not wholly unexpected ways. Some looted what was left of shops and factories, although it went against their nature to cut loose and run amok. Most bowed before their conquerors and played along, at least in daylight and in public. Thousands who'd survived the Nagasaki bombing lay suffering in hospitals where 90 percent of all doctors and nurses had died during Fat Man's explosion. Pregnant women who'd lived through it wondered if their infants would be stillborn or emerge into the new world as blighted monsters.

When an American reporter stuck his microphone in Nolan's face and asked his take on Nagasaki, Nolan told him, "It's a filthy, stinking, wrecked hole, and the sooner we get out the better we'll all like it."

While O'Hara waited to escape, he joined in advance parties, shepherding specialized staff officers to liaise with Japanese civil and military authorities, coordinating transportation, taking inventory of arms and supplies, locating ammo dumps and installations. Every member of his squad was fully armed, but no one had to fire a shot. Even the teenagers and street urchins who glared at the marines with hollow eyes refrained from any move that might've got them killed.

The major enemies were filth, vermin, disease, and leftover explosive ordinance. Nolan's commanders had decided that the Japanese themselves should deal with bombs and ammo, while marines observed them from a wary distance. Ordinance would be dumped at sea or detonated on wasteland if feasible. Non-lethal metal items were declared surplus and left for use as scrap, while food and other stores were doled out to civilians by authorities with whom they could communicate.

Another chore: interrogating and processing military personnel and civilians returning from the far-flung outposts of Japan's defunct Empire. At repatriations centers, those hundreds of thousands were sprayed with DDT, examined and inoculated for diseases including typhus and smallpox, with suspected war criminals detained and the rest passed on to their final destinations. More thousands— Korean and Chinese prisoners, along with conscript laborers and brutalized "comfort women"—would be sent back to their homelands, aboard Japanese ships whenever possible.

And the flood of supplies to Japan from abroad seemed unending. Lieutenant Colonel Jacob Goldberg told the press, "We are building up a mountain of supplies consisting of items we will never be able to use and I can foresee the day when we just leave it all for the Japs. Everyone in the Pacific is apparently getting rid of their excess material by shipping it to Japan, regardless of whether anyone in Japan needs it. One word describes the situation: SNAFU."

Even the U.S. military couldn't get it right. Marines ate C- and K-rations day after day until, as Major Norman Hatch declared, "They're getting fed up with this, and occasionally a big refrigerator ship would come in and everybody would say, 'Now we'll get some fresh food,' but we'd find that the cold lockers were loaded with barbed wire, ping pong balls, things of that nature. What we would do with barbed wire in Japan nobody had the slightest idea."

And that defined a SNAFU: Situation Normal, All Fucked-Up.

Over time, in late September and October, the 2nd Marine Division expanded its hold on southern Kyushu from Nagasaki to occupy the prefectures of Kagoshima, Kumamato and Miyazaki, receiving supply flights on an airstrip dubbed "Atomic Field." By early November, Nolan had begun to think he'd spend his Christmas in Japan, but then the word came down: he would be shipping out aboard the light cruiser USS *Mobile* sailing as part of "Operation Magic Carpet" for the two-week journey home.

He took a jealous razzing from his buddies in the 2nd, most of whom were staying on, but Nolan couldn't tell them why he'd been selected, since he didn't have a clue. The captain who had given him his orders spoke of "something special" waiting for O'Hara in the States when he arrived, but that was it.

O'Hara's shipmates, when he boarded at Sasebo on December 6, were mostly from the 5th Marine Division's 27th Regiment, top-heavy with survivors of Iwo Jima. Now, as the *Mobile* prepared to offload at Naval Base San Diego, Nolan stood at the rail in fresh fatigues, wearing his M1941 Light Marching Pack, minus the knapsack that he'd slung beneath it during battle or the rifle that had saved his life while snuffing out others. He scanned the pier, wishing he had binoculars as he searched for familiar faces in the gathered crowd—and suddenly, against all odds, he found them.

Keely stood at quayside, looking absolutely marvelous, beaming at the *Mobile,* likely deafened by a brass band belting out John Philip Sousa's "Hands Across the Sea," while Ryan—twenty-even months old now—squirmed on her hip.

Before the gangplank fell, Nolan imagined he could feel her arms around him, taste her lips, their son mashed in between them and bewildered by it all.

And for the first time in three years, he felt truly alive.

# CHAPTER 6

AT LAST, the blessed moment had arrived. Darya Sokolva had presented Leonid Babin with a son on March 8, delivered at his dacha by Dr. Lazar Serbsky and a private nurse he'd brought along with him from Moscow. Both had been reminded that their future fortunes and survival would depend upon how tight-lipped they could be.

Not that survival was assured, by any means.

The infant had arrived nearly on time, only a single day's delay from Darya's estimate of when he was conceived, tipping the scale at seven pounds nine ounces on delivery. He had a small topknot of blond hair, although Dr. Serbsky warned it might darken with age—a point of absolute indifference to Babin, although Darya seemed to think a blond child meant good luck.

*Women.*

The baby's birth certificate was incomplete, lacking both parents' names in violation of established law. Babin could always fill it out later if he saw fit, although the document itself was unimportant to him—and, in fact, its revelation would invite questions that he could not afford to answer honestly.

In Babin's mind, the boy was "Stefan," translated from Russian as "crowned with laurels." If all went well and according to plan, he would be Babin's crowning achievement in life, the human instrument of his father's revenge against all who had wronged and abused him during his years in the United States.

And if plan should fail...well, a mistake of any size and age could always be eliminated.

The boy's life was already laid out in advance for him, although he couldn't know that yet, and any vague suspicions on his mother's part would never see the light of day. As for Major Serbsky, once the child was old enough to have no further need of medical attention at a moment's notice, the good doctor would be transferred to some nonexistent post and then erased from living memory. The nurse, a random choice on Serbsky's part, was gone already, one more victim of a fatal mugging in southeastern Moscow's seedy Kapotnya district, her slayer shot moments later by a passing *Militsiya* patrolman.

No loose ends. Call it two down, and that left one.

This morning, Babin sat at Darya's bedside, watching Stefan suckle at her breast. She seemed to have an innate feel for motherhood, despite knowing that it would only be a fleeting, temporary state. Watching her nurse the child, Babin was startled by a sudden flash of what it might be like to lead a normal life, divorced from treachery and murder, but he pushed that thought aside, knowing that any such dramatic sea change was impossible for him.

He'd come too far, had dared and done too much, harbored his brooding hatred for too long to turn back now.

And that was why Darya, in turn, would have to die and disappear, before their son passed on to other hands, molding him and propelling him toward his inevitable destiny.

In postwar Moscow, changes were occurring once again. Just yesterday, all of the government's existing People's Commissariats had been renamed as Ministries. The NKVD that he served was now the Ministry for State Security —*Ministerstvo Gosudarstvennoi Bezopasnosti,* or simply MGB. Its First Main Directorate was responsible for foreign intelligence; the Second Main Directorate focused on domestic counterintelligence; and the Third Main Directorate dealt with military counterintelligence.

The MGB's putative leader, still subordinate to Lavrentiy Beria at Lubyanka headquarters, was Colonel General Viktor Abakumov, wartime chief of SMERSH—*Smert' Shpionam,* "Death to Spies," named by Stalin himself—and a notoriously brutal officer known to personally torture prisoners. Some gossips whispered that Stalin had chosen Abakumov in a covert bid to curb Beria's power, but Babin wasn't counting on it, simply knowing that he had to take more care watching his own back now.

So far, the shuffle had not harmed him, though he'd undergone a change of rank on paper. At its birth, the MGB had formally adopted the Soviet military's standardized ranking system, which made Babin a Major General of State Security, still separated from the chief's position by a colonel. A small pay raise accompanied the change, but he had squirreled away sufficient wealth by now that it made little difference.

These days, Germans were catching hell on every front.

Ethnic cleansing had begun in Eastern Europe, with an end goal of some 14 million persons slated for expulsion or execution. On a more modest scale, watching the Nuremberg Tribunal from a distance through the updates from Soviet judges Major General Iona Nikitchenko and Lieutenant Colonel Alexander Volchkov, Babin had tracked the testimony of accused war criminals Otto Ohlendorf, former head of Einsatzgruppe D, who'd casually admitted killing 90,000 Jews; Dieter Wisliceny, architect of occupied Europe's ghettos; former SS-*Obergruppenführer* Erich von dem Bach-Zelewski, confessing mass murder of Jews in the USSR; and ex-Field Marshal Friedrich Paulus, sketching the plan for Hitler's war of aggression worldwide. The Soviet Union's chief prosecutor, Lieutenant General Roman Rudenko, had done his best to blame Nazis for the Katyn Massacre of 1940, but Babin didn't know if that would sell.

He'd been involved in the Byelorussian bloodletting himself, under NKVD Chief Executioner and Commander Vasily Blokhin, but he had no fear of his own name surfacing in Nuremberg testimony. Babin hadn't shared his name with any SS soldiers present at the massacre, and while one may have picked it up in passing, enough had happened to the *proklyatyye nemtsy* in the past five years to wipe it from a Nazi's mind, if he were even still alive.

No, he would not fear Nuremberg. The future lay in front of Babin and his newborn son, and while he could not read it perfectly, despite his best-laid plans, Babin would focus on survival for them both until his goals had been achieved.

———

*LITTLE ITALY, Manhattan: May 21, 1946*

DAVE JORDAN STOOD outside Biondi's Social Club on Mulberry Street, leaning on his polished walnut cane, and listened to the sounds of laughter and a jukebox emanating from behind its sturdy door. The box was playing Frank Sinatra, crooning out "Five Minutes More," begging his lover for a bit more time because "this evening seemed to go so awfully fast."

And don't they always, when a boy's in love or simply horny? Dave could answer to the second part of that, but as to love, whatever that was meant to be, he couldn't say.

*May as well get this over with,* he thought, then almost turned away to seek a taxi that would take him to his parents' place instead.

He'd put that off until he eyeballed Cousin Dominic, had words with him, and found out how he'd fared without a helmet and a rifle during wartime, ducking lead from total strangers on some foreign battlefield. Dave had a hunch how that would go, but he still had to see and hear it for himself, before he took his parents by surprise, then moved on to his sister Gemma and her groom.

Dave had been back the best part of a week already, keeping to himself while he arranged his application to Columbia. With any luck, if it got squared away, he'd be living on campus, which sprawled over thirty-two acres in Morningside Heights. Room enough for one gimp, as he still saw himself, and Jordan had no doubt he' find a part-time job to make up any shortfall from the G.I. Bill. He saw no problem to it, buckle down, nose to the grindstone, all that happy shit.

But first came family.

He was starting slow with Cousin Dom, least likely to

ask pointed questions, always pleased to talk about himself whenever possible. There'd be some basic cripple jokes at first, of course, but Dave could live with that and get it cleared away. Turning the conversation back on Dom and family should do the trick.

Dave pushed in through Biondi's door and let the music wrap around him, with the welcome scent of beer. Sinatra wound it up, Perry Como right behind him on the jukebox with "Surrender."

Jordan spotted Cousin Dom against the bar with half a dozen of his friends. He recognized Rocco D'Onofrio and Eddie Scarpa, but the others weren't familiar to him, even though they had a common look: hair combed in wavy pompadours, the shiny two-piece suits, loud ties and two-tone Oxford shoes. Most of them smoked, including Dom, and made a big deal out of it, convinced it made them cool.

Scarpa saw Jordan first, a grin cracking his usually sullen face. "Hey, hey!" he said to no one in particular. "The war hero!"

Dom spotted David then and blinked once in surprise, clueless like all the rest of Jordan's family that he'd returned from Massachusetts days ago. Dom shoved past his companions, crossed the floor, and stood before his cousin, looking David up and down, before he smiled in turn and stuck a hand out.

"Man, you're home. 'Bout friggin' time, eh? And still walkin' with the stick."

"I limp less with it. Anyway, it feels like less."

"You look awright, considerin'."

The others flocked around him now, asking their questions all at once—"How many fuckin' Krauts you kill? What're the women like?"—until Dom pushed a couple of them back and said, "For Chrissakes, let 'im breathe, will ya?"

When they were seated at a table with a beer in front of Dave, his cousin asked, "You seen your folks yet? Gemma an' that square she married?"

"No," Dave said. "I came straight here." A small lie, but it suited him.

"That's somethin' with your sister and the kid, yeah?"

"Kid?"

"Aw, shit. You didn't know?"

"I've been away," Jordan reminded him.

"Well, yeah. But they got mail and telephones, ya know? Jesus, I guess I stepped in it."

"You may as well go on."

"They say she's due in August sometime. You do the arithmetic about a January wedding, eh?"

So it had been a *shotgun* wedding, maybe literally, Jordan thought. At least the kid would have a legal name.

Dom seemed to think he was uncomfortable, shifting gears. "Hey, didja hear about the plane crash?"

"Hard to miss," said Jordan. Only yesterday, an Army Air Force twin-engine C-45 Expeditor had plowed into the Bank of Manhattan Trust Building's fifty-eighth floor on Wall Street, ending its flight from Louisiana to Newark Airport prematurely, killing all five persons aboard. The fuselage and one wing plummeted forty-six stories, then hung up on the twelfth-floor ledge for firemen to handle.

"Yeah, some show," Dom said, already losing interest.

"So what else has been going on?" Dave asked.

"The fuckin' PRs," Rocco interjected. "They're what's goin' on around here."

"Puerto Ricans?" Jordan ventured.

"Yeah," Dominic confirmed. "They're fillin' up East

Harlem, callin' it *El Barrio.* They bop with us and with the niggers."

"Spics can't get along with anybody," Eddie offered, grinning while he lit another Lucky Strike.

Dom shrugged. "It's what we live with," he allowed. "Our grandfathers and fathers had the micks, now we got spics."

"And niggers, don't forget," said Rocco.

"Like they'd let me. So, Cuz, what've you got goin on?"

"Just signing up for school—" The whole bunch of them moaned in unison. Dave overrode it, rising with aid from his cane and finishing his beer. "I'd better go around and see the folks."

"We'll catch up later, yeah?" Dom said, one hand on Jordan's shoulder now. "And hey, don't tell 'em that I spilled the beans on Gemma, eh?"

"I wouldn't rat you out, Cousin."

"My man!"

Jordan left Biondi's, looking for a cab and wondering what else had changed while he was gone.

———

*FBI Headquarters: July 9, 1946*

THE SIS WAS HISTORY, wrapped up and done. During the war years, it had rooted out 887 Axis spies, 340 shady undercover agents, 281 peddlers of fascist propaganda, 222 smugglers moving critical war materials, plus more than 100 would-be saboteurs. Agents had also silenced twenty-four covert Axis radio stations, seizing forty transmitters and eighteen receivers, with Declan O'Hara in the thick of it.

Against that epic haul, they'd lost only three men, all

killed in airplane crashes. None had been picked off by hostile spies, nor by secret police in hotbeds of pro-Nazi sentiment like Paraguay and Argentina.

For a while, there'd been some argument over the future of the SIS, whether it would continue operating, where, and for how long. The first step toward dissolution had come in January, with President Truman's creation of the National Intelligence Authority, a four-man outfit composed of the Secretaries of State, War, and the Navy, plus the president's chief of staff. J. Edgar Hoover had opposed that move, complaining to Attorney General Clark that the NIA might trespass on domestic security matters. Truman had taken notice, ordering that "no police, law enforcement or internal security functions shall be exercised under this directive," and that "nothing herein shall be construed to authorize the making of investigations inside the continental limits of the United States and its possessions, except as provided by law and Presidential directives."

Problem solved? Not quite.

In April, FBI leaders considered assuming responsibility for international intelligence coverage, with most supporting the plan. Only Clyde Tolson and Assistant Director Quinn Tamm dissented, leaving Hoover to predictably side with his alter ego. Speed's memo to his troops read: "I share the minority view and think we should not take on the foreign intelligence and only handle Western Hemisphere for time being. I have so advised the Attorney General and he wishes to speak to President before finally deciding."

Clark fell in line with Hoover, but he added a proviso to avoid antagonizing Truman: "However, if it is suggested that, in view of the Department's available facilities, rather than as a duty to participate in the Intelligence Program, I feel felt that the Department should request that a program outlining the nature and extent of its participation be submitted before any final agreement was reached."

Hoover had hit the roof, firing off a memo to his boss that read: "What is to be the purpose of this? It looks like just another position being created. There is no use providing for FBI to take over or assume worldwide intelligence coverage for we are not going to do it. The most I will agree to now is to stay in Western Hemisphere for one year. I am more and more certain that this is a project we must get out of."

And so it was, Chief Hoover dictating to Clark and Truman that the SIS would cease all operations on the final day of June.

That was another irritant between the president and Hoover, but it suited Declan fine. He'd missed his wife, his children—although both adults now—and their home in Fairlawn. South America, for all of its adventure and its overstated flavor of romance, was wearing thin for him. He spoke passable Spanish now, not that he'd ever use it in D.C., but all his foreign odyssey had left Declan were memories, the bulk of them nothing that he could talk about with Abigail.

Some of those memories were classified, others simply embarrassing. Declan had filed them with the echoes of pursuing "public enemies" and hoped the new ones that replaced them would be more uplifting, now that he was one year past his first half-century.

And how much longer did he have? Not fifty years, for damned sure.

Was it sheer ingratitude that made O'Hara grateful for that knowledge now?

―――――

*2430 E S*TREET *N*ORTHWEST*, Washington, DC: July 24, 1946*

THE OSS HAD NOT PASSED SILENTLY into its long goodnight. President Truman never liked Bill Donovan, had mocked him in his diaries and private conversations, pleased as punch in September 1945, when the Budget Bureau floated a plan to dissolve the Service. Donovan protested but the president ignored him, ordering Budget to "proceed with the dissolution of Donovan's outfit even if Donovan didn't like it."

Executive Order 9621, issued on September 20, made the demise official, but an oversight gave Donovan ten days to wrap things up before the curtain fell. He'd microfilmed all of his office files, then bade his troops farewell on September 28, at a converted skating rink down the hill from his E Street headquarters.

Colby Gantt was present for that speech and had it nearly memorized. Wild Bill proclaimed, "We have come to the end of an unusual experiment. This experiment was to determine whether a group of Americans constituting a cross section of racial origins, of abilities, temperaments and talents could meet and risk an encounter with the long-established and well-trained enemy organizations. You can go with the assurance that you have made a beginning in showing the people of America that only by decisions of national policy based upon accurate information can we have the chance of a peace that will endure."

No problem there. Come peace or war, Colby already had another job.

When Truman launched the National Intelligence

Authority in January, he'd also created a Central Intelligence Group as its operational arm, with Rear Admiral Sidney Souers—former Deputy Chief of Naval Intelligence—appointed to serve as the first Director of Central Intelligence. He'd retired on June 10, succeeded by Lieutenant General Hoyt Vandenberg of the U.S. Army Air Forces, once described by the *Washington Post* as "the most impossibly handsome man on the entire Washington scene."

Gantt couldn't see the attraction, himself, but he'd applied two days after the CIG was launched, accepted without question on the basis of his wartime record.

And in the process, he'd found himself a wife.

Eileen Brisbois was three years Colby's junior, twenty-one and ravishing, sporting a figure that could rival any wartime pinup girl's. She hailed from Minnesota with her widowed mother, part of the migration that had nearly doubled D.C.'s population through the war years. Mother Marjorie earned money cleaning richer people's houses, while Eileen had been a cipher clerk at OSS headquarters and was helping with the takedown when she'd met Colby, a chance encounter at the office coffee urn. They'd hit it off and she'd agreed to marry him in April, although neither one of them had any pressing plans to start a family.

Eileen wasn't a virgin when they met, and that was fine with Colby, since he'd never placed a premium on so-called "virtue" for its own sake. They had tied the knot at All Souls Unitarian on Harvard Street NW, the first time Gantt had been to church since heading off from home to Yale, and if it proved to be his last time, that was also fine.

The CIG was operating out of Donovan's old headquarters, familiar turf for Colby and Eileen, since she'd be staying on the new agency's payroll in her previous capacity. Colby wasn't sure what he'd be doing yet, beyond the CIG's broad mandate to coordinate, evaluate and disseminate intelligence on an international scale. That included clandestine collection plus independent research and analysis—key features since it wasn't just assessing data gleaned from other agencies, but would produce its own intelligence, expanding monumentally. The sole taboo was running operations on the home front, and Colby already knew there were a thousand ways to get around that ban.

Meanwhile, there was enough to do outside the States, and Vietnam, as Colby had surmised, was shaping up into a hotspot with a crackling fuse. In March, Hồ Chí Minh had approved an Allied compromise to accept "temporary" return of 15,000 French troops, while British and Indian soldiers departed, Chiang Kai-shek's KMT forces indulging in one final orgy of looting before they decamped for China and a new face-off with Mao Zedong's People's Liberation Army. Hồ's Việt Minh braced for a fresh struggle with the French, while Hồ continued reaching out to Washington and elsewhere in his quest for aid.

He'd written to President Truman again in January, requesting U.S. intervention to halt French atrocities, but the White House ignored him once more. A second letter to Truman, one month later, also evoked stony silence. Next, Hồ wrote an open letter to the governments of the U.S., Britain, China and Russia, reiterating crimes committed by the French, declaring that "democracy has been established on solid foundations" in Vietnam's northern sector. When none replied, he sent a telegram to Truman, yet again with no response.

The brooding fear in Washington was communism, given a name on March 5 when Winston Churchill addressed Westminster College in Fulton, Missouri, warning that in Europe, "From Stettin in the Baltic to Trieste in the Adriatic, an iron curtain has descended across the continent." Prospects looked little better in China, where a second civil war between the KMT and Reds had erupted on March 31, now raging with no end in sight.

Only yesterday, the CIG had released its first assessment of the Soviet Union, echoing published remarks from George Kennan, *chargé d'affaires* of the mission in Moscow, framed in his now-famous "long telegram" of February, addressed to Secretary of State Byrnes. CIG analysts agreed with Kennan that "the Russian people are, by and large, friendly to the outside world, eager for experience of it, eager to measure against it talents they are conscious of possessing, eager above all to live in peace and enjoy fruits of their own labor." Those laudable goals, however, were hampered by "Oriental secretiveness and conspiracy," coupled with "the Kremlin's neurotic view of world affairs and instinctive Russian sense of insecurity." Stalin required foreign hostility "as a justification for the Soviet Union's instinctive fear of the outside world, for the dictatorship without which they do not know how to rule, for cruelties they do not dare not to inflict, for sacrifice they feel bound to demand. Today they cannot dispense with it. It is the fig leaf of their moral and intellectual respectability." Soviet pressure to promote conflict and overrun its non-communist neighbors "may only be contained by the adroit and vigilant application of counterforce at a series of constantly shifting geographical and political points."

In sum, what George Orwell had dubbed the "Cold War" in October 1945 would carry on indefinitely, heating up from time to time at global pressure points where military intervention or its covert counterpart might be required.

*And that,* thought Colby, smiling to himself, *sounds like a guarantee of job security.*

---

*FBI FIELD OFFICE, Los Angeles: November 6, 1946*

CAMILLE WAS SIX MONTHS PREGNANT, and Devon Gantt blamed Agent Randall Dukes. Dukes hadn't screwed her, but he'd thrown a bash in May for Mother's Day—ironic, that—with barbecue and alcohol for families associated with the Bureau. Afterward, a tipsy homecoming, he and Camille had carelessly indulged in sex without a rubber and *voila!*

The kid was due in February, Devon still not sure exactly how he felt about it. Oh, he loved his wife all right, no question, but a small voice in his head kept saying that a baby felt like being trapped, pinned down and hogtied in a way the rigors of the Bureau never seemed to make him feel.

Something to think about, as if he needed any more right now.

Fever against the Reds was heating up throughout the Golden State, and most particularly in L.A., focused on Hollywood. Bill Wilkerson was one of the prime instigators, with his weekly "Billy's Column" in *The Hollywood Reporter,* listing anyone within the movie industry whom he suspected of collaborating somehow with the CPUSA.

But alas for Billy, he'd run into problems with The Bug over their grand Flamingo in Las Vegas. Siegel had revised their contract, giving himself total control over the new joint's gambling, entertainment, booze and food. When Wilkerson complained, Bugsy threatened to blow his brains out—not a simile in Siegel's case. Wilkerson took it on the lam to Paris and went into hiding, after marrying his fifth wife, Vivian DuBois, whose two films had been 1942's *I*

*Married an Angel* and 1944's *Lost in a Harem*. Before Paris she was going nowhere, both small roles uncredited, but now she had Wilkerson's checkbook and his whole estate if Bugsy followed up on his prediction of a sudden funeral.

Meanwhile, in politics, the fear of communists had stirred a boiling pot in California's 12th congressional district, covering L.A. County. Liberal Democrat Jerry Voorhis had represented the 12th since 1937 but Republicans were sick of him. They'd tried to gerrymander him out of office in 1941 but failed, and he'd bounced back to kick their asses in 1942 and '44. Finally, this year, they'd found a go-getter in Richard Milhous Nixon.

Nixon was a local Quaker out of Whittier who doted on his mother, didn't drink or smoke, but seemed to have no moral compass otherwise. During his last semester at Duke University Law School, in 1937, he'd burglarized a dean's office to steal critical test answers. Later that same year, back him in California, he'd botched a civil case so badly that Judge Alfred Paonessa threatened disbarment, but he'd never followed through. In 1946, after Nixon's discharge from the navy as a lieutenant commander, GOP leaders chose him as the candidate they needed to eliminate Voorhis. During the campaign, Nixon linked Jerry to a CIO political action committee, which he branded "a gigantic slush fund" promoting "communist principles." His backers passed out 25,000 thimbles reading: "Nixon for Congress/Put the needle in the P.A.C." On Election Day, Voorhis had trailed by close to 16,000 votes, and Nixon packed his bags for Washington.

Devon thought the FBI could use a guy like that some-day, particularly since he knew Nixon lusted to join the House Committee on Un-American Activities under Chairman Edward Hart. A good Red-hunter on Capitol Hill could be helpful, even if his motives were as phony as a seven-dollar bill.

And if Devon befriended him, promoted him at head-quarters...well, he could always use a pay hike, with an unexpected ankle-biter on the way.

———

*FEDERAL BUREAU of Narcotics Field Office, Manhattan: December 16, 1946*

IF IKE SAWYER believed the memos covering his desk, the war against narcotics traffickers was heating up again.

Just five days earlier, meeting at Lake Success in New York's Nassau County, signatories of a brand-new protocol had shifted duties of the old League of Nations' Advisory Committee on Traffic in Opium and Other Dangerous Drugs to a new Commission on Narcotic Drugs, appointed by the United Nations' Economic and Social Council. Ostensibly, the new group would administer the "estimate system," banning UN member nations from producing or importing more narcotics than their ailing citizens required, but Sawyer doubted whether it would have much more success than the League had achieved since 1920.

Meanwhile, the global amphetamine epidemic was growing by leaps and bounds. By December 1945, two major rival firms were churning out come 40 million tablets monthly, and a court had affirmed Smith, Kline & French's patent monopoly earlier this year, boosting sales of Benzadrine and Dexedrine to $2.9 million. Up to 16 million military veterans were self-medicating as they saw fit, with no legal limits imposed, no one to monitor their unpredictable mood swings, stimulant psychosis, or random violence.

On a more positive note, an International Military Tribunal for the Far East had convened in Tokyo on April 29, with judges from the U.S. and Canada, Great Britain, France, Holland, Australia, New Zealand, India, the Philippines, China and the USSR. Seventy-eight former Japanese military and political leaders stood accused of various war crimes, but the count that interested Sawyer most was "Subject No. 5," referring to "Atrocities connected with Japanese Military Aggression in China and the Traffic in Opium & Narcotics."

As one journalist summarized that case, "Japan's real purpose for engaging in drug traffic was far more sinister than even the debauchery of Chinese people. Having signed and ratified the opium conventions, Japan was bound not to engage in drug traffic, but she found in the alleged but false independence of Manchukuo a convenient opportunity to carry on a worldwide drug traffic and cast the guilt upon that puppet state. In 1937, it was pointed out in the League of Nations that 90% of all illicit white drugs in the world were of Japanese origin."

Specifically, a Manchurian Affairs Bureau had been created to manage affairs in what the Japanese called "Manchukuo," encompassing Northeast China and Inner Mongolia. Presidents of the bureau had included Tokyo defendants General Seishirō Itagaki, Field Marshal Shunroku Hata, and General Tōjō; defendants Rear Admiral Takasumi Oka and Lieutenant Colonel Kenryō Satō were former bureau secretaries; while bureau councilors at sundry times included defendants Oka, Satō, Tōjō, Minister of Finance Okinori Kaya, General Akira Mutō, Minister of

Foreign Affairs Mamoru Shigemitsu, and General Yoshijirō Umezu.

Outside the formal structure of the bureau, two other tribunal defendants included on drug-dealing charges were Chief Cabinet Secretary Naoki Hoshino and General Kuniaki Koiso, governor-general of Korea from 1942 to '44.

All faced the gallows if convicted.

One witness who could've sealed the deal was Henry Pu Yi, aka Xuantong, who originally took China's throne as its last Qing Dynasty emperor at age three, in 1908, then was deposed in 1912, restored in 1917, and dumped again after a brief twelve days. In 1932 the Japanese appointed him as puppet ruler of Manchuoko and their fall guy for whatever crimes they perpetrated there. In Tokyo, he testified that "Japan made opium addicts of Manchurians to keep down revolt and was planning an invasion of Soviet Russia," but beyond that, he'd begun to fall apart, once whining to a prosecutor, "Please don't ask me any more about the question of dates." The same went for most other specifics of his sham rule in Manchukuo spanning thirteen years.

For all Ike knew, the whole damned trial could be a wash.

At home, the year had been another bad one for Ike's people stuck below the Mason-Dixon Line. On February 8, honorably discharged Negro marine Timothy Hood removed the Jim Crow sign from a trolley in Brighton, Alabama, whereupon the driver shot him five times, then Police Chief G. B. Fant arrived, arrested Hood, and finished him off with a head shot in the backseat of Fant's patrol car. Hood was unarmed, but the coroner still returned a finding of "justifiable homicide."

Four days later, only hours after being honorably

discharged, still in uniform, Negro Sergeant Isaac Woodard Jr. took a bus from Georgia's Camp Gordon to rejoin his family in North Carolina. Before pulling out of Augusta, he'd used the depot's restroom, then faced arrest by officers including Chief Lynwood Shull at a stop in Batesburg, South Carolina. The white cops beat him senseless in an alley, then again in jail, where Chief Shull gouged out both of Woodard's eyes with a nightstick, leaving him permanently blind. At trial in federal court, Shull confessed his crime, but his lawyer secured acquittal by raving to the all-white jury, "If you rule against Shull, then let this South Carolina secede again."

One day after Woodward's blinding, masked Klansmen kidnapped Hugh Johnson, a Negro navy veteran working as a bellboy in Atlanta, and drove him into woodland where they laid on fifty lashes for alleged "familiarity" with white hotel guests. The police, as usual, made no arrests.

Bloody February ended with wholesale mayhem in Columbia, Tennessee, where Negro navy veteran James Stephenson accompanied his mother to a local store. The white proprietor slapped Mrs. Stephenson when she complained of shoddy service, and her son had shoved him through a plate glass window. Police arrested both shoppers, who paid a $50-fine, but would-be lynchers were dissatisfied with that result. A white mob had descended on the black ghetto called Mink Slide, trading shots with barricaded residents. Four white cops suffered minor wounds, and then all hell broke loose, white rioters and state police randomly firing into Negro homes and stores, committing wholesale acts of vandalism, jailing more than 100 "suspects" and seizing some 300 weapons. Before the smoke cleared, police machine-gunned three unarmed black prisoners behind closed doors, while they were being "questioned," killing two and wounding one.

Skip forward to July, when Negro army veteran Maceo Snipes returned from overseas to farm his father's land in Taylor County, Georgia. His mistake was voting in the July's Democratic gubernatorial primary. Next day, several whites arrived to threaten him but white veteran Edward Williamson got carried away, shooting Snipes and leaving him to stagger several miles before he died. At trial, jurors believe the lie that Williamson had gone out to "collect a debt" and only fired "in self-defense" when Snipes pulled out a knife.

Five days after Snipes died in Georgia, Mississippi lynchers killed Leon McAtee, a tenant farmer on a white planter's land whom they accused of stealing a saddle, afterward dumping his corpse in a bayou. At trial in October, one murderer confessed and implicated four accomplices— including McAtee's landlord and the planter's son, but Judge S. F. Davis acquitted two defendants from the bench. White jurors only took ten minutes to release the other three.

The South's worst lynching of the year occurred three days after McAtee's murder, at Moore's Ford, outside Monroe, Georgia. Victim George Dorsey was another Negro veteran, home less than nine months from the Pacific, his wife Mae seven months pregnant. With friend Roger Malcom, Dorsey sharecropped on J. Loy Harrison's land with wife Dorothy. Two weeks before the lynchings, Roger supposedly stabbed a white man in a brawl and was jailed in Monroe. On July 25, Harrison drove Mae and the Dorseys into Monroe, where he paid Roger's $600 bail and set out for home with his four passengers. In transit, he found the Moore's Ford bridge blocked by a couple dozen white men led by one in a double-breasted suit. The mob took all four Negroes at gunpoint, tied them to trees and riddled them with lead before one ghoul cut Mae Malcom's fetus from her body with a knife.

Although Governor Ellis Arnall told reporters that "fifteen to twenty members of the mob are known by name," FBI agents claimed they could find no evidence. U.S. District Judge Thomas Davis convened a federal grand jury but admitted that he had no jurisdiction in the case. The panel wound up indicting one white man for perjury but he never faced trial.

August was just as bad. Black veterans Alonza Brooks and Richard Gordon died in Texas after labor disputes with white bosses, Brooks strangled, Gordon's throat cut before his killers dragged him behind a car. In Louisiana, Negro veteran John Jones allegedly peeped through a white man's window, prompting a mob to kidnap him and teenage cousin Albert Harris—who survived, bearing scars, while Jones was slaughtered. Two days later, a white mob of 2,000 ran amok in Athens, Alabama, after two of their friends were jailed for beating a Negro. The toll there: more than fifty Negroes injured and sixteen whites arrested, none brought to trial. In North Carolina, a week after that, Negro veteran J. C. Farmer made the fatal mistake of laughing at a bus stop. When officers tried to arrest him he protested, "forcing" them to pistol-whip him until one clumsy cop accidentally shot himself. Within the hour, a lynch mob had claimed Farmer's life.

In such an atmosphere, Ike wasn't shocked to find the Klan growing like Georgia kudzu, Dr. Green burning a 200-foot cross atop Stone Mountain, his group spreading into Alabama, Florida, and Tennessee so far. *Life* magazine sent a reporter to record his thoughts on "uppity niggahs" and an America "flooded with Jewish refugees." The House Committee on Un-American Activities considered investigating but voted against it, deciding there was insufficient evidence of any wrongdoing.

In the private sector, famed Negro singer and activist Paul Robeson led the American Crusade Against Lynching, created on the anniversary of the Emancipation Proclamation. NAACP leader Walter White, ironically Caucasian, viewed the ACAL as "competition" and refused to support it, although his own group had protested lynching since the First World War. It made no sense, but Ike had seen the way black folks fell out and undercut each other when they had a common cause. In Washington, Hoover's G-men ranked Robeson and many of his group's members—including immigrant genius Albert Einstein—as communist sympathizers, building files on all of them.

One ray of hope, though dim, had come from the Supreme Court back in June, with the case of *Morgan v. Virginia*, when seven justices declared the Old Dominion's segregation of interstate buses unconstitutional. It sounded like a breakthrough, but Dixie just shrugged and went on with business as usual.

Finally, in early December, Harry Truman had issued Executive Order 9808, establishing a fifteen-member President's Committee on Civil Rights to learn how government at all levels "may be strengthened and improved to safeguard the civil rights of the people." Their report was due within next year, but Sawyer wondered whether they'd have anything to say that really changed a goddamned thing.

———

*Fairlawn, Southeast Washington, D.C.: December 25, 1946*

IT WAS Nolan's first Christmas at home with family since he'd enlisted in the Corps, five years ago. Revenge against Japan was all the rage back then, but now that memory was blurred for most Americans—civilians, anyhow—and they seemed anxious to forget.

*All right by me,* O'Hara thought, grateful he'd come through it alive and well.

His parents and Fiona seemed to love Keely on sight, and Nolan's mom kept leaking tears over her grandson and the presence of her eldest child, a certified survivor who'd turned twenty-five in April, having come through all the worst Hideki Tōjō's troops could throw at him.

"I can't believe you actually *jumped* on top of a *grenade*," she scolded softly, not wanting to agitate young Ryan on her lap, already three years late to stop Nolan's impulsive act.

"That's what *I* said," Keely chimed in, resting a hand on Nolan's knee. "Of course, by then—"

"Seemed like the thing to do," Nolan horned in. "I didn't know it was a dud, but it worked out okay."

"You should've had a medal for a thing like that," his Dad opined.

"Well, now you mention it, they've got a little thing lined up for after New Year's."

"A *little* thing?" This time, his missus slapped the knee that she'd been stroking. "Well, if you won't tell it properly—"

"Okay, okay. So here's the deal..."

He told it all, beginning with his expedited discharge at Camp Pendleton, getting a virtual bum rush through their streamlined separation battalion. There'd been lectures on the benefits and pitfalls of postwar civilian life, pressing of brand-new uniforms with the addition of insignia and decorations, tips on job placement from the U.S. Employment

Service, even Red Cross aid with disability claims for those who required it. Five days after he'd disembarked from the *Mobile,* Nolan was holding discharge papers and his final paycheck from the Corps, together with a pamphlet that explained the G.I. Bill. He'd spent part of his payoff on a 1940 Chrysler New Yorker convertible and aimed it eastward, trundling his little family across the continent.

"Before I left, though," Nolan finished, "I got called into this full-bird colonel's office and he tells me that I've got another medal coming on top of the Silver Star I had already, but I have to get it from the president."

His father nearly choked on that. "The president? But that means—"

Keely beat him to it, almost squealing, so that little Ryan peered at her, bemused. "The Congressional Medal of Honor! That's right, for his crazy stunt with the bomb!"

Next thing Nolan knew, his dad was standing over him, slapping him on the back and grinning like he'd won a medal, Mom was tearing up again, Fiona leaving lipstick on his cheek, and Ryan couldn't figure what in hell to make of it.

When he could get a word in edgewise, Nolan said, "So, if you don't have any plans for the day after New Year's, there's this ceremony at the White House."

"Son," his father said, "we wouldn't miss it for the world."

Now all O'Hara had to figure out was what he planned on doing for the rest of his civilian life. He had a few ideas, but nothing he could bank on yet.

Right now, just being with his family was victory enough.

———

*LITTLE ITALY, Manhattan: December 28, 1946*

GREG JORDAN WAS RELIEVED to have Christmas behind him
this year, even though he had received two unexpected gifts.
David was home at last, though definitely altered by the war,
and daughter Gemma had belatedly revealed to all and
sundry that her first child should arrive in August.

*Grandkids,* Jordan thought, shaking his head. *Jesus.*

What kind of city, and what kind of world, were they
inheriting?

At his inauguration, New Year's Day, Mayor O'Dwyer
celebrated with a mob of 700 backers to the strains of "It's a
Great Day for the Irish." Two months later, he'd disbanded
Mayor La Guardia's anti-corruption squad at NYPD headquarters, presumably part of his pledge to "do good work."

Two days after O'Dwyer took his oath of office, Governor
Dewey "reluctantly" commuted Charley Luciano's sentence
to time served, on condition that he be deported. Lucky
spent a week on Ellis Island waiting until February 10, when
he'd embarked for Italy aboard the SS *Laura Keene*. The
night before it sailed, Greg and his brother Carlo joined a
throng of other *mafiosi* and some top men from the Jewish
"Kosher Nostra" for a *bon voyage* party aboard, reporters held
at a respectful distance by longshoremen armed with
bailing hooks. The ship arrived in Naples seventeen days
later, shortly before Lucky visited Palermo for a friendly
meet with *Don* Calogero Vizzini.

Jordan knew that Luciano was already planning his
return to the U.S., while Vito Genovese went through the
motions with his murder case in Brooklyn. Trial convened
before Judge Samuel Leibowitz on June 5, Vito's petition for
a directed verdict of acquittal swiftly rejected. Ernie Rupolo

appeared for the state, calling himself a gambler. "And a killer?" Leibowitz inquired. "Oh, sure," Ernie replied, as if it might've slipped his mind.

Four days in, New Jersey police found late parolee witness Jerry Esposito murdered near the state border. Next morning, Leibowitz dismissed the case for lack of evidence, Genovese smirking as the judge said, "I cannot speak for the jury, but I believe if there were even a shred of corroborating evidence, you would have been condemned to the electric chair. By devious means, among which were the terrorizing of witnesses, kidnapping them, yes, even murdering those who would give evidence against you, you have thwarted justice time and time again."

Which came as news to no one with a brain.

Jordan's brother Carlo attended a *Cosa Nostra* meeting at Atlantic City, in July, and returned to say that while Vito retained control of his Greenwich Village *regime,* his further rise was momentarily obstructed by opponents Frank Costello and Willie Moretti.

News was also breaking in Chicago, where Mickey McBride had sold Continental Press in 1943 to James Ragen Sr., a longtime associate of Moe Annenberg and founding father of Ragen's Colts, an Irish gang that had merged with Al Capone's network in Prohibition. When Ragen refused the Outfit a piece of the action, they'd created R & H Publishing in 1945 to compete with Continental. Ragen tried to buy it out, then threatened to have a chin-wag with the FCC, maybe even the FBI. Soon, R & H morphed into Trans-American Publishing and News Service. Ben Siegel handled its action out west, with Mickey Cohen strong-arming bookies to sign up or else. In April 1946, after Outfit gunmen killed bookie Red Richmond and barely missed Ragen, Ragen briefed Cook County's D.A., preparing affidavits that accused Frank Nitti and company of plotting Annenberg's murder before he dumped the National News Service back in 1939. Ragen also warned that if he turned up dead, the prime suspects should be Tony Accardo, Jake Guzik, and Murray Humphreys.

On the side, Ragen called columnist Drew Pearson and laid out his story in detail. Pearson referred Ragen to Attorney General Tom Clark and the FBI moved in, debriefing Ragen and opening a special "CAPGA" filed— short for "*Capone Gang*"—on his allegations. Meanwhile, Pearson did his own digging, reporting that the trail led "to very high places," including Chicago billionaire industrialist Henry Crown (né Krinsky), who got his start in 1919, selling gravel, lime and sand to Chi-Town builders.

Ragen's luck ran out when drive-by gunners blasted him with shotguns in June, on Chicago's South Side. He survived multiple wounds and emergency kidney surgery at Michael Reese Hospital, naming one of his killers as ex-Ragen's Colts member David "Yiddles" Miller, now running his own that included Jacob Rubenstein, alias "Jack Ruby." It seemed that Ragen might recover, but he died on August 15 from a massive dose of mercury doctors couldn't explain. Tom Clark immediately closed the Bureau's CAPGA probe and J. Edgar Hoover went back to pretending that the Syndicate didn't exist.

Was anyone surprised? Not in Chicago, where Murray Humphreys bragged that Clark "was always 100 percent for doing favors." Clark had proved that in October 1945, when Phil D'Andrea filed a complaint against Atlanta prison warden Joseph Sanford, an alleged Klansman who hated Italians and Catholics in general. Sanford allegedly beat up D'Andrea, placing him and his fellow IATSE defendants in fear of death. Missouri lawyer Paul Dillon requested a transfer for all concerned to Leavenworth—200 miles closer to Chicago—and Clark pushed it through, despite objections from Sanford and Leavenworth's warden, prompting Lou Campagna to call it "an act of God."

Clark didn't only help the Mob, though; on occasion he'd been known to cover up for fascists, too. One sore spot there was Oetje Rogge, head of the Justice Department's Criminal Division in 1940, when FDR complained to Attorney General Robert Jackson that Rogge was an "overbearing self-seeker." Jackson pressured Rogge into quitting, but the pest returned in 1943 as a special assistant to the Attorney General Francis Biddle and prosecuted homegrown Nazis in 1944's dead-end sedition trial. In October 1946 Rogge told a New York audience, "The removal of Hitler and Mussolini and a few of their collaborators does not mean that fascism is dead. Now the fascists can take a more subtle disguise, they can come forward and simply say, 'I am anti-Communist'." Clark fired him soon afterward, claiming Rogge had "willfully violated the long-standing rules and regulations" of Justice "by revealing the contents of internal documents."

Those sideshows paled, however, by comparison with Lucky Luciano's near miss homecoming. In late September he'd secured a passport in his birth name—Salvatore Lucania—with visas for Mexico, Cuba, and several South American countries. A month later, he landed at Caracas, bounced to Mexico City, then finally disembarked at Havana.

He moved into the Hotel Nacional de Cuba, overlooking Havana Harbor from atop Taganana Hill in Vedado, the capital's main business district. Meyer Lansky and Fulgencio Batista owned the lavish hotel and casino, easily persuading Lucky to buy a $150,000 share for himself. Invitations went out to Syndicate leaders nationwide for the largest gathering since Atlantic City in 1929, beginning on Friday, December 20.

Christmas plans were placed on hold, Greg flying into José Martí Airport with brother Carlo to represent their family. Lucky and Meyer played hosts, while New York and New Jersey sent the largest group: Frank Costello, Willie Moretti, Vito Genovese, Joe Adonis, Anthony Carfano, Michele Miranda, Al Anastasia, Joe Bonanno, Tommy Lucchese, Joe Profaci and his brother-in-law, Joe Magliocco. Stefano Magaddino came from Buffalo. Chicago's top ranks were depleted, but Tony Accardo showed up with Charles Fischetti and Sam Giancana, a hitman turned *capo regime*. Carlos Marcello spoke for New Orleans, and Santo Trafficante Sr. for Tampa. Jewish bosses aside from Lansky included Moe Dalitz, Longy Zwillman, Doc Stacher, and Dandy Phil Kastel.

The entertainment, when they got around to it, would include Havana's classiest hookers and Jersey crooner Frank Sinatra. He'd been riding high all year with hits including "Day by Day," "That Old Black Magic" and "September Song," but what he really wanted was to wake up in the morning as a reborn *mafioso*. He had all the arrogance and sass required to be a mobster, but "Ol' Blue Eyes" had to settle for reflected glory from the guys who let him hang around when they had nothing more important to pursue.

After the delegates gave Luciano "Christmas presents" adding up to something like $2 million, they got down to business. Lucky opened with a statement clearly aimed at Genovese, who'd been fuming from his Greenwich Village roost and plotting to expand. Luciano had heard talk, like all the rest present, of Vito lusting to be crowned the Boss of Bosses, and he wasn't having it. Recalling Salvatore Maranzano—dead since 1931, Greg Jordan one of those who'd put him own—Lucky declared that there would never be another *capo di tuttu capi*, but only a union of equals. Everyone nodded at that except Vito, who looked like he was chewing broken glass. When Anastasia nominated Luciano as their "chairman of the board," Lucky pretended to consider it, then nodded, saying, "Awright. I can live with that."

Next up was dope, and while the Giordanos had no hand in that, Greg listened closely to the details. Shipments would be coming out of Europe through the so-called "Caneba Network," supervised from Sicily by Nicola Gentile and by Antonio Farina on the Italian mainland. Major ports handling the traffic would be New York City, Tampa, and New Orleans. A secondary route, overseen by Johnny Papalia and Alberto Agueci in Ontario, would funnel more smack through Detroit and on from there, to Joe Zerilli in Detroit, John Scalish in Cleveland, Stefano Magaddino in Buffalo, and Chicago's Outfit.

The last major item on the agenda was Benny Siegel, not invited to the gathering. Problems with Trans-America had cleared up out west since James Ragen's death, but that still left the Flamingo in Las Vegas bleeding cash that Siegel had borrowed from the Syndicate, promising to reimburse them "in his own good time." Moe Dalitz had been sent to scout the Vegas operation out, and he reported what Lansky already knew: the lavish joint was some $3.5 million over budget, with no end in sight. The only question left: was Bugsy skimming on his own account, or was his paramour Virginia Hill the culprit, hauling Mob cash to a numbered bank account in Switzerland on her sporadic "skiing trips"?

Lansky voted for Hill—"that bitch," as he described her —but the other delegates were split, many believing that the

Alabama floozy wouldn't take such an irrevocable step without Siegel's okay. Meyer persuaded those who wanted Siegel hit immediately to hold off and see what happened after the Flamingo's scheduled opening, December 26.

What happened was a mess.

It started out with heavy rain grounding Ben's charter flights from L.A. International. Still, some celebrities showed up as planned, including Clark Gable, Cesar Romero, Lana Turner, Judy Garland, Joan Crawford, George Raft, June Haver, Vivian Blaine, Sonny Tufts, Brian Donleavy and Charles Coburn. On stage, Xavier Cugat's band provided backup for comedians George Jessel, Rose Marie, and Jimmy Durante. The casino and showrooms were operational, but many of the hotel's rooms were incomplete, its lobby draped with drop cloths, while construction racket vied with Cugat's band. Opening weekend was a financial disaster and Bugsy lived up to his hated nickname, raging at employees and guests alike.

Lansky argued for time, allowing Benny to regroup and literally get his house in order for New Year's, but as a hedge, the delegates gave Chicago a prospective contract, passed on to Siegel's mortal adversary in L.A., Jack Dragna. Whoever pulled the trigger, if it happened, would be Dragna's call—and doubtless would delight him to no end.

Before the delegates dispersed—and before a startled nun arrived with wide eyed Cuban Girl Guides to give Sinatra a token of their esteem, catching him with twelve naked showgirls—Luciano had a semi-private meet with Vito Genovese, Al Anastasia standing by and later happy to relate what happened with the three of them in Lucky's suite.

It started off with Luciano standing over Genovese, repeating what he'd told the whole convention: "There ain't no Boss of Bosses. I turned it down in front of everybody. If I ever change my mind, I'll take the title, but it won't be up to you. Right now, *you* work for *me* and I ain't in the mood to retire. Don't you *ever* let me hear this shit again, or I'll lose my temper."

*Don* Vito, going mealy-mouthed, warned Lucky that the feds knew all about him being in Havana and were turning up the heat on Cuba to expel him. That set Luciano off, cursing and lighting into Genovese, beating him down and kicking him around the room, cracking three ribs. When he was done, with Anastasia's aid, they'd trundled Genovese off to the airport, loaded him aboard the next flight home, and cautioned that a bullet would be his reward for telling anyone about their little chat.

Jordan and Carlo hadn't talked about it on the flight back to La Guardia, afraid that even in first-class somebody might be eavesdropping, but getting home allowed Greg to forget about the Syndicate, its growing rifts, if only for a little while. What waited for them after New Year's Day was anybody's guess, but he would meet it as he'd met all problems since he'd been shipped off to France: head-on.

———

*FBI HEADQUARTERS: December 31, 1946*

ANOTHER NEW YEAR'S Day was coming up, and this made twenty-nine for Aloysius Gantt with the Bureau under its several names since he'd signed on. Son Colby and his bride, Eileen, were in D.C., however briefly, working for the CIG, while Devon and Camille were looking forward to the birth of their first child out in L.A.

Well, *she* was looking forward to it, anyway. From Devon's tone on the long-distance line, filling his father in, his mood as dad-to-be was still up in the air.

Meanwhile, the FBI's duties kept piling up. Congress had passed a new Atomic Energy Act in July, handing the Bureau full responsibility for investigating all persons with access to restricted nuclear data, plus responsibility for arresting any leakers. Harry Truman signed the law on August 1, and while he personally disliked J. Edgar Hoover, calling the FBI a potential "citizen spy system," he'd accepted Tom Clark's recommendation that FDR's wartime letter authorizing wiretaps remain in effect. One obstacle had been removed with Larry Fly's departure from the FCC, but now Fly had emerged from private practice in New York to serve as director of the American Civil Liberties Union.

*More stormy seas ahead,* Gantt thought, and wondered whether he should dread it or just sit and watch the show while Hoover and Clyde Tolson worked themselves into a lather.

On his own time, he'd been wading through the latest and hopefully last Pearl Harbor report, which proved to be no easy task. Senator Alben Barkley's joint congressional committee had delivered its findings on June 21, stretching testimony from forty-three witnesses out to 5,000 pages, plus 14,000 printed exhibits. The eight-man majority's conclusion, after much heated—sometimes furious—debate: "The ultimate responsibility for the attack and its results rests upon Japan," while "the diplomatic policies and actions of the United States provided no justifiable provocation whatever for the attack by Japan on this Nation." Dissenting Senators Owen Brewster and Homer Ferguson penned a minority report, stating, "When all the testimony, papers, documents, exhibits, and other evidence duly laid before the Committee are reviewed, it becomes apparent that the record is far from complete."

More proof, in Gantt's opinion, for the view advanced by one of Admiral Kimmel's lawyers that "Pearl Harbor never dies, and no living person has seen the end of it."

And so, with nothing settled about its beginning, still no mention of Hoover and Duško Popov, President Truman was calling it quits. That very morning, over radio, he'd told the nation and the world, "Although a state of war still exists, it is at this time possible to declare, and I find it to be in the public interest to declare, that hostilities have terminated. Now, therefore, I, Harry S. Truman, President of the United States of America, do hereby proclaim the cessation of hostilities of World War II, effective twelve o'clock noon, December 31, 1946."

*But what about peace in our time?* Gantt wondered. Neville Chamberlain had promised it in 1938, at Munich, when he'd handed Czechoslovakia to Hitler. Nineteen years before he put his foot in that cow patty, some other damned fool had called World War I "the war to end all wars." Now, the American monopoly on A-bombs was said to make another war "unthinkable," but Gantt knew that Britain had already drawn up plans for a surprise attack on Russian troops in Eastern Europe to "impose the will of the Western Allies" on Stalin, vaguely qualified as a "square deal for Poland."

The plan's code name: "Operation Unthinkable."

*So, no peace in our time after all,* Gantt thought. *Only a new and wider war.*

Where would he and his sons fit in?

## EPILOGUE

CORPORAL NOLAN O'HARA stood tall and proud in his dress blue uniform, resplendent from its white peaked cap to his gleaming spit-shined shoes. Keely beamed at Nolan from the front row of some twenty folding chairs assembled for the ceremony, with three-year-old Ryan beside her, a solemn frown on his face. Next to Ryan, Nolan's parents and sister fairly glowed with pride.

To Nolan's left, beyond his line of sight, a four-piece brass ensemble struck up "Hail to the Chief," announcing President Truman's entrance, trailed by Secretary of the Navy Forrestal. The audience rose *en masse*, Keely lifting Ryan in her arms, while Ryan snapped off a salute and held it until Truman asked them all to please sit down, reminding Nolan of a judge entering court.

This time, O'Hara had been judged before the gathering began.

After the president thanked everyone for coming and

some news cameras flashed around the room, Secretary Forrestal stepped forward with a piece of velum in his hand. His voice caught when he started reading, but he cleared it and began again.

"Corporal Nolan O'Hara has been enthusiastically recommended for the Medal of Honor for conspicuous gallantry at the risk of his life while serving with the 2nd Marine Division, 6th Marine Regiment, on Tarawa in the Gilbert Islands. On the afternoon of 23 November 1943, at approximately 14:00, Corporal O'Hara and a group of eight to ten other marines were advancing under fire toward enemy entrenchments when a hand grenade was hurled into their midst. Without hesitation, Corporal O'Hara threw himself on top of the grenade to spare his fellow marines from death or grievous injury. Thankfully, the defective bomb failed to explode. Corporal O'Hara's extraordinary demonstration of bravery, decisiveness, and loyalty to his fellow marines embody the Marine Corps' values of honor, courage and commitment. His total disregard for his own personal safety displayed gallantry and intrepidity at the risk of life and beyond the call of duty while engaged in an action against an enemy of the United States."

As Forrestal finished his spiel, President Truman approached Nolan, smiling and holding a square velvet box in one hand. Nolan saluted once more, waited while the president returned it, then removed his cap and clamped it underneath his left arm, just above the cast-brass hilt of his sheathed noncommissioned officer's sword, with its half-basket guard and leather-wrapped grip bound with twisted brass wire.

President Truman smiled up at Nolan, some four inches shorter than Nolan's six feet, his blue eyes almost sparkling behind spectacles with translucent full-rim plastic frames.

Reaching for Nolan's hand, he pumped it twice while saying, "Corporal, it's my *great* pleasure to present our nation's top award for valor, authorized by Congress for your heroism in the face of hostile action on that godforsaken hunk of coral."

Feeling pressed to say something, Nolan responded, "Thank you, Mr. President."

"No, son. Thank *you*."

Truman opened the velvet box, removed its contents, and held the empty out left-handed until Forrestal stepped up and took it from him. Suspended from a light blue moiré silk ribbon 21¾ inches long, the U.S. Navy's version of the medal was a five-pointed bronze star tipped with trefoils containing a crown of laurel and oak. At its center, Minerva —the ancient goddess of war—stood with her left hand clutching a fasces, her right brandishing a shield emblazoned with the U.S. coat of arms to repel Discord, embodied by an adversary holding snakes. The brass flukes of an anchor attached the inverted star to its ribbon, which displayed thirteen stars in the form of a chevron.

Reaching up with both hands, Truman draped the ribbon over Nolan's bowed head, shook his hand again with even greater vigor than before. "This is my honor," Corporal," he said. "I don't mind saying I could use a hero of your caliber with the Secret Service, covering my back."

"I'm grateful, Mr. President," Nolan replied, "but I already have my heart set on the FBI, my father's service since the last World War."

"A G-man, eh? I know the head man over there and wouldn't be surprised if we can make that happen for you soon."

"That's much appreciated, Mr. President."

Leaning in closer, lowering his voice, Truman half-whispered to O'Hara, "Son, if I could turn back time, I'd rather have this medal than be president."

Turning back toward the audience, Truman declared, "I have said on several different occasions that this is the most pleasant and the most honorable job that a President of the United States has to do, to pin the medals on the heroes who have made the country great. That is the reason I am not uneasy or alarmed about the future of the United States of America. Good day to you all, looking forward to great days ahead."

Nolan donned his cap, saluting once more as the president and Forrestal withdrew to more strains from the brass band that had greeted them, then everyone was standing, moving forward, and he stepped into his wife's arms while his father clapped him on the back, his mother and Fiona shedding happy tears.

Great days ahead, Truman had told the crowd.

And Nolan planned to be a part of them.

**TO BE CONTINUED....**

In Book V of *The Bureau—Code of Honor*—a grim "Cold War" settles in to replace the recent global conflagration, spawning a Red Scare at home and abroad surpassing the postwar paranoia of 1919-20. Declan O'Hara returns to FBI headquarters from service in Latin America, to find Aloysius Gantt still striving to curry J. Edgar Hoover's favor. Devon Gantt serves the Bureau in Los Angeles until he, too, is recalled to Washington at the peak of the Red-hunting 1950s. Richard Nixon and Joseph McCarthy leave their indelible marks on a country afraid of its own lurking shadows. When President Truman dissolves the wartime OSS, Colby Gantt transfers to its successor, the Central Intelligence Agency, joining in subversion of "dangerous" governments abroad. Ike Sawyer nears mandatory retirement age at the Federal Bureau of Narcotics, but remains determined to make his last years on the job count for something, while son Payton joins the New York City Police Department, beginning a career that parallels his father's early war against black "radicals." As the USSR goes through traumatic changes, climaxed with the death of Joseph Stalin,

*To Be Continued....*

Leonid Babin pursues his campaign to raise a son who will become a sleeper agent in America and infiltrate the FBI, destroying it from within. Their courses converge during conflicts in Korea and Indochina, while Greg Jordan and his Syndicate associates plant their flags in Cuba, launching a new age of gambling and drug smuggling into the United States, with incipient warfare brewing inside *Cosa Nostra*.

*COMING SEPTEMBER 2018 MICHAEL NEWTON AND WOLFPACK PUBLISHING*